Harry pulled out the hand grenade and knotted his hand around the dark gray bulb.

"This is an antipersonnel grenade. Ever seen what happens when one of these goes off? Oh, it's terrible. All I have to do is yank this, and the shrapnel will cut this place up like everybody was tissue paper."

"Harry..." Jeff said, watching the pin slowly being eased from its safety tube. "Harry, for Christ's sake. What you'll do is destroy the entire cab. You can kill us, but if the tower goes black, what about all those jets out there? We'll have a dozen midairs, Harry! It won't be just us, but all those passengers. Think of them."

"I am thinking of them. That's why you're going to do exactly what I say. If you don't, I'm releasing the trigger. I won't be killing the people out there, *you* will."

CONTROL TOWER

Robert P. Davis

FAWCETT CREST • NEW YORK

CONTROL TOWER

This book contains the complete text of the original hardcover
edition.

Published by Fawcett Crest Books, a unit of CBS Publications, the Consumer Publishing Division of CBS Inc., by ar-
rangement with G. P. Putnam's Sons

ISBN: 0-449-24470-9

Printed in the United States of America

First Fawcett Crest printing: December 1981

10 9 8 7 6 5 4 3 2 1

FOR MY GODSON:

SHANE O'Kelly

ACKNOWLEDGMENTS

The author wishes to thank Captain Lawrence Raab for his technical assistance; Lawrence Montgomery, perhaps one of the best STOL pilots in the world, who assisted with the design and performance data of the Helio Courier aircraft; Buck Christian, Chief Meteorologist, National Weather Service, West Palm Beach Station; and William McLean, Facility Chief of the FAA control tower, Palm Beach International Airport.

AUTHOR'S NOTE

Thanks to supersaver fares, almost everyone is taking to the air these days, but not without heated frustrations: reservations are tight, terminals are jammed, and there are extended lines both at ticket counters and along the taxiways as squads of high-tailed jets inch toward the active runway.

While some confusion and delay on the ground is to be expected, it must be asked: are the air-traffic controllers keeping pace, and does enough air space remain to handle each flight?

Fortunately, there is plenty of air space left, much of it still unused. That is not the problem. But a crisis in air-traffic control (ATC) is beginning to develop around some major airports, as painfully proved by the recent midair collision over San Diego, as well as the repeated near-misses over New York City.

A busy air terminal does not function in the same way as its counterpart, the big railroad station. Trains usually arrive via two tracks, but as they near the station the rails spread out into many sidings. The airport, on the other hand, functions on an inverse principle of traffic flow: hundreds of en-route airways gradually narrow down and finally end up on *one* single track, the runway; in that sense, the airport might be considered a funnel.

Compounding the growing airport dilemma is the limited maneuverability of airplanes in flight; they are the only vehicles of transportation that cannot stop or back up.

All of this places inordinate demands and grave responsibilities on the terminal controllers. Whenever the Federal Aviation Agency (FAA) is asked how well the present ATC system handles traffic at major U.S. airports, the agency usually makes a boiler-plate statement, which is often read from an agency directive. "We have the finest air-traffic control system in the world.... With our computer-assisted radar, plus collision-avoidance systems, some planned, others operational, we [the FAA] are handling our mission efficiently, providing the highest standards of safety for the millions of Americans who fly in our controlled air space."

That is the official FAA grammar.

The unofficial report is not so comforting.

"Systems errors," the euphemism for an ATC mistake, such as a near-collision in the vicinity of a busy airport, occur frequently, and a few control towers at major terminals are now pressed beyond capacity. If air travel continues to grow at the present rate—about 20 percent in recent years—some control towers will be pushed to the breaking point.

This is the story of one such tower operating beyond its capacity and the man in charge who dared to buck the government and tell the truth. The story is set in the near future at Miami International Airport in a new control tower constructed to handle the escalating air traffic coming into southern Florida from all directions.

While much of the novel is based upon facts about air traffic control, it is still a work of fiction, and the characters are not intended to portray actual controllers or FAA officials. Celtic Airlines is not intended to portray any existing air carrier.

I wish to thank all those controllers who helped me; many of their "off-the-record" ideas and complaints are included in this work. They are a valiant bunch of men and women working long hours in a job where one small mistake can result in a holocaust.

Their job may be the unbearable profession.

ROBERT P. DAVIS

Palm Beach, Florida
February 1979

It was a sunless day in Miami, chilly even for February. The producer of a live interview show on WTRM-TV welcomed the weather, for his ratings went up when people remained inside on Sunday afternoon.

"Five minutes to air time," the director said to his floor manager.

"Where the hell is the guest?" the producer asked the men yawning in the control room.

"He's on his way," a production assistant said.

"Cutting it damn close," the producer muttered.

The interviewer, a slick Miami newsman, paced back and forth, deepening his voice and studying the questions jotted down for him on small bits of paper.

The doors at the end of the studio opened and a tall, thin man in his early forties with a thatch of ginger hair walked in. He wore Levi's, an old tweed coat, and a University of Miami tie.

"Is that Sutton?" the producer asked.

"That's him," someone said.

The producer, a nervous man in his mid-twenties, sprang out of the control room and jumped over the studio floor cables.

"I'm the producer," he greeted the guest. "Why the hell are you so late?"

"I'm sorry," Jeff Sutton said in a slow-paced Kansas accent, "but I'm in charge of a control tower. I couldn't get here any earlier."

"Of course, of course," the producer said.

"Three minutes to air time," the director announced over the P.A.

"We don't have much time to prepare," the producer chirped.

"I know what I'm going to say," Jeff assured him, "and I prepared some introductory material."

The interviewer looked over Jeff's notes and questions as the sound man hooked up a neck microphone. The producer went back to the control room and stood behind the director.

"Live TV is bad enough...and now we have to wing it."

"No one watches this show anyhow. What difference does it make?" the director said, blowing out smoke rings from his cigar.

There was a round of laughter. Then the director went back to his work.

"Stand by on the billboard. Roll tape...and up on two."

For twenty seconds scenes of Miami dissolved from one to another; a pompous musical theme stressing the importance of the public-affairs show ran under the glossy shots of the city.

"Stand by on three and cue the announcer."

"We come again to *Miami Weekend*. Our guest is Jeffrey Sutton, facility chief of the control tower at Miami International Airport. Our subject...air-traffic control in the busy skies over the Sun City."

The interviewer was announced, and he went through his opening statement, ending on a somber note.

"Since the tragedy at San Diego, over 491 Americans have been killed in similar midair collisions, Mr. Sutton. Congress and large segments of the American people have lost faith in our ability to separate traffic. Is air traffic control *out* of control?"

Jeff Sutton's handsome, bony face was on camera.

"Do you mean the whole country or the airways around Miami?"

"Miami."

"Air-traffic control's a donnybrook, in my opinion.

12

If people knew what went on in my control tower, half of them wouldn't fly."

The producer popped to his feet and pushed his nose toward the monitor in the control room.

"Am I hearing him right?"

"You sure are," the director said.

"Perhaps you should qualify that statement," the interviewer said, regaining his breath.

"First of all, I have one hundred and seventy men in that tower. Ninety-one are controllers, which sounds like a big enough group. But some of them are kids...'developmentals,' we call them; they're learning on the job. And they're scared of their job. I have borderline alcoholics in there controlling planes...a great many men with ulcers and constant headaches, and these men are handling too many airplanes at once. You see, our business is the only one in the world where the margin for error is zero."

The phone rang in the control room.

"This is Warren, station manager for Pan Am. What the hell is that guy talking about? Our board is lighting up. Tell him to cool it."

"What can I do? The show is live," the producer said.

Jeff Sutton must have known the controversy he was creating, but he went on.

"At first we didn't feel the crunch of increased traffic. Even though more people than ever are traveling by air, the widebody planes are bigger, so for a while we had fewer operations. Then every two-cent airline in the world began coming in here with smaller planes, and the traffic load gradually exceeded our capacity to handle it safely. Our airport now serves ninety-seven airlines."

"Are you saying it's not safe to fly in and out of Miami?"

"It's risky during some peak traffic periods. We had two near-misses last week alone."

"Where does the fault rest, Mr. Sutton?"

"With the FAA. They're an underfinanced agency

...full of bureaucracy...and they historically act after the fact."

"Which facts?" the interviewer asked quickly.

"After the San Diego midair the FAA initiated new rules for heavily trafficked control zones, but they *should* have seen the problem before hundreds were killed. And take the DC-10 crash at Chicago. The FAA knew there were problems with those planes...the cargo door deficiency had already killed 346 people near Paris. It would have to be asked...how do faulty design and slack DC-10 maintenance programs get by the FAA?"

"How do they?"

"The agency, I feel, has acted in collusion with big business...the airlines...the aircraft manufacturers ...and the result? Mass murder!"

"That Sutton will be fired for this. He's flipped!" the producer said.

"It's the best show you ever had, Bert," the director said, smiling. "Be happy with the guest."

The phones continued to ring.

"This is Delta public relations. We've gotten ten calls so far...cancellations all over the place."

"Mr. Sutton is the head of the Miami control tower. We are not endorsing his comments."

The other phone buzzed. It was the station manager.

"Did you know this Sutton was going to pop off?"

"No, sir. He came in late," the producer said.

"No rehearsal?"

"We don't edit the comments anyhow."

"But the station is getting flak from the airlines. There may be a liability question here."

"I'll put in a disclaimer after we hit the commercial."

"During the break, you go out there and tell him to soften up."

"What if he's right?"

"Right or not, don't you know that these airlines represent one of our strongest revenue shares? The commercials pay your salary...mine, too. That guy should have been screened."

The producer had no sooner put the phone down than another one lighted up.

The station manager's fears were already realized.

"This is Reid, Trans-Continental Airlines. Tell your spot sales department that we just cancelled our commercial schedule. As of today."

Jeff Sutton's control tower was one of the most modern and efficient in the country. To counter public criticism of its safety record, the FAA had built the "ultimate" forty-million-dollar terminal facility at Miami International Aiport. It shot up like a lone flower out of a grassy plain between the two fourteen-thousand-foot runways. Built of red river stone flecked with quartz crystals, the MIA control tower sparkled in the sharp Florida sun. The locals called it the "tulip" because of its shape—a narrow tower blossoming at the top into several layers of glass-sided control rooms—but those who worked inside the two-hundred-foot structure had other names for it: the "skinny loony bin" or the "tower of babble." It was packed with every conceivable gadget for separating air traffic and even had a computer that was designed to talk to pilots.

Jeff Sutton, the chief "psychiatrist" of the tulip, had said what he needed to say. But then, from the very first day he entered the Miami control tower, he had run counter to the government grain, for while most of the controllers kept their mouths shut and their heads low to protect their jobs, Jeff could not be stilled when he recognized tower conditions that were risking lives.

The AP picked up part of Jeff's TV outburst, and quotes appeared in newspapers all over the world. The airlines serving Miami immediately phoned the FAA authorities, not only in Florida, but up in Atlanta, also, where the agency's southeastern regional office was located.

"Has that guy Sutton gone crazy?" the airlines asked.

"We don't know what happened, or why it happened.

But it's an untrue, totally irresponsible statement. The Miami tower is the finest terminal facility in the country, and don't worry...we'll discipline Mr. Sutton."

The FAA did not have to deal with Jeff Sutton. Shortly after the TV broadcast, Jeff wrote the southeastern regional director a letter that said, in part: "The agency believes the answer to separating aircraft is computer systems, but the human element has been largely disregarded. Therefore, I am tendering my resignation and wish to be separated from the FAA at the earliest possible time."

The resignation was accepted with pleasure.

Jeff's condemnation of his own tower occurred on February 9; his resignation reached the FAA regional office the following day, and late on the afternoon of February 12, Dr. Laura Montours, an industrial psychologist, arrived from Chicago to see the FAA administrator in his Washington office.

Employing over 62,000 men and women, the agency was one of the largest in the government and represented the highest personnel share of the Department of Transportation. The administrator, Ed Morrison, was an interstate-bus executive who had drifted into government after becoming active on various state and national political campaigns. A cheery, tub-bellied man, Ed was well liked because he echoed the government line and told most of the politicians just what they wished to hear, but his aviation background was minimal: the man knew little about air-traffic control except on a cursory administrative level.

Laura Montours walked into the administrator's office on the tenth floor of the FAA building at 4:40 P.M.

"This is Dr. Montours," the secretary said as she ushered the woman into Ed Morrison's office.

He looked up, smiled, and shoved out his beefy hand.

"Good afternoon," he said, spreading his smile from ear to ear. His visitor looked more like the society women his wife followed in the pages of *Town and*

Country than an industrial psychologist. "Good of you to come so quickly, Dr. Montours."

"How are you, sir?"

They traded the usual banalities, mostly about the frigid Washington weather, and after Laura had been served a cup of lukewarm government coffee, Ed got right to the point.

"Did your office explain the nature of this assignment, Doctor?"

"We only had time to touch upon the highlights, and I must be quite honest with you, Mr. Morrison. Our firm is involved in middle-management and production-line efficiency from the psychological viewpoint. We have no knowledge of air-traffic control."

A priority phone call from the Secretary of Transportation interrupted the conversation. As the secretary talked, Ed Morrison eyed the woman before him. She might be thirty-five, he figured, perhaps older, but again, one never knew when a woman had obviously spent money on her appearance and clothes. Her hair was coal black, her skin slightly olive. French, maybe? Yes, it was a French name, but her complexion was a little too dark; she might be part Portuguese. When the phone call ended, Ed Morrison could no longer check his curiosity.

"Dr. Montours, I hope you don't mind me asking you a personal question."

"That depends upon how personal it is," she said, flashing a wide smile for the first time, so the administrator could see her perfect white teeth.

"Are you French?"

"Everyone asks me that. Yes, partly French and partly American Indian. I'm originally from New Orleans, where I graduated from a Catholic girls' convent; then I went on to the University of Chicago for my B.S. and my Ph.D. My family was in the shrimp business. I'm unmarried...and I've just earned my pilot's license. That's why the firm sent me here. So, now you know everything—or almost everything. But again, Mr. Morrison, my credentials for evaluating air-traffic

17

controllers are limited, maybe nonexistent. I think Dr. Barnes told you that."

"He did," the administrator said as he moved out from behind his large desk and sat beside the woman on the couch. "But that's an advantage. I mean, not knowing too much about air-traffic control. In that way, you won't be prejudiced, will you?"

"Oh, but I am."

The administrator stiffened and looked at the beautiful woman before him with his puffy lips hanging half-open.

"What do you mean by that?"

"When I left Chicago last night, I looked over at the O'Hare tower and studied the building for the first time. I know what Mr. Sutton said on TV. His remarks were printed in the Chicago *Tribune*. Rather frightening, Mr. Morrison."

The administrator pushed to his feet and padded about the office.

"First of all, there's not a word of truth in Sutton's accusations. Of course, there are deficiencies in our air-traffic-control system, but it's the best in the world. Our overall record of serving the public speaks for itself. There's just an epidemic of panic right now. It'll pass...always does."

Laura looked down at the beige rug and then drifted her dark brown eyes toward the administrator.

"But there have been a lot of accidents."

"There have, and we think the pilots have abdicated their responsibilities. The tapes show it."

"The pilots say these accidents were caused by confused instructions from various controllers," Laura responded.

"Their side of the story," the administrator said, his face becoming cherry red. "Dr. Montours, we did not employ your firm to evaluate our air-traffic-control system or criticize our operations."

"What is my assignment?" she said, retreating.

"This agency, with the help of the private sector, has developed a new computer radar which we call CORAD—

18

Computer Overall Radar. The system is now installed on an experimental basis in the Miami control tower. Basically, we feel it's the air-traffic tool of the future. It not only predicts an upcoming conflict between aircraft, but through an electronic voice, the radar system warns pilots. If communication *is* our problem, misunderstandings between the controllers and the pilots, then CORAD will eliminate that."

"A talking radar?" she said, smiling.

"Yes," the administrator said, returning to the couch. "It not only talks, but it thinks. It can reason. While we admit the controller can make a mistake, the computer cannot."

"Sounds very exotic, but I am in no position to evaluate such a system. I deal with real brains, not electronic ones."

"Of course. But let me continue. The Secretary of Transportation, Mr. Cranston, and I are visiting the Miami tower day after tomorrow. The purpose of the visit is to let the secretary see this new CORAD in operation. He's a powerful man, Dr. Montours, and he has influence on the Hill. If the secretary believes in this radar as I do, we'll get appropriations to install CORAD in other control towers and air-traffic-control centers. But the secretary is concerned about this particular tower; some people feel it's operating beyond its capacity."

"Is it?"

"No. Jeff Sutton, the head of the tower, has condemned the new radar. But the outspoken Mr. Sutton is on the side of the local air-traffic controllers' union. So he sees CORAD as replacing his men. He's a dissident, Dr. Montours. There's no room for such people in civil service. If he wants to change things, he should enter politics."

"All government is politics in one way or another," she said.

"That's not the subject, Doctor."

"You're right. But will the new radar replace controllers?"

19

"Not necessarily. It's merely a backup...a system of checks and balances."

"What exactly am I supposed to do at the Miami tower?"

"Make sure the house is in order. Evaluate Mr. Sutton."

"Calm him down for the secretary's arrival?" she said sardonically.

"Yes. I also want you to make a preliminary evaluation as to whether or not these controllers are at the psychological breaking point, as Sutton claims. But time is very short."

"Too short for an in-depth study," she agreed. "Mainly I'm to spy on Mr. Sutton?"

"Let's not put it that way. Actually, I want you to reassure the secretary that the controllers are *not* coming apart."

"Why don't you just move Mr. Sutton out of the tower?"

"He has already resigned, but we feel it would be wise to keep him on for the secretary's visit. He knows the operation, and besides, his blowup only happened a couple of days ago. We can't replace him this quickly."

"But aren't you afraid he'll embarrass you in front of the secretary...seize the opportunity to fire a parting shot?"

"He might, but I'm counting on you to give us the drift of the wind, so to speak. This is very important, Dr. Montours."

She was silent for a few moments, then said, "I'm supposed to soothe Mr. Sutton?"

"Yes, and a lady as attractive as yourself can certainly...ah...bring the man to a more rational viewpoint."

"That's dirty work, Mr. Morrison...entirely unprofessional."

"Well, I could say that what Sutton did to us was unprofessional, if you want to put it on that basis." He paused, and then continued in a very earnest tone, "Dr.

Montours, believe me, your contribution is necessary and vital to air-traffic safety."

Laura walked out into the wind blasting down Independence Avenue. She pulled her mink coat collar up around her ears and got a cab for the Madison Hotel, where she immediately called her office in Chicago.

"Dr. Barnes, I've just had a chat with the administrator. Frankly, sir, I don't like this assignment. We're *not* evaluating psychological pressure in the tower. I'm going down there to tranquilize this Mr. Sutton, who's scared everybody to death. We're acting as peacemakers."

"Yes, yes, I felt that, too. But Senator Marlin, who's been a friend of this firm for years, asked us to handle this as a personal favor. Apparently he's known Morrison since the man was in the private sector."

"Well, I still don't like it."

"Dr. Montours, indulge me, please. I need your support."

There was a long sigh from the other end of the phone. "All right, I'll do it, but only under protest."

"Protest registered. Keep me informed from Miami."

Laura Montours had considered taking a flight down that night, but she was exhausted and decided instead to have a leisurely dinner and book the earliest plane out in the morning.

It was Laura's first visit to Miami, and as the jet landed, she looked over at the cinnamon-colored tower and began to fantasize about the man who ran it: a disturbed union sympathizer, maybe in his late fifties, a lug who was trying to make his mark in life through a splash of outrageous PR. He was probably fat, bald, and wore cheap shirts.

After checking into the Ramada Inn near the airport, Laura called Jeff Sutton to say that she had arrived.

"Dr. Montours," Jeff said, "the tower, as you probably saw, is located in the center of the field. Take a cab along Thirty-sixth Street until you see a sign with the words

'FAA Control Tower.' There's a gate at the entrance. Simply pick up the telephone and call security. I'll leave word with them to expect you."

Laura had never been to a control tower before, and she had no idea what to expect. The taxi took her to the gate; she announced her arrival on the phone, and a second later the gate slid open along its greased tracks.

"Place is like gettin' into a prison, huh, lady?" the driver said.

"Sure is."

They drove down a glistening tunnel of arched cinderblocks painted creamy white. Thirty seconds later the car arrived at an underground parking lot crowded with cars and soaked in a harsh fluorescent light. She walked to a gray steel door marked "Authorized Personnel Only," and above it there was a TV scanner. She noticed that the outside of the door had no handle and could be opened only from the inside; it swung slowly on its creaky hinges, and a small pink-skinned man who looked to be in his sixties peered out and said, "Dr. Montours? I'm Ted, the security guard. Welcome to the Miami tower."

She said hello and stepped inside the security station, a small bare room with a metal desk and two green plastic chairs. Ted waddled over to another door and unlocked it, and she noticed the handgun hanging off his belt.

"Do all towers have this kind of security?"

"Oh, no, but this is supposed to be the tower of tomorrow. The government thinks control-tower security will be important in the future. But do you want to know something?" Ted whispered. "Look at my right hand. You see, I had to retire from the Toledo Police Department because my paws were arthritic. So, actually, I couldn't shoot the gun anyhow."

"Well, I hope you don't have to."

"Not much chance... no one's ever tried to break in. I just sit here and play my electronic chess game and count the days till retirement."

She thanked Ted and walked down a sterile corridor

22

which was chilly and so functional with its government-green linoleum floor and cinderblock walls that Laura felt depressed, as if she were on her way to the morgue or the gas chamber. Halfway down the corridor there was a long glass panel and inside she could see a battery of secretaries. To the far side was a row of cubicles for the tower's administrative staff.

"Mr. Sutton is in the last office," the gum-chewing secretary said, pointing her thickly painted fingernail.

As Laura moved toward the office, Jeff Sutton came out to meet her. He was not at all what she had imagined. Sutton was a much younger man, and the reddish curls that flopped down on his tan forehead made him look both boyish and handsome. He was dressed very casually and there was an engaging smile upon his face.

For a moment she studied the "dissident" facility chief, trying to think whom he looked like. The "Marlboro man," she concluded: the eternal cowboy who rides the range, smoking while his eyes become more crinkled each year from looking into the blast of the sun.

"I'm Dr. Montours...ah...just call me Laura," she amended. She usually found that it helped to start out with her professional title, but her instinct told her the facility chief would only be amused by a cold, formal approach.

"And I'm Jeff," he said, showing her into his office.

In her work of interviewing middle-management executives, Laura had discovered that she could learn something about them from the look and neatness of their offices. A man's props told much of his story. But she was completely baffled by Jeff Sutton's office.

The rest of the cubicles along the same concrete wall were plain and austere: gray metal desks, plastic green chairs, and the sickly overretouched photographs of the President and the one of Ed Morrison sitting in front of the American flag looking as if he had just come from a high-caloried luncheon in the Senate dining room.

Sutton's office was a total contrast.

23

In the center was an old-fashioned rolltop desk which smelled of lemon oil; papers were stuffed neatly in the cubicles, and behind the desk was a wooden roller chair, the kind railroad telegraphers had used at one time. Laura was an antique collector and recognized the desk and the chair as authentic pieces, not cheap reproductions. And along the walls were small well-framed oil paintings of old steam locomotives, rendered with a love of detail and fondness for the subject.

She thought it was curious that a man in aviation would style his office like a railroad stationmaster's, reflecting another age.

Jeff's place told her quite a bit about the man she was supposed to calm down. He was an individualist, and not one to acquiesce to the cheap governmental metal desks and official prints of the superiors.

"Do you like my office?" Sutton asked, a slight note of pride in his voice.

She held back her answer. Not only did she like the office, but she immediately liked the tenant. Jeff Sutton was no ordinary man, and she knew at once that it had been a mistake to come to Miami.

Nothing would soften Jeff Sutton.

"Well, now, I know what you're thinking, Laura," Jeff said when she didn't respond. "You're a psychologist and you're wondering: how the hell did this guy get an office like this? Whose furniture is it, and why does he have it in here in a government installation?"

She laughed out loud. "Yes, that's precisely what I'm thinking."

"Well, sit down and I'll tell you."

"There must be a story behind it."

"Sure," Jeff said, rolling the top of his desk open and shut. "I used to work in the cab."

"You drove a cab?" she asked, confused.

Jeff sat down and wheeled around in his stationmaster's chair, smiling at Laura.

"You know nothing about our business."

"Frankly, no."

"Well, the cab is the glass part on top of the tower.
24

We'll go up there for the tour. About the desk... When I was appointed deputy chief down here, I couldn't stand this subbasement. No windows, all the offices looking alike. So I asked the tower facility chief if I could bring in my own gear. This desk has been in my family since 1854. My great-great-grandfather was an artillery captain stationed at Fort Scott, Kansas. See, it still has the old army serial number burnt into the back."

Jeff got up and showed Laura the faint remains of the serial number.

"I wrote my request up to the regional head in Atlanta, telling him the story. He wrote back and gave me permission to bring the desk in—only because it was originally army issue."

A warmer feeling flowed over Laura Montours and she began to understand how this man might have said the things he did on TV.

"And the pictures?" she asked.

"My hobby is oil painting. Those were some of the locomotives that used to steam past our acreage in Logan County, Kansas. Painted them myself, mostly from memory... but sometimes I sent away for those old nostalgic photos and used them to go by. An old controller told me one time, 'If you don't have a hobby, something to take your mind off this job, you'll go crazy.'"

Then Jeff Sutton's expression changed. His eyes narrowed, becoming almost pinched, as if the reflective glare of the range had gotten to him.

"Why are you here? No... don't answer. I know."

"Then tell me."

"Morrison sent you. He wants to make sure that things in this tower are straightened out for the secretary. No touchy moments. And since they couldn't kick me out on such short notice, you're supposed to do a little number on me... unwrinkle the cloth... turn off my ovens."

Laura got up, lit a cigarette, and said, "Colorful way of expressing it, but you're right, that's part of it, Jeff. But on a long-range basis we're trying to study the psychological pressures on controllers, and I hope you'll cooperate—even though you've resigned, I understand."

"Yep, I'm going. Tomorrow's my last day in this asylum. Then I'm heading back out west with my daughter." He stared at her with a steady gaze. "I have no reason to withhold any information at this point."

There was a short pause, then Laura said, "That was some attack on TV the other day."

He shrugged. "I was only trying to shock the agency into doing something. If you can grasp the situation here, maybe you can convince the bureaucratic priests that we're sitting on a time bomb."

Jeff stopped and thought a moment. "I might have lost my head a little on TV, but the administrator will send out what we call a 'massage' message. 'The head of our Miami tower was a disgruntled, baleful employee suffering hidden emotional traumas, but the FAA has now corrected the situation.'"

"You *are* a government hater, aren't you?" she said.

"Yeah, and I used to be a government lover."

"What the hell does that mean?"

"Tell you later. Long story, but it has to do with this tower. Now, what do you know about ATC...where do we start?"

"At the beginning, please. I have a private license, three hundred hours, and I've talked to controllers, of course, but I've never been in a tower before today."

"Okay, let's work our way up from here."

Jeff gave Laura a quick tour of the administrative level, and each of the forty-two windowless, sterile offices was about the same: bare, neat, functional.

"What's your entire tower complement?" she asked as they proceeded down the corridor.

"One hundred and seventy."

"All controllers?"

"Oh, no. We have ninety-one controllers and a hell of a lot of support and management people. Four training officers, seven assistant chiefs, sixteen team supervisors, and then, there's the airways facility sector.

They maintain the radar. And there are six data-systems specialists who program our computers. But I don't know who programs those guys."

"How many women in here?"

"Fourteen. Five of them are controllers and the rest are secretaries and support personnel."

"And what does it cost the government to run a facility like this?"

"About fourteen million a year, considering the salaries, supplies, and everything."

Then they stepped into the elevator for the higher levels, where the traffic was controlled. On the way up, Laura asked a routine question she had often used in her evaluations of the private sector.

"What makes a good controller?" she asked.

Jeff smiled and said, "Well, one of the fellows who trained me when I came to the old Miami tower said, 'Show me a good short-order cook and I'll show you a good controller.'"

"Meaning?"

"He has to be calm, fast, and store a bunch of orders in his head. In our case, it's planes and numbers."

A couple of seconds later they stepped off the high-speed elevator onto the radar level, with its waxed green linoleum floors and cinderblock walls. The tower had been completed only nine months before, and the halls still smelled faintly of resin.

Jeff showed her the conference room and said, "This is where we explain to the visiting girl scouts what they're going to see in the cab."

He took her across the hall to the ready room, a lounge with three government-issued couches, a TV set, a hot plate, and a refrigerator. A small table in the corner was piled high with magazines, and along one wall there was a bank of dispensing machines. One unit carried nothing but medicinal supplies: antiacid pills, cold and headache remedies, Wash 'n Dri, tissues, toothpaste, breath fresheners, nosedrops, and Visine for the tired eyes.

"That's a good seller," Jeff said, seeing Laura study the eyedrops bin.

Laura thought the look and feel of the ready room mirrored that of a factory recreational facility, except that the squad of men in there, some eating, some watching TV, were better dressed and all of them were relatively young.

"What's the average age of a controller at MIA?" she asked.

"About twenty-nine," Jeff said.

And that told Laura something about the job. She had not seen an old man in the facility except for a few of the supervisors down on the administrative level.

"Do they go out for lunch?" she asked.

"No. Technically, there's no lunch break. Most of them get about forty minutes to grab a sandwich in here, and sometimes one of the fellows goes out to a fast-food place and brings back hamburgers for the others. On days when we're working at capacity, the men may not eat at all."

"That's bad for the head and the body."

"I know. There have been occasions when a man has worked his entire shift without food."

They left the ready room and crossed the hall to another gray steel door, marked "Approach Radar," and Jeff unlocked it.

"Most towers have just one radar room. We have two, one for departing traffic and this one for inbounds."

The room was dim, bathed in the sickly green light flowing off the bank of radarscopes along one wall. There was a clatter of mixed voices. The scopes were speckled with whitish targets, and beside each blip was a small tag telling the controller the flight's identification, its altitude and speed.

Above this electronic emporium were blinking lights and beside each scope was a forest of thumb-dirty computer-terminal buttons. As Laura's eyes adjusted to the faint green glare, she began to see the controllers hunched over their scopes. Each man seemed to be permanently arched with a twisted spine. They looked

28

ghostly and their faces were vacant as their mouths flipped open and shut with machine-gun-like orders.

At first the radar room seemed rank and chilly as the air conditioner pumped and sucked out the humidity. Then she began to smell the scents: electronic equipment with its metallic odor; the light stench of human sweat creeping through the thick layers of underarm deodorant. The radar room, she concluded, smelled like an expensive gym.

"How much do you want to know about the operation in here?" Jeff asked.

"Not too much of the technical stuff, please."

"Well, what you're seeing are radar targets, or flights, in our controlled air space. Some flights are transitioning, meaning they're just passing by. The others are being handed over to us by the en-route control center. We put them in a sequence, and when they're about five miles from the field, we hand them off upstairs to one of the local controllers. He gives them their landing instructions. The difference between this room and the one upstairs is our visual reference. Here we see the flights as radar targets, and up in the cab, or the glass part of the tower, we usually see the traffic by eye…in good flying weather, that is."

Even though Laura had spoken to radar controllers before from the cockpit of her Beech Bonanza, she had never imagined that they worked under such deplorable conditions, like moles in a dark covey.

Inhuman, she thought. What came to mind were pictures she had seen of women bent over the clack of fast-moving giggers, trying to keep pace with the machinery in the worst years of the industrial revolution. But in this dim chamber the product was not shirtwaists, but human lives. Each radar target on the scope represented hundreds of people located in a cigarshaped tube flying around in the skies.

The supervisors, most of them in their mid-thirties, stood in back of the seated controllers. Laura realized she was older than almost everyone else in the room.

How could young men work under these conditions, some without a meal in eight hours, each of them burdened with the knowledge that he could *not* make a mistake?

She wanted to escape that diabolical room. Outside she leaned against the sweating wall and asked, "What could go wrong in there?"

Jeff rattled it off. "A training flight could stumble into the area without cockpit equipment to give us an altitude tag...in bad weather the drug pushers pour in here and cut right through our control zone. Then, of course, we have radar failures. All of a sudden a foreign target pops up, or we see a plane in four places at once. At other times the computer breaks down, and that really causes heart attacks. But mainly we just have too much traffic."

"What happens if you exceed your capacity?"

"We don't let the planes in. The computer knows just what we can handle. It sends a message out to gate-hold a flight or delay it en route by a speed reduction. Haven't you ever heard a pilot say that your flight will be delayed while they check out something?"

"Sure."

"Usually they're not checking a damn thing. We've informed the carrier to gate-hold until the computer says that MIA traffic sequencing will accept the flight."

They climbed the black metal stairs to the cab, and Laura immediately sensed the change in climate from the hellish room below. Morning light flowed in through the tinted windows; the men working the local traffic seemed less sallow and sweaty; and from their high perch, the entire airport could be clearly seen.

The airplanes on the taxiways formed one solid line of high tails, like a long line of patient birds waiting their turn to fly away. The azure sky was dabbed with dark spots which occasionally glistened and flashed in the bright sun as the flocks of arriving and departing jets let out their black kerosene trails, turning the once-pure air into a smoking grid of crisscrossing aircraft.

She stood staring out the window, transfixed by the sight, and at first Laura did not notice Jeff walk away toward a young man working the local north runway.

His name was Nick Cozzoli; he was twenty-five, with a cap of shiny black hair, and he wore a T-shirt inscribed: "God Is A Stock Car Driver."

Laura edged over toward the control station as she heard the sudden outburst.

"Look at that son of a bitch!" Nick was yelling above the chatter of the cab.

An old DC-4 cargo plane, a "cockroach," was struggling in for a landing, and the pilot, a South American by the way he spoke over the radio, had landed his plane too high; it dropped, bounced, and the pilot who should have applied power for a go-around, was simply fighting the controls to stick his old, rattling hulk onto the runway. He rolled out and then stopped just short of the taxiway turnoff.

Suddenly the cab speaker boomed, "Tower...Eastern 89. I see a guy directly ahead of me...on the runway. Am I cleared to land or not?"

"You're cleared," Nick yelled into his boom mike, sucking on an old half-chewed cigar.

"Nick, you can't get away with that!" Jeff blasted. "Send him around."

"I gotta pinch my traffic, Mr. Sutton. You know that."

"Give the banana jockey a call...tell Eastern to get out of there!"

"Get that load off the active!" Nick snapped into his mike.

"Ah...my nose-wheel steering has problems, sir," the Spanish-accented voice came back.

"I don't give a damn! Roll it off on the grass ...*immediately!*" Nick demanded, and then he said, "Eastern 89, go around..."

But Nick's transmission was interrupted by the airline captain.

"There's a guy down there in a DC...something... with his tail hanging out on the runway...."

The DC-4 taxied sluggishly onto the grass infield.

"Eastern 89, cleared to land," Nick yelled.

"That's cutting it too close, mister," the pilot said when he was on the ground and had reversed his thrust.

"So, what else is new—what did you want me to do, put you back in the sequence?"

"No, thank you," the captain answered, blowing out a long, frustrated breath.

"Goddamn it, Nick, that captain's right! I told you to send Eastern around."

"I was going to, Mr. Sutton. You heard me. But if we went by the book on horizontal separations, this traffic would be backed up to Orlando. That skipper was willing to chance it. Sending him around would have delayed him forty minutes, he knows that."

Jeff flashed a quick look at Laura, whose face was drained of blood.

He hunched his shoulders. "Just another day in the ward," he said.

Jeff introduced her to the cab complement, telling them that she was a consultant with the FAA.

"Dr. Montours is a shrink, so don't tell her about your ulcers or hives. She's not carrying any pills or liniment."

There was a ring of laughter, and at last Laura saw some normal human reactions in the hot tower.

About five minutes later an older man entered the cab. He was neatly dressed, paunchy, but his eyes, his complexion, and his hair seemed drained of color, and there was a pall of grayness about him, as if he were walking around proving that the dead could move.

Jeff introduced him to Laura. "This is Harry Boyle, the man who's going to demonstrate CORAD, the new radar, for the secretary tomorrow."

Harry extended Laura a weak, moist hand as Jeff pointed out to her the large triple radarscopes which sat enthroned on a raised platform in the center of the cab.

Jeff glanced at his watch and then said, "Laura, would you like to stay up here and sop up some more of the action? Harry and I have to go downstairs for a few minutes. Feel free to ask questions...if you can catch somebody between planes. The boys don't usually have such good-looking company, so I'm sure they'll cooperate."

It was time for Jeff and Harry Boyle to go to work downstairs on the departure radar station. In most towers the facility chief and other supervisors did not take radar positions, but in the tulip Jeff had initiated a policy which provided that all management should be current on each tower position. This, he felt, enabled them to become working partners with the men rather than aloof bosses.

As the two men left the cab, they could hear the eager voices of the controllers already talking to Laura.

Several minutes later Harry and Jeff unlocked the metal door to the departure radar room. Four controllers were departing planes to the north and south, and between them was a data clerk and hand-off man, who passed the traffic on to Miami Center, the control facility that guided the flights up to a line south of Jacksonville.

The radar controllers oriented Jeff and Harry to the traffic, and then Jeff excused everybody from the room except Hoagy Washington, the hand-off controller, an old black man with frizzled white hair, impeccably dressed in a neat three-piece suit.

For about ten minutes Jeff and Harry worked their traffic. As soon as the local controller upstairs cleared a flight off the runway, the plane came up as a grayish-white target with an identification tag on one of the two scopes headed either north or south.

"Lufthansa 890," Jeff said. "Radar contact. Continue to climb on present heading 090 and report leaving three for four."

Jeff worked the German departure and five others for a minute or two, and just as he was saying, "Lufthansa 890...contact Miami Center now on 128.75. Good day," he noticed that Harry was staring at his scope, his mouth drooped wide open, his eyes glaring like two glass balls.

The man had frozen.

"Harry!" Jeff yelled. "Harry!"

"Mr. Boyle," Hoagy said, shaking the motionless controller.

Nothing.

Jeff knew that at least four targets were not being handled and he couldn't possibly work both scopes.

"Harry!" he yelled again. "What's the matter? Harry ...Harry!"

Boyle didn't answer, but continued to watch the scope, his muscles paralyzed.

Jeff picked up the phone, at the same time flipping a button beneath his scope. This signaled the cab and the security desk downstairs that an "Emergency One" existed. The "goose button," they called it.

"We've got a serious problem," Jeff said over the phone to the cab. "Go to Emergency One. Hold all departures."

Radar freeze-ups were nothing new to the FAA. Although they were never discussed, a procedure had been developed, an experimental MO in this tower, and it was swiftly put into motion.

Nick Cozzoli responded immediately, picking up his mike. "MIA local control to all departing operations. A tower radar emergency exists. Repeat: a radar emergency exists. All departures expect delays. Departing operations connect Miami center on 128.75."

When a control failure occurred in this tower, the airport was partially and in some cases completely shut down as a safety precaution. It was always inferred by the pilots who were being guided by this nerve center that the failure was mechanical, not human: a radarscope on the blitz, a short circuit, a fire. The tower traffic was handed off to center immediately.

Luckily, the departures were accounted for; the flock was all there, and forty seconds later, the red light flashed on Nick's panel: center was satisfied. The traffic had identified themselves one by one.

The next step, according to the tower's blue book marked "Confidential," was to activate the emergency diesel generators in the subbasement of the tower. Nick pushed an automatic start button under the lip of his worktable: both GM generator sets hummed into action. Had those generators been damaged somehow, another set would have been activated. The tower had six power options.

The whole procedure from the time Jeff declared the emergency until the shutdown list was completed took one minute and nine seconds. The efficiency was not surprising. Twice a month the tower practiced its emergency procedures, and no other tower in the world had such contingency plans or backups. In other towers, if a radar went black, the men worked around it, sending the traffic to a holding pattern while the problem was corrected.

The failure of any control position in a tower, especially a Class Five facility working heavy traffic, was considered a critical situation. But since Miami was supposed to be the tower for the 1980s, when air traffic would be dramatically increased, they could not risk any shutdown without taking immediate emergency measures.

All this well-thought-out procedure was developed for one reason: an FAA tower study had concluded that the most important aspect of an emergency was to hand off the aircraft to avoid midair collisions. Saving the air traffic was the prime mission, and with that secured, they would then turn their attention to the blackout.

And they did. Two men in the cab rushed downstairs, and the four others in the lounge ran across the hall as old Ted sprang from the elevator door with his gun ready. There had been situations when controllers cracking up on the job became violent.

Inside the radar room Harry was shouting. "Why did you hit the goose button, Jeff?"

"Harry, you were *frozen.*"

There was pounding on the door.

"What's wrong?" Ted screamed.

"We're all right," said Harry. "Just the radar...be with you in a minute."

"Get out of this tower, Harry. Right now."

"I just...just had a short blackout."

"That's one too many."

"Please, Jeff. I can handle every position."

"You can't handle *one* position."

"Jeff...oh, Christ, don't let the others know. Hoagy, you shut up, hear?"

"Won't say a thing," the old black man responded.

"Report in sick to the office and go home," Jeff said.

"I can still handle CORAD tomorrow."

"No, Harry, you can't. Now, go quietly."

Harry suddenly lunged for the fire ax on the wall. He took it down and held it out toward Jeff.

"I could kill you...you know I could kill you."

Jeff was not a man to be intimidated. He walked up to Harry, grabbed the ax, and slowly replaced it on its two red holders.

"Don't *ever* threaten me again. Now, get your ass out of the tower!"

Minutes passed, and still Harry stood there. There were pounds on the door.

"You all right in there?" Ted shouted. "What's wrong?"

"We're okay, just a little breakdown," Jeff called. "Have to check a few things."

The pounding on the metal door reverberated through the darkened, stilled radar room. There were more heavy footsteps and commotion out in the hall.

Harry's voice was frantic. "Cover for me, Jeff. Fire me if you have to, but cover for me, *please*."

Jeff knew what Harry was talking about. There was nothing worse than a controller being fired on the spot in front of his co-workers.

"Mr. Sutton," Nick called through the door. "What's going on?"

Jeff glanced at Hoagy, then sighed. "Okay, it was a radar foul...unusual clutter."

"Thanks, buddy," Harry said, placing his arm about Jeff's shoulder. "But I can operate CORAD . . . the whole tower. I feel fine now."

"Stop bullshitting me!" Jeff said as he moved toward the door and slid back the heavy cast-iron bolt.

Nick stuck his head into the room slowly. "What happened?"

"The radar went loony."

"All of a sudden it was cluttered up," Harry said confidently, leaning against the scope and slowly taking out his cigarettes as if nothing were wrong.

"What do you mean?" Nick asked.

"We were losing targets," Jeff said. "Didn't like the situation."

"Had a few bad moments," Harry added quite calmly, darting a quick look toward Hoagy.

"That's right," Hoagy said.

Joe Redmond, the lead radar-maintenance man who had arrived immediately on the scene, spoke up. "Mr. Sutton, did you switch to the B power option?"

"Yes," Jeff answered.

"Same problem?" Joe asked.

"Exactly," Harry chimed in.

"Did you switch circuits?"

"Oh, yes," Harry said.

Joe studied the sweeps on the radarscopes, the single green lines circling the scopes, and they looked normal. He tuned one slightly and then hunched his shoulders. The other technicians quickly put their test equipment on each of the scopes, and when they were satisfied, Joe turned to Jeff.

"Mr. Sutton, doesn't seem to be anything wrong with these scopes or the circuits, but I'll check it out some more."

"Thanks, Joe. Okay, everybody, let's get this facility back on the line," Jeff said briskly.

The tower was back in full operation just seven minutes after Jeff had kicked the goose button. Joe Redmond went down to the switchgear room, wondering what to put on his report, and he said to his associate, a man named Tillis, "You know, Leroy, I've been working with radar for twenty-two years, most of those in the navy, and they just don't go out for no reason. Now, this might happen again. So you and I are going to start looking through these trunk cables one by one. It might take us a week, but we've got to troubleshoot this thing."

The assistant radar technician agreed with a nod of his head.

Thirty minutes later, Jeff drove Laura Montours back along Thirty-sixth Street. They rode in silence past the cavernous hangars of Pan Am and Eastern, and Laura's mind was a confused blur. If this is the ultimate tower, what happens in an ordinary one? she thought.

"Hey, you still alive?" Jeff asked, looking over toward her.

"Barely. Are we going to be truthful with each other?" she asked.

"Why not?"

"What happened in that radar room with Mr. Boyle?"

"The scope suddenly went black."

"Did it really? There were a lot of rumors in the cab."

"There are always rumors in control towers. It's a condensed society with cliques, gossip, and hatreds, and people have to work and exist together somehow. Someone once told me that a control tower was similar to a submarine tipped up on its end."

"But what happened to Harry?"

"I told you."

"I don't believe your story."

"Well, why don't you have dinner with me at my house tonight, and maybe I can come up with another story."

She looked over at the lanky red-haired man, and they crossed smiles.

"All right," she said. "Just for business purposes."

"Good," Jeff said, patting her on the hand, and for a

moment she hoped he would not remove his warm fingers. Then she chided herself for thinking these thoughts and accepting a dinner invitation from the man she was supposed to evaluate for the administrator.

As Laura was getting out of the car in front of the Ramada Inn, Jeff said suddenly, "Have an idea...I own this rebuilt Waco, an open-cockpit biplane. How about taking a ride around the traffic pattern with me this afternoon? You'll be able to see this bees' nest from the sky."

"How old is the plane?" she asked.

"Nineteen-twenty-eight. My father and I rebuilt it years ago, but she's the safest bird going. I have a radio and an engine that sings the right tune."

"Sounds great."

"I'll pick you up at three, then. Oh, bring a sweater. Might get a little cool up there."

2

As Laura Montours entered her room, the red light on the phone was blinking. The administrator had left a message asking her to phone Washington immediately.

"Thank you for calling me back so quickly, Dr. Montours," Morrison said. "I understand you were in the tower this morning."

"Yes, I spent about two hours there."

"What happened in the radar room with Mr. Boyle?" the administrator asked in a rapid-fire sentence, his words edged with authority.

"How did you know about that?"

"Doesn't matter," he said just as sharply, but then he eased off. "Well, I received a call from our ATC man in Atlanta. Mr. Boyle was thrown out of the tower by this Sutton, who accused him of blacking out on a radarscope. Mr. Boyle is one of the tower veterans, and is very much in favor of our new CORAD. Sutton detests the radar. Maybe he's taking it out on this man. Anyhow, what did Sutton say about Boyle?"

"He claims there was a radar mechanical failure."

"Now, Dr. Montours," the administrator continued in his official tone, "I don't want anyone's personal feelings about the radar to upset our demonstration for the secretary. I told you how important his visit is to that tower in terms of future budgeting. Sutton will *not* allow Boyle to operate CORAD...he told the man he was burnt out, an emotional piece of wreckage, or some such thing. Two assignments, Dr. Montours: find out what happened and evaluate Boyle."

"I can talk to Mr. Boyle, certainly, but how can I find out what really went on in that radar room?"

"Was anyone else there when this happened?"

"Let me see. Yes, when I came down from the cab with the others, a black man named Washington stepped out of the radar room with Sutton and Boyle."

"What did he say?"

"Same thing...a radar failure of some kind."

"Well, I'll have the regional ATC head send Mr. Washington over to your hotel right away. You get the facts, Dr. Montours. But I don't want Sutton to know what we're doing."

"I understand."

"How did you find Sutton...angry?"

"He has a few chips on his shoulder."

"But is he going to raise hell tomorrow?"

"I don't know yet. I'm just trying to ease into this...get him on my side. I'll know more later."

"One other point. Our FAA flight surgeon, Dr. Striker, is coming into the tower to speak with Sutton and Boyle tomorrow morning at nine o'clock. We won't arrive there until after lunch, but I'd like you to sit in on that evaluation and report directly back to me. Boyle has to operate the radar. Sutton will never give it a fair test."

"I understand your concern, Mr. Morrison, but frankly, I don't like getting into the middle of the situation."

"What do you mean?"

"This is tower politics, sir. I'm not sure it's connected with psychological pressures...and we really don't have much time."

"That's why we have to move quickly, Doctor. I'm very concerned about this development. Didn't expect it."

"I'll call you back as soon as I've spoken to Mr. Washington."

Laura was already exhausted, drained just by visiting the tower. She sent down for lunch, and by 1:30 she was asleep. The phone woke her up twenty minutes later.

"Dr. Montours, there's a Mr. Washington down here."

"Send him up, please."

Laura brushed her hair quickly, took out her notepad and then came the knock.

"Come in, Mr. Washington," she said brightly, opening the door. "Thanks for coming."

The old black man was diffident and slightly wary as he walked into the room and took a seat by the window.

"The office told me it was an emergency," he said.

"Can I order you lunch or some coffee, perhaps?" Laura asked.

"No, I'm fine."

"The administrator is concerned about what happened in the tower this morning," she said, studying the man closely.

His deep brown eyes didn't flicker, nor did his white eyebrows move. He was clearly not reacting. Laura decided to ease into her questions, and she backtracked.

"I'm here on assignment from the administrator."

41

"I heard that, Dr. Montours. What are you trying to find out?"

"We're studying psychological pressures in the tower," she said weakly, covering her version of the truth.

"How can I help you?" Hoagy said, half under his breath, still uneasy from having been ordered out of the tower by the Atlanta office for a hasty interview with a psychologist.

He thought *he* was being evaluated.

"Mr. Washington, what happened in the radar room?" Laura asked, deciding to get it out hastily.

"One of the scopes went black."

He rushed his words, and she immediately knew that he was lying. Hoagy Washington was a good controller and a terrible liar.

"Let me put it this way," Laura said, sharpening her words. "The administrator wants the *truth!*"

"Then he can go and look at the report."

She got up and strolled around the room, trying to establish where his allegiance lay: with Jeff Sutton or Harry Boyle, and why was he holding back? Laura, who was trained in people's reactions under questioning, decided not to press the subject at the moment, because she realized that the man was being pushed into something he abhorred.

"I see," she said, tucking a smile into her face. "You've been in the system a long time, haven't you, Mr. Washington?"

"Yes. I started as an air controller back when our tools were just blackboards and telephones," Hoagy said nostalgically and proudly. "We had to look out the window to see where the DC-3's were. That was up on the old Greensboro–High Point field in North Carolina. It was only a grass strip then."

"Do you think the ATC system works, Mr. Washington?"

"Yes, but the airports are behind the air-travel boom. Too many planes to handle."

"And what would you suggest?"

"More controllers...better-trained men, maybe. I

just do my job. I'm not a visionary like Mr. Sutton...
or a fighter."

"And what about this business of burnt-out controllers? Do you feel the pressure is too great?"

"I've been controlling aircraft for forty years, and I sleep every night without pills and I don't take stomach medicine. Depends upon the person, Dr. Montours. Some people just can't take the job. But then, maybe they couldn't take any pressure to begin with."

Laura was not getting the answers. She paused and asked quietly, "How do you feel about Mr. Sutton?"

"He's one of the best facility chiefs I've ever worked with," Hoagy said unhesitatingly. "Very loyal to his men."

Laura nodded. "I understand he's pro-union."

"Yes, but that's not what I mean. Mr. Sutton treats us like we were his own family. He remembers our birthdays with greeting cards...even knows the names of our pets. And on holidays he brings this microwave oven into the tower and cooks up a Thanksgiving or Christmas dinner with a special stuffing he does, and homemade nut bread. We're mighty sorry to lose him. He's like a father to us."

"Doesn't he have a family of his own?"

"He did, but his wife left him few years back—married an Englishman, I think—and she took along their only daughter, Honey. Mr. Sutton lives by himself. I think he's a lonely man, and he's made the tower his whole life."

"But he's deserting you now, isn't he?"

The old man shook his head. "Mr. Sutton's gotta do what's right for him. He says he can't live with all the conflict...protecting us and the passengers at the same time." Hoagy paused. "Maybe I shouldn't say this to you, but Mr. Sutton thinks the FAA system is sluggish. He always uses that word 'sluggish.'"

"And Mr. Boyle?" she asked.

"He's a very fine controller. I believe he's the oldest man in the tower. Came here, they told me, in 1953. Sure knows these airways, Dr. Montours."

43

Laura thought she had gone through enough pacifiers now, and she sprang her question again.

"Mr. Washington, what happened in that radar room?"

"Told you."

"You're protecting someone, but I already understand what took place in there."

"Then why are you asking me, Dr. Montours?"

"Because you were there. I want it from your point of view. Did Harry Boyle black out on his departure scope?"

Hoagy Washington ran his finger around his neck, recrossed his legs, and Laura noticed the sweat breaking out on his hairline where the light black of his skin met his sugar-white hair. The old man got up and moved to the window. He looked out for a while, watching the jets lift off from his field, and when he turned back toward Laura, there were tears in his eyes.

Sensing his embarrassment, Laura crossed to him and placed her arm about the old man's shoulder. "It's all right, Mr. Washington."

"For years Harry was the best man we had in the tower," he said mechanically.

"But he did fold up this morning?"

"Yes." Hoagy let out a big sigh. "Harry blacked out on the scope. He grabbed a fire ax and went after Mr. Sutton."

Laura could feel the breath drain out of her, and it was a full twenty seconds before she could speak again. She regained her own composure and said, "Why did Mr. Sutton cover for him?"

"Because he's decent. He never wants to embarrass a man in front of the others."

"But Mr. Sutton told Harry he couldn't operate the CORAD for the secretary. Everyone in the tower would figure it out anyway, wouldn't they?"

"Maybe. But everyone doesn't know about Harry. It's been kind of hidden. Started two years ago, and Mr. Sutton has suffered a lot for Harry's sake. Didn't want to put him out on the street. Yet, the man isn't able to control planes anymore. That's what's tearing Mr. Sutton apart. He won't risk people's lives with a man like that on the scope—no, sir—but Mr. Sutton never could be hard-nosed. He's tried to help Harry. He sits up all night with him sometimes. He got him to private psychiatrists, and I think Mr. Sutton paid for some of those visits himself."

Hoagy seemed on the verge of tears again. "That's why he's leaving, Dr. Montours, but unfortunately, there's other Harry Boyles in that tower."

The old man wiped his eyes, and it was obvious that he didn't want to continue. Laura patted him on the back and thanked him for coming. Ten minutes and two Scotches after he left, she called the administrator.

"I just spoke to Mr. Washington. Harry Boyle *did* black out on the scope. He picked up a fire ax and went after Jeff Sutton."

There was a pause punctuated by heavy breathing.

"Whose side is that black man on, anyhow?"

"The side of safety, I suppose."

"I just had a conference call with Boyle and the head of ATC in Atlanta."

"And what's his version?" Laura asked.

"Well, he admitted the fire-ax business, but he claims he was only kidding."

"Kidding around with a fire ax?"

"Yes, yes, I know, but Boyle also says he didn't black out. He says he just took a brief pause, and he *was* controlling his targets."

"That's not Mr. Washington's recollection."

"All right. You talk to Dr. Striker, Sutton and Boyle in the morning, and call me before I leave Andrews Air Force Base at nine. I'm not going to play games with safety. We can get another man in there if Boyle is crazy. I don't want anything to go wrong in that tower."

"It won't," Laura said.

Thirty minutes later, Jeff Sutton picked up Laura in his gray interagency station wagon, and she asked almost immediately, "Jeff, are you going to tell me what happened in the radar room?"

"You already know. Hoagy Washington's been over to see you."

"You miss nothing, do you?"

"I'm facility chief. I have to know the little turns and twists of tower politics."

"You said we were going to be totally honest, so to keep my end of the bargain, I'll tell you now that Harry Boyle is going to be evaluated tomorrow by a Dr. Striker." She paused. "And I called the administrator. He's very upset about this Boyle situation. Morrison doesn't think you'll give the radar a fair test."

"All right, let's make a deal," Jeff said. "You've learned something about the tower already, right?"

"Yes, and I don't like what I saw, or, let's say, what I felt in there."

"Okay. We'll take a short trip in my bird, and you can view the situation from the sky. If you truly feel we're in trouble controlling the Miami traffic, tell the administrator I've been pacified. If not, tell the boss to get me out quick!"

"I'm supposed to mislead Morrison...deliberately?" she said slowly, trying to think through the ramifications of his suggestion.

"I have a chance to get the secretary's ear, and that's far more vital than embarrassing Morrison."

Laura thought again of the scene she had witnessed that morning in the cab when the Eastern captain had almost collided with a cargo plane...Hoagy's revelations about the incident in the radar room... the sweating faces of the youthful controllers. If she continued to fly, her own life might be at stake one day, if this man was right. Finally, she nodded.

The deal was made.

A few minutes later they arrived at the National hangar, where Jeff's sparkling deep-blue Waco biplane was fitted in between the mammoth jets. Jeff cranked over the engine and in five minutes the tower had slot-

46

ted the facility chief onto an active runway, and the ancient flying machine lifted off quickly.

The air cooled. The breeze shuffled past Laura's face, and sitting outside, hearing the air zing along the strut wires, she realized that this was flying in its purest form, the subtlest relationship between air and man, the way it all started.

Above, below, behind, in front, left, and right of the Waco, the Miami skies were dotted with big jets and small planes weaving between one another, banking left and right, as they took their orders from the tower cab and radar room, that frantic greenish place that was still imprinted upon Laura's mind.

Jeff was right, she thought. The air-traffic swarm was too squeezed. And Laura realized immediately how the San Diego and other midair collisions could have happened: far off in the west, the sky had turned coppery as the sun lowered, and the whole celestial expanse was dotted black with air traffic, as if a giant hamburger bun had been sprinkled with coarse pepper.

They banked back toward MIA and flew low over Thirty-sixth Street; Jeff pointed out row after row of private planes that had to be slotted into the snarl of terminal traffic. He dipped one wing low, easing back on his throttle, and then slid the Waco into the traffic pattern.

They were on the runway less than a minute before he pulled off, and they taxied far up to the northwest corner of the field to the "cockroach," or corrosion, corner.

It was an airplane graveyard.

The place consisted of a grease- and oil-stained ramp with grass popping up between the macadam cracks. In this area, once-proud airliners came to die as they corroded and rusted in the torrid salty air of Miami. While furniture and fine paintings may age with grace, ambering and taking on a patina, old airliners become as wretched as swiftly decomposing bodies. Their innards begin to smell and stain; their tires go soft and collapse as the rubber heats, and the aluminum skin becomes brittle and falls away, revealing the framework of bones.

As soon as Laura climbed out of the cockpit, she smelled the rot and decay.

"Why does a modern airport put up with an eyesore like this?" she asked, trying to fight the nausea building in her stomach.

Jeff moved around the old hulks as he explained how the graveyard began.

"Originally these old airliners were towed here to be broken up for junk. Then all of a sudden the air-cargo rates to South America shot up and a few opportunists thought: Why should we junk this fleet? We'll put these babies to work. So, with secondhand parts and a lot of prayers, probably, these wornout birds began humming again. The cockroaches are overloaded, misloaded, often flown by pilots who are either too young, too old, or too boozed-out to know what they're doing. As a matter of fact, these crates drop out of the sky all the time...on the runways...around the airport. About a month ago one of them came down on runway nine left over there. Seventy-four goats in the old passenger section were crushed to death, but the pilots walked away. We have so many mechanical failures around here that the Miami crash crews are the best-trained in the world."

"Can't the FAA keep those guys out?" Laura asked, studying the sickly old planes.

"Our jurisdiction over them is limited but we're getting tougher."

"Summing it up, then," Laura said, "you definitely need another airport. I saw that from the air. You should get these cockroaches out, as well as the small planes."

"Yes. We have acute traffic-mix problems. The Pipers land at fifty knots; others, like these wrecks, at a hundred. Then the big jets come in at one hundred and forty-five, and the Concorde sits down at one hundred and sixty knots. Think of a highway, Laura. What would it be like if some cars went along at twenty miles an hour and others at seventy in the same lane?"

"Eventually they'd all pile up."

They looked past the wrecks, and far beyond they could see the big and little planes coming into Miami; Jeff didn't have to detail the problem further.

Ten minutes later they were back in the air and Jeff headed his cherished old biplane southwest into the sun, which was now cuddled by long layers of gray-and-crimson clouds.

Soon the white specks of the cinderblock houses below thinned out and verdant patches of scrub pines and palmettos took over. Then, thirty miles west, they were out on the rim of the Everglades, where the lush Gold Coast slips back in time to a primeval land pocked with swamp ponds, occasional hardwood hummocks, and all girded by a sea of waving turtle and saw grass.

It was a frightening and alien place. The occupants were poisonous snakes, alligators, and fat mosquitoes.

Ahead Laura saw the sun pick up speckles from the liver-colored swamp ponds, and she wondered why they were flying into nowhere. Suddenly Jeff banked the plane and made a 180-degree turn back toward civilization and in seconds the throttle was chopped and the Waco was heading down toward a grass strip ringed by palmettos and palm savannas.

He feather-landed the plane and Laura did not get a good look at the surroundings because her eyes were pinned to an elderly woman standing like a statue on the far side of the grass strip. Jeff, who seemed to know who she was, taxied up to her and chopped his throttle.

"You might as well meet her," he yelled back to Laura as they climbed out of their divided cockpit.

"Who is she?"

"Harry Boyle's wife."

Jeff introduced Laura to the woman, who looked about as worn and lifeless as her husband.

"Want to come up to the house, Clara?" Jeff asked.

"No, Mr. Sutton, I'm in a hurry. Have to get

back...Harry will wonder where I am."

"Problems again?" Jeff asked mechanically, as if an old tale were continuing.

"Yes. I heard what happened this morning. Harry thinks you're against him," she said dully.

"That's not true, Clara. I've been his friend ...supported the man all these years."

"I know." She nodded. "About the evaluation tomorrow—you might as well forget it. Harry is in no shape to operate a radar." She sighed and began again. "This morning the thunderstorm woke me up and I heard our kitchen disposal running. When I went downstairs I saw Harry feeding a pile of grapefruit into the garbage disposal. They were all fresh grapefruit from the little tree by the side of our driveway. He went out in his pajamas in all that rain and picked the tree bare. He loves grapefruit," she added almost as an aside.

"Did you ask him why he was doing it, Mrs. Boyle?" Laura interrupted.

"Yes. He said that he had to destroy everything because of fruit bugs. But that's not true. We never have insects on our trees. It's hard for me to come here, Mr. Sutton, but I thought it was my duty to tell you. Harry's whole life has been controlling planes, but he's too sick now. I wanted you to know."

"Thank you, Clara," Jeff said, clasping the woman's hand. "I've known it for some time."

The plainly dressed woman said no more, and in a second she spun around and walked briskly toward her old Nova parked to the side of the grass strip. Jeff stood looking after her.

"Sad, isn't it?" he said.

"Very. But why didn't she just call you rather than drive out here?"

"I have no phone...and I make my own electricity."

"Good Lord," Laura said.

As they moved toward the house in the background, more of Jeff Sutton emerged in Laura's mind. For her the complicated parts of this man were forming a picture, or at least the outline of one; she realized already that she would never be able to satisfactorily slot or catalog Jeff.

The man was socketed into another age, some un-invaded time when problems were fewer and, perhaps, more basic.

His desk had been one clue, his house was another.

It was atypical for Florida: a two-storied clapboard structure with scroll boards along the vault of the roof and a tilting shade porch surrounded by a mock entablature and mail-order columns, the sort of prairie-Gothic house which might have formed an acceptable backdrop for a Grant Wood painting. The katydids were screaming away now and the swamp bugs sang their tune, but no other sounds could be heard, not even a distant car horn or the throaty whistle of a train.

"Used to be a lemon grove here in the twenties," he said. "The lemons died along with a lot of other South Florida dreams. I bought the acreage cheap."

"Must be lonely."

"Reminds me a little of Kansas," he answered quickly.

"What's the story behind your electrical boycott?"

"I found out I was being conned by the public utility company. Overcharged. I told them to get their lines the hell out of here."

"What do you have, gas lamps?"

"Oh, no." Jeff pointed to the far side of the landing strip. "Those two windmills give me enough power for the lights, and then I have a diesel generator for the air conditioner, plus extra AC loads."

"But you have to put oil in the generators?"

"Sure, but I get it for nothing."

"How?"

"Well, every other Saturday I go around to a bunch of gas stations and pick up the oil they drain out of cars. I have barrels of used oil...burns okay in the diesel generator. Not the best, but I strain the goop before I dump it in."

"But how do you possibly manage without a telephone?"

"Have a damn good base radio station. I can phone the Miami mobile operator—that's how the tower gets me—and I talked most of my friends out of using phones. In the long run, the radio is cheaper. You don't have to pay for line charges; the airwaves are free."

"You make Silas Marner look like a spender." She laughed.

"I'm not really cheap." Jeff flushed. "It's just that I don't like to be held up by public utilities. They're making a fortune on deals with the government, buying oil at one price and announcing another to their customers. I won't be lied to, and being a farm boy, I never had to 'take back,' as we used to say. There are always other solutions. No utility company is going to have me by the tail."

The inside of the house was neat and plain. Cooler fans hung from the ceiling, and the furniture was comfortable but functional, probably all sent east from Kansas. The kitchen looked like a set from a TV western. There was a pump for a water spigot, a large white pine table in the center, a big black wood stove for cooking, and the only concession to modernity was an icebox, circa 1937, with the cooling coils on top.

"It's kind of damp and chilly in here," Laura said, shivering a bit.

"I'll fix that in a second," Jeff said as he dumped a load of small cypress blocks in the stove and lit the crushed paper balls. Next, in the living room, decorated with more oil paintings of steam locomotives, he started the fire under the well-prepared bank of cypress logs.

In a matter of minutes the house was warm, and a mellow smell of well-dried wood drifted into the air.

"How about a toot?" Jeff asked.

"You mean you actually drink?" she asked, taunting him slightly.

"Sure."

He built two martinis and then they went into the

kitchen, where Jeff removed the cloth from two loaves of dough and placed them in the wood-burning oven.

Laura sat at the table studying the most interesting man she had ever met, one who confused her, for he bristled with so many convictions, some practical, some not. The question was not how Jeff Sutton existed in civil service, but how he managed life in the late twentieth century.

"Why didn't you become a railroad engineer?" she asked.

"I almost did. You see, we lived on this corn-producing acreage in Logan County, Kansas. My family went out there as homesteaders just after my great-great-grandfather was separated from the Union Army. The big thing every afternoon just at four-fifty was the coming of the Western's number sixty-two, pulled by a beautiful old four-eight-four...largest one on the line. It had to haul its thirty cars up the brow of the Rockies to Denver. The train didn't stop in Logan, but just outside of town it took on water from one of those overhead towers. Well, all through my youth I used to walk over there through the corn sections to see my four-eight-four."

"What does that mean, four-eight-four?"

"That's how the wheels were arranged. Anyhow, Snapper and I—that was my collie, kind of a medium-priced Lassie—used to go over to the roadbed and I'd put my ear to the track. I could hear the iron monster five miles away by the rail rumbles. Then she'd come through, all painted up royal blue, and the engineer and fireman would wave. We sort of knew each other. The embers floated out over the corn sections, and the clacks of the rail joints had their special melody. I thought the guy in there was a hero, driving the hell out of that big old thing. I wanted to be like that man when I grew up, but one day when I was fourteen the whistle sounded different, and Snapper and I rushed to the roadbeds, and do you know what?"

Laura shook her head, moved by the sweetness of Jeff's simple story.

"My four-eight-four was gone. They had a new diesel on the run, and the engineer didn't even wave at me...a different crew. A whole age passed that afternoon. But I got back at them."

"Did you dynamite the tracks?" she asked.

"No, I simply switched my allegiance from trains to planes. Come on, let's go into the living room."

They settled themselves in front of the crackling fire, and Laura said, "And that's how you got into air-traffic control?"

"Well, not exactly. After we rebuilt the biplane, I took my private and commercial tickets over at the Logan County Airport, and after a couple of years in the army, I headed the family bird down to Tulsa to sign up for American Airlines. They weren't ready for me," he said ruefully as he got up and paced.

"I would have been two thousandth in line. The man told me about air-traffic control. He said, 'Son, keeping the planes apart will be more important than flying them.' I wanted to control something, the way my family had always controlled its land. They were all fighters...heroes, in their own opinion."

Laura leaned back against the pillows of the couch and sipped her drink.

"Were they real heroes?" she asked.

"Well, they all came on with epic proportions, as if they were dumped out of the age of Pericles. My great-great-grandfather became a sodbuster after the Civil War, but we fought in all sorts of other wars—against the Spanish in 1898, the Germans in two wars, the North Koreans. None of the family ever made it to Vietnam."

"That's good."

"But we battled natural wars, too—droughts, blizzards, tornadoes, floods, corn bugs, and every other damn thing that gets to a small Kansas corn producer. We usually won. My grandfather had half his shoulder shot off in the battle of the Marne, and my father's whole back was a valley of shrapnel wounds from World

War Two. But do you know my father's greatest accomplishment in the war?"

"Well, let's see, he must have received plenty of medals...disability checks...."

Jeff took a gulp of his martini and returned to sit next to Laura.

"Sure, but that wasn't it. His greatest moment came before the war, or just when it started. He used to tell me this over and over again. 'You see, Jeff, Spivey Johnson'—he was our closest neighbor seven miles away—'well, Spivey and I were too old for World War Two. I was thirty-eight, he was forty. And they wouldn't take overage farmers with kids. So, Spivey and I pooled ninety bucks between us and we took the bus into Salina and we had this printer forge birth certificates saying we were only thirty-four. Then we joined up. Spivey got killed at Guadalcanal, poor guy, and I took a load of mortar fragments on Iwo, but, Jeff, we did our job. It needed doing.' So, that's how I was brought up. I thought air-traffic control needed doing, and I guess I wanted to be a hero like all the other Suttons."

He got up to watch his bread, and she followed him into the kitchen.

"You said you were a government lover, then a government hater. Why?"

"I came out of Kansas thinking that government was good. What mythology!"

"Well, I'd say it's necessary, but not necessarily good."

"I only met two government people when I was on the farm. One man came from the Department of Agriculture to find out why our corn crop was top-singed. He spent four days and never charged a thing. About two years later the FAA inspector came around to sign off our Waco. He stayed three days realigning the control cables, which my Dad and I had kind of screwed up. We tried to give the guy something for his trouble, but he said no thanks and just left the farm. Well, he did take two bags of fresh-picked Golden Bantam."

They picked up their drinks and moved back to the living room.

"All I knew about the government then was those two guys," Jeff said.

He moved closer to her on the couch, and they looked at the cypress fire for a long time, saying nothing, and then their hands were clasping each other. She turned to look at him, and there was hardly a second's delay before they embraced and their tongues were mingling sweetly, and she whispered, "I'm beginning to feel the wrong things."

"Why wrong?" he asked.

"I've never kissed a subject before."

"Is that what I am?"

"Technically."

They held each other again, and he could feel her firm breasts pressed against him.

"It's so damn unprofessional," she said, "and do you know what? I think I'm about to do something unprofessional...lie."

Ten minutes later Laura Montours was speaking to Ed Morrison through his private number in Georgetown.

"You sound funny, Dr. Montours," he said.

"I'm coming through on a radio-telephone system."

"Oh. What's the situation down there now?"

"Well, sir, I believe the last thing Mr. Sutton wants to do is embarrass you or the secretary tomorrow."

"That's a load off my mind. And what about Harry Boyle?"

"Sutton is going to let Dr. Striker make the evaluation along with me."

"I've spoken to Striker," the administrator said. "He feels that Boyle is tired but okay. I'm sure you'll back that up. I mean, Dr. Striker *is* the flight surgeon. He's aware of Boyle's...ah...shall we say, temporary stress."

"Yes, of course. I'll respect the doctor's opinion."

"Good. Well, I feel very relieved. But call me again before we take off from Andrews in the morning. I just want to be absolutely sure everything's okay."

"I will. Good night, sir."

"That was a beautiful lie," Jeff said, clearing the frequency and turning off the power.

After a roast-beef dinner, ringed by home-grown vegetables, home-baked sourdough bread, and coffee which had been ground in Jeff's kitchen from fresh beans, he said, "On the way back you'll be able to see the traffic around here in terms of blinking strobe lights."

"Isn't it a little touchy flying an old biplane around MIA at night?"

"No. A lot of small planes have only very little equipment, but mine's okay. It's completely equipped with Mode C—that's the transponder which sends out a signal to radar. Plus I have one of those encoding altimeters which tells them my altitude."

At 11:10 on the evening of the thirteenth, the biplane lifted off from Jeff's grass strip. They were only in the air about five minutes when Laura looked north and saw the sky smeared with moving lights, and she thought again of the men in the dark, locked radar room, those young men trying to keep the targets apart while the supervisors looked over their shoulders and the chatter went on and on, and the sweeps of the radar lazily circled the scopes. All night...all day...forty hours a week for each man, and maybe extra hours added to that...no official meal breaks...no windows... and a place that smelled like a locker room and looked like an institution.

In the inky-black sky, Laura, a woman whose emotions were usually subject to her professional training, was suddenly afraid to be up there in the swarm of aircraft all winding their way about in the darkness. She was going to ask Jeff to turn back, but something saved her from the embarrassing show of fear.

They suddenly flew into a chilly rain shower and the sky to the east and south of them was an avalanche of tumbling black clouds tinted on the high edges by the chromelike glare from the Miami skyline.

"I'm getting kind of cold and wet up here," she said

57

into her boom mike. "Have a guest room back on the farm?"

"Sure...but I can drive you home."

"That would mean a sixty-mile trip for you, Jeff, and tomorrow is a big day."

Jeff banked the Waco around and they headed back toward the small strip. In five minutes she saw his landing lights, standing out from the blackness like a thin, welcoming ally.

3

Jeff Sutton had married an ambitious woman from Coral Gables who eventually wanted much more from life than a husband limited to civil-service pay scales, and she felt little comfort living on the hem of a great swamp with a man who found victories in telling the utility companies to pull their lines out.

She discovered a wealthy English businessman who promised a lusher life outside London. When she announced her departure one night, Jeff was shocked; as a Catholic, perhaps he had taken the permanence of his marriage too much for granted. What rattled the Kansan more, though, was the loss of his daughter, Honey, a bright, beautiful girl whom he had taught to fly and change spark plugs and repair the diesel generator set.

Honey was only fourteen years old when Gloria Sutton took her to England, but she remained more her father's child than her mother's. She disliked the foreign food and weather, and she had no friends there who knew about the things her father had taught her. Finally, after three years of living in England and visiting Florida during the summer months, Honey wrote Jeff begging to come home permanently. And tired of trying to please her daughter and adjust her own social schedule to accommodate her, Jeff's ex-wife agreed.

Honey was flying into Miami on the fourteenth of February, and Jeff had picked that day for three reasons. It was St. Valentine's Day and the reunion would truly be a hearts-and-flowers occasion for him. It was also the date Jeff had scheduled for his annual vacation. Honey and Jeff would climb into their Waco with a few personal belongings and take an open-cockpit tour of the United States, seeing the cornfields of his youth and the national parks of the Southwest.

The trip was still planned, but it was no longer a "flying vacation," for Jeff Sutton was never returning to the tower. The fourteenth of February had also been chosen because Jeff's old friend Lou Griffis was skippering the Concorde in from London that day with Honey aboard.

Lou was a big, burly Australian whom Jeff had met in Miami when Celtic Airlines, a maverick airline, was planning its London-South Florida service. The founder of Celtic was a glib, outspoken route analyst who had been employed by several European airlines and dismissed by each because management could not come to terms with the man's abrasive personality.

Just as the 1973 energy crisis began, Roger Smith addressed an association of airline executives and said:

"I believe in the future of supersonic flight, but the Concorde is too small, its range too limited. The plane's a fuel gobbler, burning as much kerosene as a 747, and the Concorde can only lift one-third the payload. Now, the economic projections for this plane were worked out when aviation fuel was selling at eleven cents a gallon. What would happen if fuel went to one dollar a gallon?"

They all laughed. But the chuckles died out. Smith was right.

Still, he continued secretly to love the Concorde. He looked for an opening, some route structure where the SST could turn a healthy profit, and *he* could be that profiteer.

To the dismay of Jeff Sutton and a few others, Miami was quickly becoming a popular new gateway to the United States. International flights arrived from all directions—Europe, South America, Central America and Canada—and MIA's share of overseas traffic was escalating at a rate of twenty-six percent a year.

Smith spent months in Miami reviewing the load factors to and from London and Buenos Aires. Then he employed a research firm to establish how many of the passengers who regularly traveled between the city pairs would pay a high premium for supersonic service. The results were established and run on a computer which forecast the future passenger traffic.

Smith found his niche.

If a Concorde left London in the morning for Miami and then refueled for an afternoon flight to Buenos Aires, the seat demand would ensure a profitable operation.

Smith returned to London and met with formidable lending institutions. He said to one financial group:

"Now, the figures show the London–Miami and Miami–Buenos Aires are high-density routes, but each segment takes over eight grueling hours in a conventional jet. I want to put long-range Concordes on the service and I'll achieve my market share because I'll deliver happy, well-rested passengers in just under four hours on each leg."

"What would you charge on the London–Miami run?" a banker asked.

"One thousand six hundred and fifty dollars per seat."

"One way?"

"One way—no discounts."

"Nobody would pay that price for a ticket with all the cut-rate fares today."

"Yes, they would," Smith answered. "There are just

enough executives and wealthy people who would come up with the extra fare. They value their time more than their wallets."

"Mr. Smith," another banker said, "we've monitored the Concorde as a possible investment for years. You cannot reach Miami from Heathrow without a fuel stop, and that increases your time."

Smith smiled. "I'm not planning a fuel stop. The British and French airframe manufacturers tell me they can add additional fuel tanks if I give up some seats—plus, they'll improve the engines."

The banker shook his head. "Mr. Smith, in all my years of dealing with informed airline executives, this has to be the most outrageous proposal I've ever heard!"

Smith was tenacious.

For months, over wine and dinner, he begged, pleaded, coerced, and bribed every lender who would listen to him. In the end, Celtic Airlines was capitalized.

Three retrofitted SSTs began their London–Miami service, continuing on to Buenos Aires. Within six months Celtic was serving three additional cities from the Miami hub: Rio de Janeiro, São Paulo, and Paris. People who had the money stood in line for Celtic reservations. Smith's all-supersonic airline proved itself to be a brilliant marketing coup.

While Smith and the lenders were elated, the Celtic pilots, including Lou Griffis, were not. International regulations said that a flight had to arrive in the air over its destination with enough fuel for a ten percent contingency in flying time. The plane also had to have enough fuel to reach its alternate landing field and circle for thirty minutes. In the case of MIA, the alternate was Fort Lauderdale, almost next door.

Technically, the Celtic SSTs were arriving over Miami from London with the correct amount of fuel remaining. But if a massive weather system were to cover the entire state of Florida and the Bahamas, closing down all airports, the Concorde would run out of fuel. The reverse leg, Miami–London, was less of a problem. At that end the Concorde had many other landing options in the event Heathrow dropped below minimums: Shannon, Dublin, Prestwich, and about five additional airports could be elected. But under certain conditions, the Concorde could get in trouble over Miami.

"Of course we're in a spot if the entire state of Florida is socked in," the chief pilot replied. "But in that case, we'll drop into Bermuda for a fuel stop and, after all, Florida has clear weather ninety-five percent of the time. Nothing to worry about. The odds are very much on our side."

But the weather odds began to break down on the night of February 13. Throughout the afternoon of that day a cold front was lying in the Florida Strait between Cuba and the Keys. It was not an unusual weather condition for South Florida during the month of February, except for one thing. At two o'clock in the morning a bulk carrier plowing up through the Gulf of Mexico inbound to Tampico radioed the meteorological station on the Yucatán Peninsula, indicating that a low pressure had formed along the front. The Yucatán meteorological office redisseminated the report to the world's weather stations, stating that the core of the low pressure read 1,009 millibars and was deepening.

When Lou Griffis pulled his Jaguar into the employees' car park at Heathrow on the morning of the fourteenth, a sky of azure blue had broken through the dove gray of the British winter, and puffy cumulus were sailing over London, rim-lighted by a strong, bright sun. It was forty-seven degrees, and as Lou lifted his six-foot-two-inch frame from this squatty motorcar, he was bolstered by the fairness of the weather.

But when Lou entered the Celtic operations, a long functional room clogged with flight crews coming and going, weather maps, teleprinters, bulletin boards, and a level of human chatter which ricocheted off the gray plaster walls, he took one look at the en-route and terminal forecasts for his flight and realized that the

Miami weather was deteriorating swiftly. As he studied the deep low pressure over the Yucatán, Charles Moran, Lou's copilot, came up and surveyed the weather board.

Charles was a suave, dark-haired, ex-RAF bomber pilot who had been with Celtic from the beginning. Outwardly the two men were discrepant: Lou was a rough-hewn "Outbacker," heavy in the midsection, and he wore his dark blue uniform poorly. The pressure of his belly against his shirt sent out waves of blue wrinkles from his middle. Charles, on the other hand, was slim and faintly aristocratic; he looked and acted like a young life peer.

But on the inside where it counted, both pilots were identical: they were air-sensitive and knew their Concorde, her operating envelope, the strengths and limitations of the droop-nose spindle.

"What do you think, Charles?" Lou said after a long pause during which his teeth bit hard on the buttonwood end of his battered pipe.

"Don't like it, sir," Charles said.

Lou nodded.

It was now three hours before flight time: 11:00 A.M. Greenwich time, 6:00 A.M. Miami time.

Lou continued to study the map and finally said to his copilot, "Have you ever met Jeff Sutton?"

"No, sir."

"Hell of a nice guy. He's facility chief of the Miami tower. We're taking his daughter, Honey, with us today. Maybe I should call Jeff about this weather situation. He's a pilot himself...knows this local South Florida weather."

"It's all on the map, isn't it?" the copilot said.

"I've learned one thing, Charles, from years in this job. Don't always trust the map or the flight manual. A lot of this business sits up here in the head."

Lou Griffin understood Jeff's radio setup, and in fact, the cheery Australian was highly fascinated by one man's mastery of electricity and communications.

Lou called the Miami tower and asked them to contact Jeff Sutton with a full weather prognosis, and ten minutes later Jeff was put through to the Celtic operations office via his radio patched into the Bell System overseas line.

"How are you, Lou?" Jeff boomed.

"Fine, Jeff. Looking forward to seeing you later today. Did the tower bring you up-to-date on the weather down there?" Lou asked quickly.

"They did. Have it all written down in front of me."

"What do you think?"

"Miami's now reporting ten thousand broken. It's forecast to deteriorate during the morning. Typical overriding situation, Lou. Cold surface air wedging in beneath warmer air."

"How do these things usually go?"

"The low pressure on the stationary front is beginning to move at around forty miles per hour. We see this situation about twice a year. Typically, these low pressures move out to sea, and we'll experience a clearing trend starting west of us. The Yucatán first, then Key West, then Miami."

"Tell me this, Jeff. What's the worst that could happen? You know I'm coming in there without too much juice in my tanks."

"I realize that. And you have a very special cargo today."

"Right. So how do you read this?"

"The worst?" Jeff sighed. "All right—the low pressure could deepen and stall along the front, say, down in the Florida Strait. The overriding situation would be massive. We'd be looking at fog, indefinite ceilings, heavy rain from here up to Jacksonville. Also, a stalled low pressure would kick off embedded thunderstorms and possibly tornadoes."

"The system would be that massive?" Lou said, rather surprised.

"Yes, under the conditions I told you about."

"How many times have you seen this, Jeff?" Lou asked with a stutter in his voice.

"In my twenty-one years around Miami, only twice.

There's only about a five-percent chance of the low pressure stalling."

"So, that's my odds."

"I'd say so."

"But if it did stall, and Nassau and the whole state of Florida were fogged in, I'd be looking at an almost impossible landing with low fuel... and not enough kerosene to get me to a clear terminal facility?"

"You'd be in trouble, Lou. No doubt about that. It's your decision. I can't tell you one way or the other, but I trust you, old buddy."

"I'm going to request a fuel stop at Bermuda. If the Florida weather deteriorates, if the five-percent margin goes against me, I'll have enough fuel in my tanks for a diversion up to Atlanta."

"Sure. The system wouldn't extend that far."

"Well, that's my decision as of now. I'll be talking to you along the way. Are you going into the tower this morning?"

"Yeah, we have the FAA administrator and the Secretary of Transportation coming down today. Looking forward to our dinner tonight, Lou."

"So am I, Jeff. I'll be in touch."

Lou immediately phoned his boss, George Hornsby. Any departure from standard procedure had to be cleared first with Hornsby, and he, in turn, would check it with Roger Smith, who, despite his position as Celtic president, kept daily tabs on every operational aspect of the SST program that was making him richer every day.

"George, I'm requesting a Bermuda fuel stop," Lou said.

"What's wrong?"

"You ought to see this prog for the U.S. Southeast ...looks like a can of worms."

"We've never experienced nonpenetrable weather on the run."

"We have it today. Come over and take a look."

"I'll be right there."

Then George Hornsby phoned Smith, who was

breakfasting at his estate nine miles northeast of Heathrow.

"Mr. Smith, we have a flight irregularity."

"What is it, Captain Hornsby?"

"Lou Griffis just phoned me from operations. He wants to land at Bermuda, sir."

"Captain Hornsby," the airline president said, as he removed the remnants of a poached egg from his lower lip, "meet me in operations in, say, one-half hour. Make no statement or express any opinion to Captain Griffis until I arrive. I'm leaving straightaway."

Forty minutes later, Hornsby, a rugged, bald six-footer in his late fifties, was studying the weather map with Lou Griffis and Smith.

"I'm not a pilot, nor a weatherman," Roger Smith said distinctly. "I don't have to be. We have experts like you people for that. But today's flight is important. Captain Griffis, earlier this week you were sent a departmental memo. Dame Margaret Corbett is flying with us today on the Concorde. Do you recall the memo?"

"I...ah...went over it rather hastily, I'm afraid, sir," Lou said, trying to figure out the significance of what Smith was saying.

"You don't seem to remember what you read," Smith said disapprovingly.

"Well, sir, I get these memos every flight. There's hardly a trip goes out that some notable isn't sitting back there."

"Of course, of course. But, Captain Griffis, let me explain about Dame Margaret. You realize, naturally, that she's England's greatest living actress. She's never been in an airplane. The woman distrusts this mode of transportation. She's eighty-one and fit as a well-fed tiger. But it's essential that Dame Margaret get to the Miami Heart Institute as soon as possible, because her brother is critically ill there. As a matter of fact, I believe he's not expected to live. More than anything else, Dame Margaret is afraid of the landings. She told me that, so we don't want to unnecessarily put down in Bermuda today if we can reach Miami. One takeoff, one landing, a quickie...that's what I promised the lady, and, of course, I thanked her for choosing Celtic. We're not BAC, but we do get to Miami faster than anyone."

"Mr. Smith," Lou said carefully. "I don't care who's in the back of my Concorde. One life is no more valuable than another. I'm concerned about what's going on up front and in my fuel tanks. You know we're pushing our fuel reserves under the best of conditions. Today we have a meteorological collapse. The situation could be critical...all I wish to do is put the odds on our side. With a Bermuda stop-off, I don't have to worry. The Concorde uses abnormally high fuel rates at subsonic speeds. Let's say, Mr. Smith, that I'm committed to my Miami destination. I get there, and the field is fogged in with a lot of rain. So I divert to Fort Lauderdale, my alternate airport, but it's closed. Where do I put down within my fuel range?"

"How about Nassau?" George Hornsby spoke up.

"I spoke to Jeff Sutton, tower chief at Miami. He says the entire state and Nassau could be closed to all operations."

"Hardly likely," Hornsby said. "All right, Lou. You can reject the flight, but do it within the next half-hour so we can ring up a standby crew. You have every right to step aside without prejudice."

Lou heard the words and smiled to himself. Of course, there would be prejudice. If the flight went off routinely, nothing would be placed in Lou Griffis' permanent file, but no one at the British carrier would look at the senior captain in quite the same way again. A pilot is really known and appreciated not for how he lands the aircraft, but for the overall judgment which is the aggregate of his skills, the reason why he's paid forty thousand pounds a year.

As Lou walked out of the conference room, however, his mind was on Honey Sutton. If he rejected the flight, she'd be in someone else's hands, unless he could convince her not to go at all. As Jeff's daughter, she of all people should be aware of the dangers of air travel, but she was really excited about the trip: she was going home at last to be with her father. No, he wouldn't be able to persuade her to play it safe.

Lou Griffis had never feared responsibility, but this time there was no book of rules, no previous experience to tell him where his real responsibility lay.

The rain had started to ping off the metal roof of Jeff's prairie-styled house, and as Laura rested next to the man in his outsized bed, the kind frontier babies are born in, she felt as if she were holed up inside a tin can.

"How do you stand the noise?" Laura asked Jeff.

"Two solutions. I pull the covers over my head, and then I make love, and the raindrops go away."

She laughed. "Do you always have someone to make love to?"

"No. You're the first one in a long time."

She leaned over and whispered in his ear, "Well, maybe we should try your solution...again."

He smiled and reached out for her. His warm hands were skillful, touching her in all the right places, and soon she was moaning, hurrying him toward a climax which, when it came, was as explosive and fulfilling as the one before. Jeff groaned and rolled over to his side of the bed. They both lay there silently as the raindrops plopped away overhead.

Jeff arose first and dressed and started his wood stove and reignited the cypress logs in the fireplace; soon the house was warm and scented by a light drifting smoke.

When Laura came downstairs wearing Jeff's bathrobe, she had had time to think and consider her own confusion: as a psychologist, she was supposed to undo other people's pressures, but this was a situation she had personally created.

"Is the weather getting you down?" Jeff asked, sensing her despondent mood.

"No, I'm getting me down."

"What's the matter? I thought it was a great odyssey last night."

"Fantastic trip," she said almost mockingly.

Laura padded about the kitchen, and under her light step the slash-pine boards creaked; the hickory chips glowing in the potbellied wood stove were spitting and crackling. The mellow noises inside formed a counterpoint with the harsher sounds outside: the peal of the wind and the pelting rain.

She felt odd and rueful.

Jeff's house seemed as out of place as if she had suddenly stepped aboard a time machine and been whisked back to rural Kansas in the late nineteenth century. And it was not only the setting which haunted her, but the man walking around the old-fashioned kitchen. He looked perfect in the setting, for he was dressed in just the trousers of his Sunday suit, and he was so lean and wiry that he had to wear suspenders over his broad, bony shoulders to hold the pants up.

But it was more than feeling she'd been dropped in another century—Laura felt a certain self-loathing.

For some reason she had panicked in the open plane the night before. She could not explain the fear, and this was curious and upsetting, for her business was human emotions and her logbook showed just over three hundred hours of flight time. Maybe it was the experience of sitting outside in an open-cockpit plane at night, seeing the streaks of fast jets clog the horizon, like a disco light show gone mad.

And compounding her strange fear were her other actions. She had lied to Morrison; she knew very well that Jeff Sutton was not going to play the agency game for the administrator. Jeff had every intention of telling the secretary just what he felt about the airport and ATC, and Laura knew it.

Besides deceiving a client, she had gone to bed with her subject, willingly and joyfully. It was the first time in her life that she had conducted herself this way. She wondered what had happened to her so quickly.

Laura looked out the window at the downpour, then turned to Jeff and said, "How is this rain going to affect the radar demonstration?"

"In a way, it's the ultimate test. In weather like this, the only way to see the planes is on a scope."

Jeff looked at Laura's face, drenched in gloom. She had not smiled that morning.

"I'm sorry about last night," he said slowly. "It was my fault."

"No, it wasn't. I was just trying to figure out why I did it."

"Maybe you love me."

She spun around and smiled for the first time. "That's arrogant!"

"I guess it is."

"You're an enigma...in love with the past...the old house here...your plane...your desk. To you, the past was better. The present stinks, and there's probably nothing wrong with the new radar. You detest it because it's new."

"No, that's not true. There has to be progress, but I can't see the wrong machine replacing a man. Today I'm going to show the secretary what radar should be. I've built a model of what I think is the proper radar for the future."

"You built a radar? Well, I'm not surprised—you are in the utility business."

"The radar doesn't really function. It's merely a mock-up."

"I'll be interested in seeing that."

"You will."

She walked about the kitchen, and Jeff started the eggs in a frying pan that looked as if it had swung off the tailgate of a horse-drawn chuck wagon.

"I suppose the eggs come from your own chickens?"

"My neighbor's. I supply him electricity and he gives me fresh milk and eggs."

"You have the whole Kansas scene going, don't you?"

"I don't like your comments this morning," Jeff said

stiffly. "I've already apologized for last night, if that's what's bothering you."

She crossed quickly and kissed him.

"Sorry, Jeff. I'm just in a foul mood. The weather, I guess, and I'm not looking forward to facing the administrator after I conned him over the phone."

"Again, that was my fault."

"What really bothers me is you."

"Why?"

"Well...you remind me of the way I used to be. I was brought up down on the Delta, and I had these enormous dreams like you. First, I was going to organize the shrimp packers because they were working for ten dollars a day. I wanted to be a fighting labor leader, and I almost went to law school. In the late sixties I marched for everything until I had calluses on my feet."

"What happened?"

"The calluses went away. After I graduated from the University of Chicago with a Ph.D. in the head business, there were only two things open. I could teach or become an industrial consultant. I suddenly forgot the shrimp packers...never went back to the Delta...never thought of it again. I was earning twenty thousand dollars, then thirty thousand, then forty thousand. And I was telling one lie after another."

"Why did you have to do that?"

"Jeff, skull inspection is big business. I was a yes-person. I used to see one production line after another raping what dignity those workers had. They got fat and drank too much and died, never really knowing why they had lived. But the corporations wanted more work out of them. So I told them what they wanted to hear. I lost my guts. I wouldn't get up there and tell them that they were operating dangerously demoralizing production lines. I'd have been out on the street if I did. Then I come down to Miami and meet a man who takes enormous risks, and I see in you something of myself the way I used to be. And I have to ask: how can you take so many career risks?"

"Because ATC deals with human lives. That's why," Jeff said rapidly.

"And you don't care what happens to you?"

"I want to be heard. In my business, you can't be a yes-man if you intend to keep your conscience. Half the men in the tower know we're operating on luck. They don't speak up. I don't blame 'em, but I'm the tower spokesman. What I say is true for them, too."

"But it all comes down to nothing. This is your last day. What does a man like you do now, stand on the corner in a blue uniform and direct traffic?"

"I don't know what I'll do. All I know is that I won't continue in that control tower. I'm not going to be a muzzled yes-man!"

"I might be out on the unemployment line with you. I can just hear Morrison getting back to my boss—'That little bitch double-crossed me!'"

"But you've seen the air-traffic conditions down here now, Laura. Are you convinced that I'm right?"

"From what I've observed so far, yes."

"Then it doesn't matter. Come out west with me and we'll set up a fruit stand together."

"There's an optimistic career goal. Seriously, Jeff, I'm going to be very interested to see what happens to you."

"I'll be interested, too," he said, flipping the eggs up and over. "But like I said, I'll never be a yes-man."

"Either you're the biggest fool I've ever met or you have totally archaic guts. Maybe both. And I think I've suddenly caught some of your craziness."

She broke into a wide smile as he crossed the creaky boards and grabbed her in a big bear hug. She pulled away for a moment and looked up at him with a playful smile.

"Maybe I do love you a little, Jeff Sutton," she said just before he kissed her again.

The rain continued to saturate the air. The wind was now swirling at twenty knots an hour, and Jeff left his

Waco tucked inside the hangar and drove Laura over to the Ramada Inn, where she changed.

They arrived at the tower at 7:50, and Jeff immediately placed a phone call to Lou Griffis.

"Lou," he said, "here's our present Miami weather— 4,000 broken, in light rain. The low pressure is deepening significantly. There's a rapid movement on the front to the northeast. It's normal progress for this sort of meteorological condition."

"I demanded a Bermuda fuel stop, but management voted me down for reasons I'll explain later."

"Lou, are you taking the flight?" Jeff asked with growing concern.

"I don't know yet."

"Make me a promise," Jeff said urgently. "If you reject the flight, get my daughter off the plane and come in tomorrow. I don't want her up there without you. If you reject the flight, Honey's not going either. That's *my* order!"

"I understand, Jeff. I'll call you back within half an hour.

Laura had put on her most conservative dress, a dark blue ultrasuede, and her glistening black hair was pulled back into a knot. Still, she did not look hard or too official until she pulled out her horn-rimmed glasses and began to read Harry Boyle's file in Jeff's office. She looked up at Jeff, smiled, and returned to the file.

"Harry sounds like he should be institutionalized. He has missed a lot of work time. Is he the oldest man in the tower...I mean, besides Mr. Washington?"

"Yes. Hoagy's way over seventy."

"Are you sure? Isn't that against the rules?"

"I have a feeling the man has sort of tickled his employment record, but Hoagy's one of those rare types who can go on controlling planes forever."

"How old is Mr. Boyle?"

"He's only fifty-one."

"My God, he looks seventy-one."

"I know."

"Jeff, did you ever look at yourself in the mirror? That suit...did you get it off some scarecrow?"

"That bad, huh?"

"Dreadful, and way out of style. I'm going to buy you some clothes."

"For my next job I may only need a bathing suit. I'm a damn good swimmer, and I could always be a life-guard."

As they laughed the door opened and a man who Laura assumed was Dr. Striker walked into the office clutching a cargo of files. He was a weary, bulky man who was nearing his government pension. Jeff introduced Laura to the man, and the three of them sat down while Harry Boyle waited outside in the reception area. The doctor opened up a bulging folder which was thumb-marked and dirty on the edges, indicating to Laura that Harry Boyle was an old and frequent patient of the FAA flight surgeon.

"I can't say, Dr. Montours, that we haven't had problems with Harry Boyle," Dr. Striker began. "Perhaps he should be out of the system, but let me inform you of this man's past. It's rather tragic in a way."

Laura shook her head and said, "Dr. Striker, we're not here to understand why Mr. Boyle is in trouble. I'm supposed to report to the administrator on one point only. Can Harry Boyle operate the radar today for the secretary?"

"He might be able to."

"If it's only 'might,' then let's forget it," Laura said swiftly.

"Dr. Striker," Jeff interrupted, "you and I have argued for years, but I'm still the head of this tower until five o'clock today, and I say Boyle is *not* handling the radar."

"You're a contradictory man, Mr. Sutton," the doctor said.

"Explain that!" Jeff thundered, his tan face turning a light red color.

"You say you're all for your men. Fine. But how

many of them are misfits? One fellow—what is his name...oh, yes, Ramsey—sucks his thumb. Another controller in this tower is a flunked-out radio announcer who thinks he's still spinning discs instead of controlling planes."

"I know who you're talking about, and that's not true. Besides, I never said I had the quality of man I needed in here."

"There's also a bunch of frauds in this place."

"I've had enough of this! You don't know a damn thing about our operation, Dr. Striker. This is only—what?—the third time in eleven years that you've been inside the tower."

"Ah, but I know what the men say to me, and I'll tell you...since you're leaving now, it doesn't matter. There are controllers in here right now who are planning nervous breakdowns. Fakes. Goddamn fakes! One man had the audacity to tell me last year, 'I'm going to go crazy. I'll collect my disability, and then my brother and I are going to open a lumberyard.' These guys are just doing their time. Like prisoners."

"That's the rare exception, Dr. Striker," Jeff said. "Most of these men are dedicated."

"May I ask you a question, Doctor?" Laura said. "From your knowledge of ATC, would you say that a controller's job is almost an impossible one at the present time?"

"No, no. These men are well paid and—"

"Not well enough," Jeff said.

"But why are most of them so young, Dr. Striker?" Laura asked.

"Well, they do tend to leave the system early...way before fifty-five," the doctor answered.

"In other words, they're burnt out?"

The doctor shifted about in his seat and pondered the question. "True, it's a young man's game. But take Boyle. He's one man who desperately wants to stick it out. Means everything to him. When he was a kid, he was the worst baseball player in the Albany Recreational League. He likes to play the guitar, and he enters the bluegrass competition down here every year, but Harry's the worst picker and stomper in South Florida. He couldn't catch a baseball and he can't make a guitar sing. But one thing Harry Boyle knows is controlling planes, and that's made up for everything else."

"Harry was great at one time," Jeff agreed. "Very steady, and he knew the picture around this terminal better than anybody."

"But now you're telling him he's finished," the doctor said.

Jeff then told the flight surgeon about the grapefruit incident and Clara Boyle's visit the evening before. About ten minutes later Harry Boyle was brought into the room, and Laura asked him how he felt.

"Fine," Boyle said quickly. But he was sweating as he spoke, and looked like a broken man.

"I see nothing wrong with Harry operating the radar," Dr. Striker said, "as long as you'll be right there, Mr. Sutton, and you'll have backups in the radar room. Do you agree, Dr. Montours?"

"I don't agree. The man is too ill."

"I'm *not!*" Harry burst out. "What do you know, coming in here for one day? You know nothing! Listen," Harry said, as if pleading for his life. "I've looked forward to this demonstration for six months. I wanted to say I was the one who showed the new radar to a man on the Cabinet level. It was me, Harry Boyle. So, I've had a bit of trouble lately, but it's only temporary. Doesn't anyone ask about my twenty-seven good years in the tower...all the planes I've brought in and departed...the passengers who got here because Harry Boyle knew exactly what he was doing. Does anybody say, 'Good work, Harry. We won't forget you.' Look, see this? It's my twenty-year pin."

Laura Montours did not know whether it was sadder to see an old controller trying to hang on for his big moment, or the young ones working for the time when they could wear their own cheap little FAA pins.

"Harry," Jeff said, placing his arm about the man's

dandruff-flecked shoulder, "I do want you in the tower when the administrator and the secretary arrive."

"To watch in the background?" Harry said. "Is that all I'm good for now?"

"No, that's not it, Harry. You can explain the CORAD operation while I actually run it."

"You're really telling me to get out because I'm too sick. Dr. Striker says I can handle it."

"But I'm the head of the tower. My authority as facility chief overrides Dr. Striker."

"Yes, Mr. Sutton, you override me," the doctor said, "but the administrator can override you."

"That's true."

"Then I suggest that we get right on the phone to the administrator now."

"I'd like to speak to Mr. Morrison myself," Harry said weakly.

"I don't think that would be appropriate, Harry. Why don't you wait outside and let us settle this?" Dr. Striker said.

"I can operate it, Jeff. You know I can."

Jeff did not react one way or the other, and when Harry left the conference room, Dr. Striker said, "Perhaps Harry has had it. But just to give the man his last little scrap of dignity isn't going to hurt a damn thing."

"That's precisely why I'm leaving this tower," Jeff said. "One side of me says give Harry a break. Be sympathetic, reward a man who has devoted his whole life to ATC. And what has he got to show for it? A little pin and, eventually, some disability checks. But the system cannot tolerate the Harry Boyles. We can't operate on past performance. It's the here and now, not the then and there. We have deteriorating weather conditions for Miami today. The boys in the tower will be on edge because the secretary and the administrator will be in the cab. I cannot let Boyle near that radar. Let's make the phone call, but hear me straight, Dr. Striker. If Harry Boyle is in charge of traffic in this tower for even five seconds, I'm not going to be here. And you take the responsibility!"

Ed Morrison was up very early that morning; he had shaved carefully and put on his new custom-made suit for the Miami trip. Morrison knew that the secretary's approval of CORAD could change his entire economic future, and the man was so certain now that he was about to succeed that the phone call from the Miami tower completely unnerved him.

Laura Montours explained what had happened so far, and finally Ed Morrison said, "I can replace Sutton. You know that."

"Of course, sir," she answered.

"But let's do this. We'll make the decision later this morning. Naturally, I don't want a sick man showing himself to the secretary, any more than I want an arrogant facility chief like Sutton spouting off with his idealistic solutions."

"Then what do you suggest?" Laura asked. "It's Harry or Mr. Sutton."

"I understand. But is Sutton going to cause trouble?"

"Only if Harry Boyle remains on duty."

"Dr. Montours, when you came to my office the other day, I told you how vital this demonstration was. It isn't easy to get the secretary down there for a personal visit."

"I'm sure it isn't."

"You could have made a small concession here. If you and Dr. Striker both concur that Boyle is fit, Sutton could hardly argue with that."

"Mr. Morrison, I'm sure you wouldn't want a man like Boyle functioning in a busy control tower. Wait until you see him."

"Well, on the other hand, it might be the best demonstration."

"Explain that, sir," Laura said quickly.

"The whole point of CORAD and our other computer anticollision systems is not only their accuracy, but the fact that the electronic brain doesn't collapse. Once we have it programmed, the computer cannot become a Harry Boyle."

"I can't comment on that, Mr. Morrison."

"Well, I'll make a few calls. Dammit...wish I could delay this trip, but I can't. I'll talk to Boyle when we get down there. You're still sure that Sutton will give us a fair test and keep his loud mouth muzzled if we go along with him on this?"

"I don't know what the man will say to the secretary, but I can assure you he wouldn't purposely dissuade the secretary with a false or prejudiced demonstration."

"That's some consolation. See you later."

Morrison put down the phone and felt his stomach weaving about; he went to the bathroom and took two tranquilizers and then attempted to read the Washington *Star*, trying to plan his next move. He could warn and prepare the secretary on the way down to Miami; he knew that, but one other call had to be made: Al Cummings, the head of the computer company that had built CORAD, had to be forewarned about what was happening in Miami that morning.

He phoned the man at his office in Chevy Chase and explained the Boyle-Sutton conflict, and then the computer executive, a raspy-sounding man, said, "Ed, you should have removed Sutton right away after that TV barrage, and somebody must have known about Boyle. What are we paying him?"

"Nothing. I don't want to take that kind of risk, Al."

"So, what's he getting as our salesman...a free lunch?"

"No, I promised him we'd bring him up to Washington for a good position in ATC. An office job on the GS-fifteen level."

"Why didn't you check him out?"

"I did. The man had a good record; nothing on his report."

"Well, why do we need Boyle? Can't somebody else do the demonstration?"

"Harry Boyle is an experienced controller, a tower veteran, and we originally thought that if a man like that argued for our radar, it would carry a lot of weight...offset some of Sutton's criticism. If we replace him at this point, there's no telling how he'll react. He might get angry and start blabbing about a lot of things in front of the secretary."

"Shit!" Al Cummings said. "Ed, we've worked on this deal a hell of a long time. Whatever you do down there, don't blow it. Based upon your say-so, we've dumped a big bundle into this developmental program, and unless the secretary is pleased, we're going to be looking at a goddamn deficit. We'll never get out of this hole unless the agency orders these radars."

"You have my word. But the budget has to come from the Hill, and the secretary is the key."

"Then you be certain that it goes off all right today. Check with me later."

The phone clicked off and Ed Morrison instinctively moved toward the medicine chest in his bathroom, but then he remembered that he had just taken two tranquilizers. So he decided he would take a walk around his block in Georgetown before driving to Andrews Air Force Base. Suddenly he saw the entire "inside deal" going sour, and he tried to rationalize the risks he was taking. Ed Morrison wished he had never heard of CORAD, Boyle, or Sutton; in fact, at that point, he desperately wished he were back in the bus business.

4

For a North Florida accountant named Sean McCafferty, the fourteenth of February meant the fulfillment of a long- and well-plotted dream. At eight o'clock on the morning of the fourteenth he walked with a puffed chest out to his amphibious float plane parked on the Tallahassee Airport ramp and climbed in with his wife, Connie, and their two daughters, Katie, seven, and Hillary, twelve.

Sean had carefully preflighted his single-engine plane, and when he checked his Miami terminal forecast, he discovered it was foul. But being a prudent man, he also studied the prognosis for the stationary front and the associated low pressure; he found it was forecasted to move out to sea, evoking a clearing trend later. Sean was *not* told that the low pressure could stall, as weather reports are based on nothing more than the best averages of what usually happens, without taking into account everything that could go wrong. The weather specialists figured that Sean's flight would take four hours and a half, for his plane moved like an overfed Canadian goose, only one hundred and twenty-five miles per hour. By the time he reached Miami, the weather would be open, with scattered ceilings through which he could sneak down. And even if MIA remained veiled and clamped in the low-pressure system, Sean knew he could always put his light plane down on a lake or a grass field if necessary. It wasn't as if he was flying a Concorde.

Sean was confident and buoyant as he took off that morning into fast-moving scattered clouds. The sun was shining dully through the high lacy clouds, and even if the wind had been howling and the precipitation down on the deck, Sean would have taken off anyhow. He *had* to fly to Miami that day.

As a boy Sean had fallen in love with airplanes, the idea of flight, its freedom and self-determination. But as a man he had been early harnessed to the pressures of bringing up a family and paying for so many necessities, and his dreams of the world of flying had been fed merely by aviation magazines. His CPA's salary with the eight-man Tallahassee firm was far too small to allow him to enter that glorious world himself.

But then Sean rationalized his dream: he would turn flying into a "necessary business venture." He knew there was an Association of Flying Accountants in the state of Florida, and each year they convened for a meeting and dinner-dance at the Eden Rock Hotel in Miami Beach. From that Sean began to construct his fantasy: he would become a pilot; he would join the association, and then one day he would fly his family down to Miami Beach for the convention. He was a fine accountant and he felt that if he mingled with partners of the big national firms in Miami, he could probably expect a job offer. After all, he would be one of them, a member of the flying accountants, an insider who might logically attract the attention of his fellow club members.

Privately, his wife thought it was a long shot, for Sean had already solicited several national accounting firms, such as Price Waterhouse and Arthur Andersen, for possible job openings, and the answers had been prompt and negative: the waiting list was too long.

But Sean was sure that the Association of Flying Accountants would give him an edge. How many other candidates for the big firms could sit down right next to a partner and have something in common?

But Sean's lift-off from Tallahassee that morning meant more than just the possibility of a better job; it was also a triumph over his own ineptitude. When he had started taking flying lessons, the analytical accountant, of far-above-average intelligence, found that for some inexplicable reason he could not land a plane. Take off, yes. Land, no. Since getting back to the ground in a controlled manner is an important aspect of safe flight, Sean went through a series of landing traumas that almost wrecked his hopes—along with a string of small training planes.

As the forty-one-year-old accountant headed his plane south that morning, he began to review just how much trouble and expense had been required to place in his wallet the small green card that certified him a private pilot with an instrument rating.

Around the Tallahassee Municipal Airport where he trained, Sean had been called the fuzzy-eyed bird, meaning that he couldn't see or judge the distance to the runway very well. Airport personnel and hangers-on always held their breath when he landed, or, more properly, made contact with concrete. When the hangar rats saw Sean's plane wriggling down on final approach, they would yell, "Here he comes! Here he comes!"

Mechanics would drop their tools; linemen would pull out their fuel nozzles; secretaries in the offices would go to the windows to watch. A few of the more sadistic types were probably hoping that someday Sean would splatter his machine all over the runway; they were the sort who attended the Demolition Derby every other Saturday night on the racetrack outside Tallahassee.

Sean often came close to breaking up his bird, but he never had an accident. Most people, including the Piper dealer on the field, said that only proved how strong and forgiving light airplanes were, and on several occasions, unknown to Sean, an engineer from Piper had come up from Vero Beach to find out how the product withstood such brutal and repeated punishment.

When he first presented himself at the Piper dealer's office on the Tallahassee field, the man at the desk said, "Mr. McCafferty, anybody can learn to fly. We'll give you a ten-dollar introductory lesson."

So the diffident accountant in a stiff-collared shirt went up that day with high hopes; he flew the plane straight and level in the practice area, and when they landed, the instructor said, "Mr. McCafferty, I've never had a first-time student who was such a natural. You'll be a fine pilot in no time. A piece of cake for an intelligent, mature guy like yourself."

Puffed up, Sean started the course: ground school and flight lessons. He passed the written ground-school examination with a grade of one hundred; he was extremely retentive and, as the instructor said, his IQ was much higher than most people's.

But Sean's air work was something else. In his first lessons he practiced stalls, held certain altitudes and course, but when they started on the landings, the instructor knew he was in for trouble. He was used to uncoordinated students. He knew that a student pilot *had* to develop a sense of depth perception, of his own proximity to the runway, so that the airplane stopped flying and touched down at approximately the same time.

But with Sean, the elements of landing a plane never came together. He was either too high or too low, too slow or too fast, and it chattered the teeth of his exhausted instructor.

"Mr. McCafferty, I think it's your eyesight. We've been practicing landings for seventeen hours and you don't seem to get it. You go from one problem to another. It's like golf. A man picks up a slice; he corrects that, then starts hooking the ball. Why don't you have your eyesight checked?"

Sean never told his wife that he couldn't land a plane. The lessons seemed to go on and on, with Connie always asking, "When are you graduating?"

"In a while," he would say, and then change the subject.

Sean went back to the FAA flight surgeon for another eye check, but his vision was far above the FAA standards. Then he talked to the owner of the flight school.

"Maybe," Sean suggested, "it's the instructor. Perhaps someone else would give me a different approach to landings."

"I think that can be arranged," the fixed-base operator said.

When the new instructor arrived, the first instructor went out on the field to greet him. "You've inherited the world's worst flier," he told his successor. "The Irishman just can't set a plane down."

"Bullshit. I've been teaching grandmothers to fly for twenty years. There's no one who can't be taught. Some people take longer than others, but I've never had a failure."

The first instructor smiled and walked away.

After six lessons with Sean McCafferty, the new instructor faced the fact that his record had been ruined. He said nothing to Sean, but one day the head of the school asked to see the accountant.

"Mr. McCafferty, I noticed by your logbook that you've had forty-seven lessons and we still can't turn you loose for a solo."

"I have a little trouble landing."

"*More* than a little trouble. You just can't do it, for some reason."

"The man told me when I signed up that anyone could learn to fly. I'm reasonably intelligent. I played high school basketball, so I'm not uncoordinated. My eyesight's fine. It must be your teaching techniques."

"No, sir. We've soloed seven hundred students here, and we enjoy a perfect safety record. But you're just not good for business. First of all, we guaranteed you a license at our package price of $1,250, but you've already spent $1,740 and we can't even solo you. Then there's the question of our insurance, Mr. McCafferty. If we let you solo and you smash up the bird, we'd have to take it out of service rather than let the insurance company raise our rates."

"What makes you think I'll break the plane up? Haven't done it yet."

"True. But each time you go up, the instructor has to take over and land for you. If you were alone, you wouldn't have that help."

"You're exaggerating," Sean said. The fear that he would never solo began to show in his broad, homely face.

"I've seen your landings. For some reason you are the one student in a million who can't get a plane down. I've heard of that...although it's never happened here. How can I take any more of your money? This could go on for years; the FAA flight inspector will think we don't know what we're doing. Why don't I just refund half your deposit and we'll call it quits? Nothing to be ashamed of. Just one of those things."

"I'm not quitting," Sean said resolutely.

"It's your cash, but Mr. McCafferty, I don't think we'll ever solo you. I mean, if you just want to take airplane rides with us at fifty-two dollars an hour, fine. We're on the field to make money. But I can't promise that you'll ever get a license. In fact, I'd say you won't."

Sean was heartbroken. He desperately wanted to solo so he could attend the accountants' convention, and it was only eight months away. He let a couple of weeks go by and then returned to the flight office.

"What if I bought my own plane?" he said. "Would you let me solo? That way, it would be my equipment, not yours."

The operator thought for a long moment. Not only would he escape a readjustment in his insurance if Sean plowed one in, but he would also make a profit on the sale.

"Mr. McCafferty, you're on. But don't forget, if you do solo and keep your plane together, you will have to pass the flight examination. We have no control over that. If the FAA inspector doesn't think you qualify, then you don't get the piece of paper."

"I realize that, but I still think I can do it. You know, all my life I've wanted to fly, to be near planes. That's why this is so strange."

"What, Mr. McCafferty?"

"For years I read aviation magazines and lived the life of a pilot vicariously because I couldn't afford lessons. Now that I do have the money, I find that I can't fly."

The fixed-base operator, a tough Texan, was touched by Sean, the pleading in his eyes, his sincerity.

"Well, I wouldn't take this as a personal defeat, Mr. McCafferty."

"But I do. I'm growing older. I feel the nudge of age, and the time is getting shorter."

"Yes." The FBO nodded, feeling a sense of responsibility for the sad man leaning on the counter before him. "Mr. McCafferty, I can't in good conscience sell you a new or a secondhand Piper. I'd make a few bucks on the deal, sure, but how would I feel if you sprayed the machinery all over the runway? You could always try another operator, of course. Any dealer will give you lessons if you buy a plane from him. But give me a little time to work on this. I want to help solve your problem."

Sean thought for a minute and finally nodded. "That's fair," he said.

He walked out into the sunlight and felt about as downcast as a man could be. His supreme desire, his obsession, had been squashed. He was moody for the next three days, but one night a call came from the FBO.

"Mr. McCafferty, I might have a solution. Could you come over in the morning?"

"How about tonight?"

"Well...ah...all right."

When Sean walked into the small office of the FBO, the man was seated beside his paper-littered desk.

"Mr. McCafferty, most people who take lessons are just numbers to me. Frankly, we're very seldom moved except by checks."

"I realize that," Sean said, sliding into a seat. "I'm an accountant."

"But I said to myself, 'Here's a special case. What kind of plane could get you through the test and not endanger your life or somebody else's?' I called a few guys in the business and told them about you. I didn't mention your name. Everyone said to me, 'The man needs a Helio Courier.'"

"A helicopter?"

"No, no. It's fixed-wing aircraft designed for STOL operations—short-field takeoffs and landings."

"Do I need that? There's plenty of runway out here."

"Well, let me explain what this plane is. It has a big wing with slats so it doesn't stall or spin. It can land at about thirty-five miles an hour under perfect control.

Originally, these Helios were developed for rough work, like bush operations where the field was nothing but a mud strip hacked out of the jungle."

"But I don't plan to operate out of the jungle."

"Yes, I know, but this aircraft is solidly built. It's tubular-constructed, very strong. It's almost impossible to get killed in one of these. The cockpit can withstand a fifteen-G load impact; the pilot is in kind of a cocoon. And with those slow landing speeds, there's not much damage you could do to the plane." He paused. "But we have problems with the Helio."

"You just said there were no problems."

"Well, most Helios have the old-fashioned wheel in the back. Conventional gear. Now, that's very difficult to land, as you know. The center of gravity is behind you, and a lot of guys who aren't experts ground-loop these birds. *You'd* ground-loop for sure; you can't even land a plane with the tri-gear, and that's much easier than a tail-dragger."

Sean nodded.

"Okay, now. There happens to be a tri-gear version of the Helio Courier available, and in your case it would smooth out your landings, because you can drop it in at thirty-five or forty...too slow for bending."

A victorious smile was beginning to spread across Sean's face.

The fixed-base operator looked at him and then said, "I called around at my own expense, and they want about seventy-five thousand for these tri-gear Helios."

"Seventy-five thousand!" Sean cried out.

"Yeah, it's a bundle."

"I can't afford that."

"Didn't think so, but, Mr. McCafferty, it's the bird for you. The only winged thing I'd advise at the moment."

Sean walked out of the FBO's office just about as dejected as he'd been the last time. But two days later the fixed-based operator called him again.

"Mr. McCafferty, I might have the answer."

At lunchtime the following day Sean showed up at the field.

"You know," the man began, "I've made about fifteen phone calls for you. This has become a real challenge. I'm going to get you up in the air, Mr. McCafferty, if I have to hang you on a hot-air balloon."

"Hope it won't come to that."

"No, no. But we were talking about this Helio Courier."

"Way out of my price range."

"Of course, but I found a Helio on amphib floats."

"I don't want a seaplane. I can't swim."

"Well, this one is offered for sale at forty-six thousand dollars by the University of Miami Marine Laboratory. They used it to find fish or something. It has wheels that come out of the floats, four of them, and they're quite far apart. So considering the Helio's low-speed landing ability and the four wide-track wheels...I can't imagine you busting it up."

"But I don't like the water."

"Well, just operate the bird as a land plane. And maybe someday you could get a float license to land on the lakes or rivers." The FBO passed his meaty hand over his face and quickly said, "No, I take that back. I wouldn't want to see you try to land on water *ever*. But, Mr. McCafferty, I think this plane is the only answer."

"What's your commission?"

"Ten percent usually, but I'll drop it to five plus my expenses."

Sean first went to his bank to secure a second mortgage on his house, and combining this with his savings he came up with the $46,000. Then he contacted the principals in Miami through the FBO and arranged to charter the aircraft for a month; there was no reason to purchase the expensive, exotic piece of equipment if he found he could not land it.

Three weeks later a strange-looking plane arrived on charter. And after two weeks of further instruction,

Sean felt that he could handle this slow-flying gooney bird.

Then one day when the weather was clear and the wind zero, his third instructor, just as frustrated as the first two, told the struggling student to come to a stop. He got out and turned to Sean.

"Mr. McCafferty, I don't know if the time has come or not, but if you're going to twist up this machine, you might as well do it now."

Sean smiled and he had no fears or doubts, for he had soloed a hundred times in his head. The instructor climbed out of the Helio, waving it good-bye forever, he thought, and he picked up his walkie-talkie and called into the FBO office.

"Charlie, the galloping Irishman is going around by himself."

The operator ran out to the hangar and screamed, "McCafferty's finally making his solo."

A cheer went up as they all raced for the door of the open hangar and stood two deep to witness what would be an ultimate triumph or a first-rate crunching. A few quick calls were made around the field, and other people poured out of offices and hangars. The flight-service station and everyone in the administrative section of the Tallahassee control tower jammed into the elevator to see the sight from the cab. Sean had become the running joke of the airport, and many had taken bets on how long it would be before the man flew alone: fifty hours, a hundred, two hundred, or never.

With the entire field watching, Sean slowly taxied his float plane alongside the active runway. He thumbed his nose at all of them.

They cheered.

"Good luck, Sean."

"Give my regards to J.C."

"Write us from China."

Sean turned his plane deftly into the wind—he was best at taxiing—and he ran up the engine to test his magnetos and exercise his variable-pitch propeller.

"Helio five-four-echo...ready for takeoff," Sean said.

"You're cleared for takeoff," the tower controller answered. "And, sir, we're all crossing our fingers up here for you. Good luck."

"Uncross them. My solo will be perfect."

He thought he heard the cackle of laughter in the tower before the mike button was clicked off. Sean fed in his throttle easily, and he began whistling, a habit which had annoyed his battery of flight instructors. His spirits lifted. He was on his own, free of those didactic, superior bullies.

Lightened up, the plane lifted off easily and pointed its nose into the morning sun. Sean was a cautious pilot, and he always stretched his neck around before turning to see if he was being invaded by traffic; when he was sure the air was clear, he banked, dipped the nose a bit, fed in some rudder, and the plane came around perfectly in a coordinated turn. At eight hundred feet he turned again downwind, with the runway and the audience off his left wing.

"Up yours," he said between his whistling.

Then he called the tower and asked permission to land.

The real test.

"Cleared to land," the controller said with a half-chuckle, his hand on the crash button.

The firemen manning the field's emergency equipment were standing ready at the hangar door.

As he turned onto his base leg, letting off the power for the descent, Sean did not feel that outpouring of sweat, even though he realized that his final minutes in the air might be the preamble to a crash. He saw the runway coming up. And he didn't remember just what he did or how he landed.

Still, it was a perfect set-down: without a bounce, a smack, a float. As he slowed down, Sean opened the door so everyone could see him, and he kept bowing right and left as he slowly taxied his plane along the ramp.

"Sorry to disappoint you... sorry to disappoint you," he chanted as he passed.

But the yelling "crash watchers" were good-humored and they all clapped and cheered for Sean.

He had done it!

But Sean's small glory was not to last.

The following day at a practice strip near Tallahassee, he almost demolished the plane with a series of bad landings. But he kept on going, not fazed by his hard contacts with the runway. Finally, after a total of eighty hours, the flight instructor said, "Well, I guest it's about time you had your check ride."

The FAA examiner had heard about Sean; his reputation had spread all over the Florida Panhandle. The check-ride landing was a frightful bounce, and the examiner wiped sweat from his brow as he said, "Mr. McCafferty, we don't expect people to be perfect, but I can't sign you off with a landing like this."

"I do have trouble getting the plane down."

"Let's forget the examination and let me show you."

The FAA man spent three hours of his own time with Sean because he wanted the man to pass, and finally, after Sean had made three barely acceptable landings in a row, the examiner got out and said, "Congratulations. You're a new pilot. But please go someplace away from here and shoot landings. You'll be laying it on like a piece of bacon someday. It just takes practice."

That night Sean, normally a conservative man, took his wife out to the most expensive restaurant in Tallahassee, and they got slightly drunk celebrating the occasion. He had a temporary private pilot's license neatly folded into a new leather wallet he had bought months ago, thinking that his certificate would be visible through the clear plastic window in a matter of weeks. Now it was really there. And that night he took it out continually and stared at the piece of paper that had cost him $55,000, including the price of the plane, the gas, and ninety-two hours of instruction. But Sean didn't mind. It was the greatest day of his routine life, even greater than the day he had opened up the letter saying he had passed the CPA test.

Two days after Sean was licensed, the crash landings resumed, but he persevered, and it cost him another $2,000 to get his instrument ticket. Being analytical, he adapted to this part of flying very well. Following the procedures of an instrument landing was nothing more than going by the book, and he was trained in the art of numbers. But after a perfect instrument approach right down the alley in thick weather, poor Sean would burst out of the clouds and bounce his little plane all over the runway. Sometimes he would even groundloop, springing the aircraft completely around, almost an impossible feat in an amphibious float plane with four widely spaced wheels.

Then one day he took his two daughters and wife up for a ride and she said, "Sean, is the plane supposed to hit the runway so hard?"

"Oh, yes," he said. "It's natural. You have to get used to it."

He wasn't deliberately lying; but this time, the Irishman was used to his cockeyed set-downs.

Sean joined the Association of Flying Accountants and enrolled for his first convention. On the fourteenth of February the group was meeting in Miami, and Sean immediately forwarded a hundred-dollar deposit to cover room accommodations for two nights. He invited his wife and children along, and the entire McCafferty family looked forward to the Miami trip and the St. Valentine's Day dance at the Eden Roc Hotel. By the end of the session he planned to have a new job, and all his flying difficulties would suddenly seem worthwhile.

Sean McCafferty's thoughts drifted back to the present, and he pointed out the window to Connie and the children.

"See over there, kids, that's Disney World."

"Can we go closer, Dad?" the girls asked.

"Sure," Sean said.

He made an easy bank to the right and the Helio

Courier flew over the park at two thousand feet and then around again.

Hillary and Katie were thrilled by their tour from the air, and Sean smiled as he straightened the plane out again and continued on his heading toward Miami.

5

It was now fifty minutes to flight time at Heathrow Airport. Lou Griffis walked out under the belly of his Concorde, watching the ground personnel prepare for the flight. He kept looking up at the spindly nose and farther back toward the cockpit, wondering if he was going to sit in the left seat that morning.

He wandered back into the Celtic operations office and called Jeff Sutton at the Miami tower.

"Jeff," Lou said, "can you hear me?"

"You're coming through fine. Are you accepting the flight?" Jeff asked, speaking slowly and distinctly.

"I don't know, but I have to make up my mind in a matter of minutes. I see the reserve captain has been called in."

"Remember, Lou," Jeff said, "if you elect to remain on the ground, my daughter stays with you."

"I know. What's the situation down there now?"

"We're looking at one thousand broken...two thousand overcast. Ceilings around central and southern Florida are deteriorating rapidly in periodic heavy rain."

"Is it going as you thought it would?"

"Yeah, Lou. The low pressure is on the move, and she'll probably go right on out to sea as forecasted."

"Are you still giving me five-percent odds on that?"

"I'd say with this constant movement that we're seeing, the odds are even less than five percent for a stalling condition, but please, Lou, I don't want to influence you."

"I know. Well, I'll call you back in a few minutes. Stay by that private number, okay?"

"I'll be waiting."

Part of Lou Griffis' hesitation that morning was rooted in the fact that he knew too much about the Concorde, much more than the average pilot, French or English, who flew the supersonic airliners. He wished for a moment he wasn't a graduate aeronautical engineer, but just a pilot whose job it was to follow the manual obediently, believing everything it said and having blind faith in the guarantees of others.

After graduating from Australia's finest technical college, Lou had gone to work for the English Bristol Company, one of many suppliers to the Anglo-French team which would later put the Concorde into the air. At the Bristol Company, Lou had assisted a brilliant aeronautical engineer, Ralph Caldwell, who was design chief for a series of fighter planes that the company had delivered to the RAF during World War Two.

As a young engineer, Lou's specialty was wing design, and he assisted Caldwell in the development of a new turbo-prop airliner for BOAC eventually named the Bristol Britannia.

When the Korean War came along, Lou left Bristol to become a fighter pilot with the Royal Australian Air Force, after which he joined Qantas as a second officer. Six years later he was sitting in the left seat as a captain on international routes for the "down-under" carrier.

In February 1960 the venerable Bristol Aeroplane Company located on the northern outskirts of Bristol became a part of British Aircraft Corporation, and it was known from then on as the BAC Filton Division. Ralph Caldwell, who was nearing his sixtieth birthday at that time, continued as chief aerodynamist for the company. Not long after the merger, word spread about that a great jump in aviation history was about to occur, and it did on November 29, 1962: on that day a series of historic aviation documents were signed.

BAC entered into an agreement with Rolls-Royce, and together the British airframe and engine manufacturers signed a bilateral contract with a group of French companies to build the free world's first supersonic airliner.

Ralph Caldwell immediately thought of Lou Griffis and his rare combination of talents: few men in the world possessed both knowledge of airframe design and experience as pilots. He wrote the Australian asking him to come back to the BAC Filton Division to work, as Ralph put it, on "one of the most challenging opportunities ever presented to a wing designer."

Lou responded at once, taking a leave of absence from Qantas, and reported to work at Bristol, taking up where he had left off with Ralph Caldwell's design group.

Then the arguments started.

What should the new Concorde wing look like?

Lou and Ralph were ardent supporters of the swing wing, or what was termed a variable geometry airfoil, and their rationale was sound. No one wing, they said, could serve the necessities of supersonic flight and still perform adequately on the lower end of the spectrum, the takeoffs and landings.

"Ever look at racing pigeons, Lou?" Ralph said one day as he hunched over his drawing table at the Bristol division.

"Not lately."

"Well, I've taken a series of slow-motion pictures of these pigeons. When they accelerate to cruise flight, the wings shift backwards towards the tail to offer the least resistance. But as they land, the wings move forward, encircling the neck in a bunch of propped-up feathers which form a speed brake. We can learn a lot from fast birds. The supersonic should have a swing wing just like the racing pigeon."

Lou laughed. "But, Ralph, we're beyond bird anatomy."

"I don't know," the old engineer answered.

"Well, all jets have their wings on the bottom. But all birds have the wings on top. So who's right? The birds or us?"

Caldwell smiled. Lou had a point.

Engineers, of course, ponder and dream in the language of ultimates. No one disagreed with the Caldwell theory of the swing wing; it had been employed successfully on supersonic military aircraft, where weight and cost did not matter.

The military supersonic was, by its very definition, a chronic money loser. Its commercial counterpart had to earn its keep. The swing wing was too heavy, too complicated, and too costly. Gradually, as the figures spewed from the computer, an alternative, the delta wing, was chosen, and even Caldwell had to go along with it.

He privately thought that the delta wing, with its precisely calculated degree of camber and taper, droops and subtle twists, was nothing but a designer's compromise. He and Lou Griffis did not disagree with the high-speed properties of the delta wing, but they remained skeptical of its ability to perform at low landing speeds.

It all came down to one statement by the chief design engineer who supervised the final shape of the Concorde wing. He told Caldwell and Griffis:

"Gentlemen, there is no such thing as a perfect wing on birds or airplanes. But I can assure you that our delta wing represents the state of the art and it will give us a stable platform at any speed. In the more accelerated supersonic ranges the wing reaches its maximum performance, but never feel that it's inadequate and undependable in the low speed ranges."

The chief design engineer was right.

When the Concorde finally became operational, it was found that the delta wing did perform well enough at reduced speeds, but according to Caldwell this was due to the aircraft's powerful engines. The SST's turbojets, four Bristol Siddeley Olympus 593s, pushed out a startling 140,320 pounds of thrust. The power-to-weight ratio was higher than that of any jet designed up to that time, and, as Smith had predicted, the fuel consumption would kill the profitability.

In 1967, long after the Concorde wing decision had been made, the Americans started their supersonic passenger-flight program at Boeing. The design they came up with was extremely ambitious. Nicknamed the "2707" by its engineers, Boeing's proposed SST was more than twice the size of the Concorde. It would travel at Mach 2.7, or 1,800 miles per hour, and the wing would swing, just as Caldwell had insisted it should.

Lou and Ralph were jubilant, but not for long. The Americans quickly retreated to the Concorde-style delta wing when they, too, discovered what the Anglo-French team had learned years before: the swing wing was a beautiful but impractical design solution, a heaven only for theorists who were immune from cost accounting.

After Lou and his group lost the wing debate, he stayed on at BAC to continue work on the Concorde program. The aircraft was one of the most thoroughly researched flying machines in the history of aviation, and every new problem to be solved cost time and money.

The thermal investigations linked to supersonic flight went on for years: how would they deal with the sudden rise of skin temperature during acceleration, the heat soak during cruise, and the quick cooling of the aircraft's surface during deceleration from supersonic flight? Thousands of questions were answered, the right materials selected, the correct design established, but the bill was so high that it ended up costing every man, woman, and child in England and France thirty dollars apiece.

Lou's dream was to fly the Concorde for one of the major airlines that had taken options on the SST, perhaps his own national carrier, Qantas.

But the sad economic facts emerged: the Concorde was a money-loser. Airline economists said it went too slow, carried too few people, and burned too much fuel. Passengers loved the Concorde; load factors were high, but developmental costs could not be overcome. Most airlines except BAC and Air France canceled their options, and Lou's hopes for a job as a Concorde captain evaporated. He went back to flying subsonic equipment for Qantas again, but his heart remained with the great plane he had helped design.

Then Roger Smith announced his Celtic Airlines. Lou Griffis was the first to apply for a position, and Smith was glad to have a man like Griffis on his team.

But now on the morning of the fourteenth, Lou Griffis struggled to come to a decision. If they tried to shoot a landing at Miami with the fog veiling the runway, but didn't make it on the first attempt, he would need one hell of a lot of kerosene to generate full thrust for a go-around. Without a stop in Bermuda, would he have enough liquid in the tanks?

But, on the other hand, it looked as if the low pressure was moving out to sea. And, after all, Jeff Sutton had said that the chances of the low pressure's stalling were now less than five percent. The odds for a safe Miami arrival seemed to be swinging in his favor.

With some trepidation, Lou Griffis accepted the flight.

He didn't want to disappoint Honey.

In front of the Heathrow terminal Lou joined the others waiting to greet Dame Margaret Corbett. When she arrived, he presented a bouquet of yellow roses to the elderly white-haired actress with the fine-lined face and clear blue eyes. The BBC camera crew interviewed them, and then Roger Smith gave his prestigious passenger a medal.

"Is that a medal for bravery?" the BBC announcer coyly asked.

Smith answered, "No, it's in appreciation of her considerable accomplishments and the fact that Dame Margaret chose Celtic Airlines for her first flight."

Just as the ceremonies were finishing, a large Bentley drove up and a slim young girl with reddish hair got out. She spoke briefly to the Celtic agent, who nodded and pointed in the direction of Lou Griffis.

"Hello, Captain Griffis. I'm Honey Sutton," she said, smiling as she approached.

"Well, how are you? Welcome...welcome."

A tall, intense-looking woman had also emerged from the car with Honey's bags. She was magnificently dressed and very urbane. As Lou watched her advance, he wondered how Jeff Sutton had ever married such a woman. They appeared to be total opposites: Jeff was a basic man, not sophisticated, suave, or worldly, and certainly not concerned with his appearance.

"Captain Griffis...I'm Gloria Fowles, Honey's mother," she said, extending a jeweled hand.

"How do you do, Mrs. Fowles."

"Honey tells me you're a friend of Jeff's."

"Yes, we met in Miami at a series of FAA conferences."

"Well, you were certainly considerate to send my daughter all that material on the Concorde. She's been studying it every night."

"We always appreciate a chance to advertise our wares," Lou said, flashing his best smile. "Would you like to join us for a tour of the Concorde, Mrs. Fowles? You can leave your motorcar right there."

"Well...I do have a luncheon appointment."

"Oh, come with us, Mummy," Honey exclaimed.

"It'll only take a short time," Lou said.

She shrugged and joined Dame Margaret and the Celtic president, who were chatting nearby, and they all walked behind Lou Griffis toward the Concorde; it was now thirty-five minutes to flight time.

Lou showed them the business end of the big Olympus engines, and then they entered the cockpit and Lou explained the innovations and control instruments. Dame Margaret was baffled and Honey was excited by the complexity of everything she saw.

When they left the cockpit, Gloria turned to Lou. "Thank you, Captain Griffis. It was very interesting. Someday my husband and I will take a trip with you. By the way, how is Jeff? I understand you saw him not long ago."

"Yes, I did. He's fine."

"Still running that control tower, I suppose?"

Lou nodded.

"He was a good man."

"He still is, Mrs. Fowles," Lou said, placing a slight edge on his voice.

"Of course," she agreed carefully. Embracing her daughter in a way that seemed to Lou rather perfunctory, she left the Concorde swiftly, pausing at the door to blow back a cursory kiss, and Honey was left standing awkwardly in the aisle. She looked around at the actress, who had settled down in a seat by the window. The clear blue eyes of Dame Margaret had missed nothing of the exchange between mother and daughter.

"Miss Sutton, how would you like to sit next to me on the trip?"

Honey's face brightened. "Oh, I'd love to, but I'm back there," she said, gesturing.

The elderly actress spoke to the Celtic agent, and since the flight was lightly booked that day, arrangements were made to change Honey's seat to 6-B. She sat down next to Dame Margaret with her load of literature about the Concorde.

"Are you interested in aviation, my dear?" the actress asked, sliding her eyes over.

"I'm going to be a commercial pilot."

"Oh, women are doing everything these days, aren't they?"

"Why not? I've already taken five flying lessons. I'm almost ready to solo."

"Aren't you afraid?"

"No, it's very safe. And there's something about flying that's free and beautiful. You're up there all on your own."

"I know the feeling, my dear. I was about your age when I went on stage for the first time. It was in Bristol...*The Workhouse Ward* by Lady Gregory. I had never felt so lonely in my life, and I wished to dash toward the wings."

"But you didn't?"

"No. Somehow I got through my lines. I had to. It seemed to be an obligation, and, of course, it was. One can't leave the other performers and disappoint the audience...not that I really gave them much of a performance in those days."

"It's the same with flying, Dame Margaret."

"The same?" the woman said, arching her perfectly shaped whitish eyebrows.

"If you're at the controls of a plane, you can't just run or pull the curtain down. You have to keep your head. Even if you're suddenly afraid, you have to keep cool."

The old lady smiled over at the young girl and wrapped her clammy hand in Honey's.

"Keep it cool, yes," she said. "How many times have I kept cool, as they say?"

They talked a bit, Honey trying to mollify the old actress's apparent fears.

"You don't sound English, my dear," Dame Margaret said.

"I'm not. I came to England to live with my mother after she divorced Dad."

"And what does your father do?"

"He's the air-traffic controller in charge of the tower at Miami International Airport," Honey said proudly. "That's where we're going to land, you know."

"That must be an interesting job," Dame Margaret

said, not knowing even vaguely what an air-traffic controller did. "Are you planning to stay long?"

"I'm going to live with Dad permanently now. It's going to be great...we have a lot in common."

Dame Margaret smiled. "Really? Aren't young ladies more like their mothers usually?"

Honey shook her head. "Not in this case. My mother likes luxury, but my father would rather be self-sufficient than comfortable. He came from a farm out in Kansas, and do you know, he can fix almost anything. Have you ever heard the term 'street sense,' Dame Margaret?"

"Of course I have. If a young lad doesn't know how to take care of himself on certain streets in London, he won't survive."

"Well, my dad has field sense."

"Is that the same thing?"

"Sort of. As he told me, out there on the farm, you couldn't simply call up and ask the repairman to come over and fix the tractor. Oh, no, you had to know how to do things yourself. And Dad learned just about everything there was to learn around the farm."

"And he taught you these things?"

"I was the only one to teach," Honey said simply. "Mom liked dressing up and going out to dinner and keeping her hands clean all the time. When I was growing up outside of Miami, my hands were always dirty. The only time I washed them was for school or when we'd go to Mass on Sunday."

There was a pause as Dame Margaret glanced out of the window, then back again toward Honey. "And you say your goal in life is to be a pilot, like Captain Griffis up there?"

Honey shifted the books on her lap. "Well, yes, but I like to fix things, too, like motors. I used to hang around the Bentley dealer in Mayfair all the time— that's where we lived. And finally this fellow, Croton, he was the chief mechanic, well, he taught me how to fix the Bentley and I bought some tools and started tuning my stepfather's car in the garage. He caught

103

me one night and exploded. I never saw anyone so mad! He called the Bentley repair shop, and Croton was almost fired. I guess the owner thought he was going to lose business if some kid like me could handle the small tune-ups at home."

Dame Margaret smiled. "What did your mother think?"

"She just said it was very, very unfeminine for a girl to be covered with grease all the time. I think she decided then that I was just as strange as my father was."

"Are you going to university?" Dame Margaret asked.

"Absolutely. My dad got a degree in computer science at the University of Miami. It took him eight years of studying at night." She paused. "I want to go to Harvard and I've already written them. They say if I keep up my A average I'll be a good candidate."

"You're a very remarkable and refreshing young girl. It's hard for me to visualize a female Harvard graduate flying an airliner, but I believe you're on the right track. And you've certainly helped calm me down."

The old actress grasped the young girl's hand, and as she did, she noticed a slight smudge under the left index fingernail. Grease, the actress said to herself, and then she smiled at Honey.

Lou Griffis went through his checklist and then ran to the telephone at the base of the Celtic jetway. Jeff Sutton picked up the call in a matter of seconds.

"Jeff, I've decided, on balance, to take the flight."

There was a long pause, and Jeff said, "Are you certain of the decision?"

"Yes. I can always put down in Bermuda if conditions warrant. What is the present situation in Miami?"

"Well, pretty bad. We have five hundred feet broken...eight hundred feet overcast in light rain and fog. There are generally indefinite ceilings...wind is southwest at fifteen. The system is extensive, covering almost all of Florida, and well out into the Atlantic. A classic overrunning condition, I'd say."

"I'm heading into hell, huh?"

"No, not necessarily. If this continues, it will deteriorate for a while, then rapidly improve. Or it *should* rapidly improve. The low pressure is now located adjacent to Key West. So I'd say come on in, and we'll have good skies for you."

Lou returned to his Concorde, smiled up at Honey and Dame Margaret, who had been silently watching for the doors to close. Now that the other passengers had boarded, Dame Margaret could think of nothing but the imminent takeoff.

Finally, to break the tension again, Honey asked why the actress had chosen to go to Miami for her first airplane ride.

"My brother is very ill, Honey. And I haven't seen him in...oh, I guess, it's twenty-eight years now, or is it twenty-nine?" She looked wide-eyed at the ceiling. "Must be twenty-nine. I remember I was in an Agatha Christie play in the West End and he went to Florida for the weather. They said the poor dear wouldn't survive if he stayed in England. Oh, it's so damp, isn't it?"

"All the time."

"He had lung trouble. The sun in Florida cleared that up, but now he's dying of a heart disease and they cabled me to come immediately. Amory never married, and he's all alone. I've sent him money to live on, but I should have been with him long before this. Life is strange. So many times we only act when it's too late, or almost too late. If I weren't so afraid of flying, I would have come to him before."

The bustle moving up and down the aisle took on the excitement of a great ship just before the final whistle blows and the deck hawsers are slipped. There was more and more movement; talk and laughter became high-pitched. Chatter was quicker and jerkier.

The moments before an ordinary subsonic flight are

routine. Bland. Aboard the Concorde it is not merely another departure, but something of an adventure, for most of the passengers will be experiencing new heights and speeds for the first time. If the cabin of the Concorde were wider, there might be bon-voyage parties, baskets of fruit maybe, and a small band playing "Auld Lang Syne" as the plane is nudged away from its ramp position.

Finally, the airplane's gangplank, the boarding stairs, is pulled away.

They are all committed.

"Oh, Honey, I'm scared," Dame Margaret said, seeing the final moments come and go.

"I'll tell you why you're afraid. There are four reasons."

"Only four?"

"Four main ones. You want to hear them?"

"Will it make me braver? I think my heart's going to leap out of my chest."

"Oh, no, it's not." Honey leaned back composedly. "Now, we know that man has been on the earth about four million years; in all that time, he never flew with the birds or swam with the fish. But over the last seventy-eight years, which isn't very much time, man has started to leave his environment. He traveled under the sea and built planes to go up in the air. His flying machines outdid the birds; this plane can go higher and faster than any bird in the world."

"That's what I'm afraid of. Maybe we weren't meant to do this."

"We *are*. But we have to adapt to it. Everyone, even the pilots, feel odd being out of place. Divers experience the same sensation as people who go up in the air. I've done both. Next, there's the feeling of being locked in here. You can't get out. There's no backstage to run to. Another fear arises from being out of control. You and I can't do a thing. The passenger has no control over his own life. The last fear comes from the thought of a crash. When a big plane goes in, usually everyone dies. We all like to think we have a chance of escaping

106

disaster, and in a car crash or a train wreck, many people do. But surviving a jet accident is not so easy."

The old actress was stunned. Honey meant to console her, but now, she realized wryly, there was even more to fear than she had originally imagined.

"You think very clearly, Honey," she said finally, blowing out a long breath. "You've figured it all out. There is, indeed, much to fear."

"Of course, but look at it is this way: the pilots know more than we do about the plane. They certainly don't want to die, and they wouldn't take the plane up if there was a chance that something would happen."

"What's that noise?" Dame Margaret interrupted.

"That's the air going into the turbines. It sounds like a swoosh. The air pressure makes the blades go around. See here...it's in my book."

Honey showed the older woman a picture of the Concorde's starting procedure.

"I'll tell you what's happening all the time throughout the flight," Honey said, folding her hands over the actress's trembling knuckles.

"You make me feel better, Honey. Very much better."

Then they heard Lou's voice come over the public-address system. He made his introductory speech welcoming the passengers aboard, but he knew it didn't have his usual bright crackle, the small corny Concorde jokes. He would be a lot more cheerful when this flight was over.

Celtic 202 was signaled off. Their flight plan was approved, and the Concorde began to roll away from the ramp toward the active runway.

"You'll hear a lot of noise, Dame Margaret," Honey was saying.

"When, my dear?"

"I'll tell you. First, we taxi out to the runway."

Five minutes later the Concorde was pointing her needle nose down the long stretch of tire-marked concrete. When she was cleared for takeoff, Lou eased the thrust levers foward.

"Now we're on our takeoff roll," Honey said as she held onto the actress's hands. "We're getting up speed for takeoff. When we reach about one hundred sixty, Captain Griffis will pull back on his wheel and the plane will go up in the air."

"I can't look...don't want to see the ground going away from me," the ancient lady whispered.

"It's an odd feeling at first. Everyone gets used to it."

"I *never* will at my age."

"Sure. You'll love it."

Dame Margaret opened one closed eye and peeked bravely at the blur of runway sliding by.

The Concorde was screaming. Lou wanted something to go wrong so he could reject the takeoff. They reached velocity one, the decision speed. Dammit! Lou thought. *Everything* was in the green. So they continued to V.R., velocity rotation. He pulled back the yoke, and the great bird lifted off into the clear blue skies over Heathrow.

They climbed out, higher and higher; Lou made the circle which would take him over the valleys of rural England. Not until they had left the coast behind would Lou begin his climb to crack the sound barrier.

Dame Margaret's eyes were clenched again, and her lips moved in silent prayer. Then the cabin attendant came by and said, "Dame Margaret, may I get you something from the bar?"

"Yes, thank you," she said, "one of everything, I should think."

She said it with a smile of bravado and Honey knew the distinguished lady had passed a great point in her rich life. She had come to terms with her fear. She had kept her head.

"Thank you," she said to Honey as she looked down on the lush English countryside from a vantage point she had never thought she would occupy. "How beautiful England is. Much greener than I ever realized."

* * *

For Lou Griffis the takeoff was the opening throw of a dice game, and only he was aware of the odds.

Were they going to make it? Would the advantage remain with them? Underneath these questions, Lou asked himself a larger one: in flying, how much should one test the odds? On that day Lou figured he was playing the percentages, and he didn't like the feeling.

6

Harry Boyle drove his Nova along Thirty-sixth Street, and the wheels furrowed the rainwater that had backed up to the center of the wide thoroughfare. The gusty wind was slinging the rain sideways, and the downpour, a result of the low pressure in the Florida Straits, was almost too heavy for the blades of Harry's worn-out windshield wipers.

He turned left at the entrance to the tower and stopped his car while he studied the tulip: it was only a soft-edged blur, as if an impressionist painter had feathered the edges; the cab was soaked up into the scud of the low ceiling, and on top of the tower the bright red anticollision beacons had melted into hazy pink dots blinking on and off with about as much brilliance as the lights on a dusty pinball machine.

Beyond, Harry could see the strobes of the aircraft landing. As they made contact with the runway, each of them sent up a high spume of grayish water. Harry looked over and talked to his dog, Jimmy, a big black Labrador who smelled slightly of rotting teeth.

"Well, Jimmy, today we're going to meet the Secretary of Transportation. He's a big man... reports directly to the President of the United States."

The dog stared at his master with sad eyes as Harry reached down and patted the hard object attached to his belt. Finally he placed his plastic card in the stanchion box; the gate slid open, and he drove his car down into the tunnel leading to the tower.

After the interview with Dr. Striker that morning, Harry had gone home, telling Jeff that he wished to change into his best suit for the visiting dignitaries.

"At least I'll be there to meet the secretary," he told his wife. "Jeff will operate CORAD, but I'll explain it."

"Harry, I think that's a good idea," Clara said, relieved. "We know you're still the best controller in the tower."

Then Harry had gone upstairs again and unlocked his bottom bureau drawer. Inside was a binful of scattered Korean War memorabilia: a picture of Harry in his air-force uniform; a picture of Harry shaking hands with the commander of the British UN forces; a shirt cardboard on which were pinned six medals, the rewards for his overseas service. Aside from the pictures and the medals, which Harry shined regularly, he had the small microphone into which he had spoken and yelled as he controlled American fighters coming and going from their missions. Underneath the nostalgic collection was a mound of other material shipped back from Korea; one of these items was bagged into a golf cover.

Harry dug his hand into the soiled mitten and slowly drew out a live hand grenade, an antipersonnel weapon that had been used by the U.S. Army until 1959. He opened another pouch and removed a bulky .38-caliber Magnum given to him by an appreciative American jet pilot whom he had talked down one night. It was freshly oiled. He held the grenade and the pistol in his hands, studying the cold blue-black metal of each; finally Harry slipped the grenade over his belt, using the clamp holder, and jammed the Magnum into his pocket along with a full box of rounds. He moved to the closet door, swung it open, and inspected himself in the full-length mirror to make sure that his ordnance didn't bulge. It did, but in a way he was sure no one would notice. Two minutes later, the controller came downstairs and kissed his wife.

"I'm going now," he said.

"Good luck, darling."

Clara thought Harry looked well. His color had returned and he was smiling. She blew him a kiss as he slipped on his raincoat and whistled to Jimmy.

Twenty minutes later Harry Boyle was re-entering the underground security section of the tower.

"Back again, huh, Mr. Boyle?" Ted said.

"Yeah, I'm supposed to meet the big officials."

Harry looked toward the radar security gate, the kind used in airport terminals, that stood on the other side of the security desk. He realized he could never carry the grenade and the Magnum into the tower without walking through the radar screen and triggering an immediate alarm.

"Oh, Ted, do me a favor. Would you ask Mr. Sutton if it's okay to bring Jimmy into the tower today? He doesn't mind usually, but I don't know if it looks right with the secretary coming in and all that."

"Here's the phone, Mr. Boyle. Ask him yourself. He's in the office."

Harry reached for the phone, but then hesitated.

"You see, Ted, Mr. Sutton and I have had some differences."

"I heard."

"So would you just go down and ask him...be my spokesman?"

The old security guard stared at Harry for a moment, and then he smiled and shrugged his shoulders. "Sure, I'll go ask. You answer the phone if it rings, Mr. Boyle."

Ted unlocked the door and disappeared into the hall, and Harry jumped over Ted's desk. When the guard returned a few minutes later, Harry was on the other side of the security scanner seated in a gray steel chair looking over one of Ted's chess magazines.

"Are you interested in chess, Mr. Boyle?" Ted said, re-entering the reception area.

"A little bit."

"We ought to play a game someday. Ah…Mr. Sutton says it's all right to bring the dog in as long as he stays downstairs."

"That was very kind of him. Thanks, Ted."

"Sure thing, Mr. Boyle. Hope that new radar works out today. I know you've put a lot of faith in it."

"It'll work."

Harry unlocked the door and disappeared down the hall toward the administration section, with his dog slowly following him.

Jeff came out of his office with Laura as Harry appeared.

"Hello, Jimmy," he said, bending down and patting the shiny black Labrador. "One thing, Harry, please don't take anything I said yesterday or today personally. I'm sorry I had to come on so strong, but I've been worried about this lousy weather."

"You have a job to do and I respect that, but you know, Jeff…the administrator might let me operate the radar."

"That could be, Harry; we'll just wait until he arrives," Jeff said, knowing well it would never go that way.

Jeff and Laura took the elevator up to the radar level. He went into the approach-radar room, picked up the latest weather report, and they returned to the visitors' lounge, which had the softest seats in the tower, those covered with real fabric instead of shiny plastic. Jeff felt exhausted, as if the administrator had already come and gone, and he flopped on the couch, looking up at the acoustical ceiling.

The phone rang, and Jeff had an idea who it was.

"Yes, Lou," he said. "Where are you?"

"We're forty minutes into the flight now…went through the sound barrier fifteen minutes ago. I'm working you through Lands End radio. What's our present prog?"

"Ceilings are down on the deck, Lou. We're still operating, and Key West radar reports a clearing trend down there. It's already stopped raining and there are partially clear skies over the Yucatán."

"Okay, so the low pressure is moving out?"

"At this point, yes."

"We'll see you in a couple of hours. Let me know if there's a change. I'll be making my refueling decision as we near Bermuda. I plan to drop in there if the low pressure stalls."

"We'll watch it for you," Jeff said.

"Jeff," Laura said after he and Lou had cleared the frequency, "I don't understand—why all these calls back and forth to England between you and the Concorde pilot?"

"Well, there's kind of a problem. The Concordes have been coming in here a little fuel-low, and if this weather doesn't improve, I'm not sure we can find my friend Captain Lou Griffis another airport."

"Isn't that risky? You told me your daughter was coming in on that flight."

"That's right."

"How much of a chance are they taking?"

"It's called a reasonable risk."

She looked at him, wondering if he were treating fate too casually, but the facility chief and the Concorde captain must have known what they were doing, so she hastily changed the subject.

"I've been thinking, Jeff. Doesn't Harry Boyle prove the case for the computer radar? That's what Morrison said. A computer can't suffer what Harry's going through."

"But it can go black, leaving the controllers with nothing to hang onto; that's why I'm against it."

"But Harry Boyle doesn't support your argument, Jeff. Look at the poor guy," Laura said.

"When Harry Boyle started, it was a different job. There were many, many fewer planes. He could see the picture without the aid of a computer or altitude and speed tags. Now computer science has taken over our collision-avoidance system. But science is too important to leave to the scientists. Somehow, there has to be a blend between the machine and the men who control planes, and I think we're depending too much on the computer. We've handed over our human responsibilities to semiconductors. Half my controllers don't trust the computers. They've seen computers make mistakes even in department-store billings, and if the temperature isn't just right in here, or if we got too much humidity in the facility rooms, the computer starts acting up. The picture goes black or it starts presenting wrong tags. Last week the computer said that a United flight was at five thousand. We confirmed the altitude with the pilot and he read off his altitude as twenty-five hundred.

"What happened?"

"We don't know. The system is so complex it would have taken a month to troubleshoot that."

"Jeff," she asked after a pause, "is your discomfort just with machines in this tower?"

"No, I think we've given our technology too much overall authority. Doctors can't prescribe without electronic diagnoses these days. Kids take hand calculators to their math classes. And airline pilots depend too much on their auto-pilots and flight directors. I'm afraid of the trend."

"Where do you think it will end?"

Jeff paced the room.

"Don't know. I was brought up in a simple land of traditional values. I guess you might call it individual freedom, and I suppose my problem started because I heard and believed in people like Harold Stassen. He always talked about individual freedom as opposed to bureaucracy."

"And you had a very deep faith in people?"

"Yes, I did," Jeff said, the rueful tone in his voice turning nostalgic. "Out there in Kansas we needed each other. When a neighbor's barn burnt down, we chipped in and built a new one; we lent each other equipment and no one asked for rental money. I thought the whole world was like that, I got one hell of an awakening. Every men for himself, and to hell with the other guy!"

"And you're terribly bitter about it?"

"I wasn't prepared," Jeff said. "I was lied to in that farm kitchen. I listened to my father with his bull about government being good... what did he know? They're all dead now, and even our farm has been plowed under by a large corporation from Wichita. And then there was my Uncle Joe, a third-rate literature professor in a little college in upstate Kansas. He used to spend summers with us, and he always came with bags of books. I started reading when I was very young, and Uncle Joe, that jackass, put life in terms of plays and novels."

"What's wrong with that?" she asked.

Jeff laughed harshly. "Nothing. But I *believed* the plays. Thornton Wilder's *Our Town,* for instance. I was very impressed because life up in Grover's Corners, New Hampshire, was very much like Logan, Kansas. You did what you were supposed to do, and if you were decent, you ended up there on that hill and sat in those chairs... kind of a heaven. Can you imagine how duped I was to think that the whole world was Logan and Grover's Corners?"

"Jeff, it was at one time, but it can't all just stop and never change."

"No, it can't," Jeff said, "but I thought progress should be slower. The worst piece of shit I read was Conrad's *Lord Jim.* Uncle Joe asked me, 'Jeff, do you know what Conrad meant?' I was only eleven and I didn't get the message. I thought it was an adventure like *Treasure Island.* Uncle Joe explained, 'Here we have this young water clerk, Jim. He wants to live a heroic life, holding the wheel in typhoons, strapping himself to masts. So Jim goes off to get his officer's certificate and he reports to an old cargo ship carrying pilgrims. About one day out, a storm hits. Jim panics and takes off with the officers, leaving the pilgrims to drown. In one weak moment Jim acts like a coward, and then spends years roaming about the East looking for lost honor. But he only finds his redemption in death. The moral of the story is never be a Lord Jim . . . never panic . . . stand up for what's right, no matter what the dangers might be, because who wants to spend the rest of his life brooding over the one moment when you behaved badly?' I remember that story very well because the next morning Uncle Joe fell over his oatmeal dead. I think God got him because even the Big Man couldn't stand Uncle Joe's message about Lord Jim."

Laura laughed. "And that was the start of your hero syndrome?"

"I suppose, but today it's better to be a Lord Jim. Be a coward and you'll get by. Speak up and you'll get killed by the system. I agree with you, Laura, we're a generation of yes-men. Guess I was just brought up with too many novels. Even my family was like that—my father bragging about forging a birth certificate to get into the army, just so he could go get his back broken up. He thought he was a hero. He was a fool and he never knew it."

Laura moved closer to Jeff and took his hand.

"Jeff," she said, "this country was built by people like the Suttons. Never be ashamed of that. There were thousands of Grover's Corners, and I'll tell you one thing— you'd never be content as a Lord Jim."

"You're right," he said with a resigned look. "You're right. That's why I blasted out on TV. Oh, did they ever hear me, and is this Secretary of Transportation going to hear me today! No, I won't be a warmed-over Lord Jim, but I'll be a loser. Because there's no room for people like me. I'm the last of the Suttons and look at me. I can't even run a control tower. I have planes barely missing each other and Harry Boyles keeping me awake at night."

Laura looked at the disillusioned man and wondered if he was right. Would anyone hear his howl, or would it echo off bureaucratic walls forever? She swung her face away quickly and felt her eyes water.

High over Andrews Air Force Base on the fourteenth the sun was masked by wispy cirrus clouds, as if it were going through a partial eclipse. A light snow had fallen the night before, and small, drifting pockets had accumulated in various nooks and cracks on the wind-blown runway. The weather in Washington gave no clue to what was happening eleven hundred miles to the southeast.

The FAA jet, a Lear 25 painted orange and white and well waxed for the private use of the administrator and his staff, stood on the Andrews apron. It was fueled and ready for the two-hour-and-fifteen-minute flight to Miami. The pilots who had reported in an hour before the 9:00 A.M. departure had routinely checked the southern weather coming up on the terminal reports in operations. They felt there would be no problem penetrating the front—the FAA plane was perhaps the best-equipped small jet in the world—so they forgot about the weather, bought coffee, and boarded their aircraft, and they sat now in the cockpit trading small talk as they waited for the VIP passengers.

The first one, Secretary of Transportation Mark Cranston, arrived half an hour early. When the pilots noticed the black car roll onto the apron, they straightened their ties and climbed out to help the fifty-five-year-old secretary carry his suitcase into the jet. Mark, a tall white-haired former business executive with Honeywell, didn't need assistance; he was trim and youthful-looking and spent his few off-hours on the squash court, continuing the game that had won him the Ivy League singles championship many years before.

"Good morning, Mr. Secretary," one of the pilots said.

Mark nodded, climbed into the jet, drank a cup of coffee, and sat back with the Washington *Star* curled in his hands.

"Gentlemen," he said in his rich Harvard voice, "I'm expecting a Mr. Rollins from a research firm to deliver a package here. Inform operations that he is to be escorted directly onto the parking ramp."

"Yes, sir."

Ten minutes later a Maserati pulled up by the Lear

jet and Bryce Rollins, a suave efficiency researcher and management consultant, emerged with a cracked leather suitcase. He entered the aircraft and moved immediately toward Mark Cranston.

Rollin's firm had been retained by the Department of Transportation to analyze and evaluate the performance of the Federal Aviation Agency. The move, very unusual in government circles, had been strenuously suggested by the powerful head of the Senate Committee for Transportation, Lewis McKim, (Dem., Indiana). It was over his state that one of the midair collisions attributed to air-traffic-control failure had occurred. And when this was followed by several other similar tragedies, the senator asked the secretary, who had his own private doubts concerning the FAA's discharge of its duties, for a highly confidential review. (Ed Morrison, who thought the review was only for the purposes of evaluating manpower utilization, helpfully made all records available to the outside firm.)

"Good morning, Bryce," Cranston said.

"Mr. Secretary, how are you today?"

"Very well. Do you have the report?"

"No, sir."

"I was promised that today," Mark said with a disappointed look.

"I understand, sir, but some of the analysts wished to dig deeper into certain areas of the review. However, we worked all night on a digest," he said, opening his case and handing a bundle of neatly bound papers to the secretary. "I can't say that you're going to like what you read, sir."

"Is it the truth?" Mark asked.

"Yes. The digest only scratches the surface, but I think you'll appreciate the overview. It will give you a sense of what's to follow next week. I would respectfully suggest, Mr. Secretary, that this be kept confidential."

"Of course."

118

There was a pause and then Rollins added, "I would not share it with the administrator, sir, for reasons that will become apparent."

"Is it that bad?"

"I'm afraid so."

Mark Cranston placed the report beside his seat and reached for another, more immediate question. The secretary knew of Jeff Sutton's TV comments, and even though Morrison was trying to shield certain facts, Mark was ahead of his FAA administrator.

"What about this fellow Sutton, who shook everybody up?" Cranston asked.

"Mr. Sutton thinks that Miami should have a second airport. That's his main contention, I believe."

"That's Dade County's problem, not ours."

"That might not be true, sir. We have made recommendations in our report on that subject," Bryce answered.

"Is Sutton an intelligent man?"

"Yes. He's a graduate of the University of Miami with a degree in computer science, but he distrusts the FAA solution to collision avoidance."

"Did we fire Sutton or did he quit?"

"He sent a resignation letter in just after that infamous TV interview. The man feels that the agency is negligent. We agree with Mr. Sutton, although he is extremely idealistic and impractical from a fiscal point of view. From what we know of Sutton, he does have some worthwhile theories, and I'm sure you'll hear them today."

"Oh, I'm looking forward to meeting that man. Any fellow who could get up on TV and make a statement like that either has to be out of his mind or some sort of FAA messiah. It's one thing to criticize the government—and who doesn't—but with the criticism there must be answers or other alternatives."

"We've tried to suggest these in our overview report, sir. They're far from complete, Mr. Secretary, so you have to appreciate that we're only touching on the high points. But I think you'll find our conclusions rather interesting...frightening, too," Bryce Rollins added solemnly.

After the consultant had left the Lear jet, Mark reached over and hefted the thin report. They must have boiled down all the statistics and research to a string of crisp declarative sentences. The secretary opened the slim volume and began reading.

Summary Report on FAA
Department of Transportation
For the Secretary's Eyes Only:

Pursuant to engagement, Harrison, Rollins, and Smith place before the Secretary of Transportation this digest of preliminary findings based upon an internal review of the Federal Aviation Administration. This report is in response to the secretary's inquiry as to the state of aviation, its air-traffic control, regulatory compliance, and other matters substantive to the progress and ultimate safety of the air-traveling public.

General Statement:
The accelerated growth of all sectors of aviation in the United States has outstripped the ability to handle the traffic pressures in terms of ATC facilities and personnel in the terminals.

General Aviation:
This sector of the U.S. air fleet consists of just over 300,000 planes, including corporate aircraft. (The air carrier fleet, or commercial airlines, presently accounts for 3,120 aircraft.) Because of the energy crisis, private flying has increased at the rate of 21 percent a year, since a single-engine plane is more fuel efficient than an automobile. Businessmen who take trips of less than four hundred miles are finding that a light plane is the answer, considering the deficiency of available fuel and the fact that the fifty-five-mile-per-hour

speed limit is now being strictly enforced along the nation's highways.

However, our findings indicate that the accident rate for private planes is increasing at an alarming rate. Most midair collisions are concerned with private aircraft, because they represent the largest segment of U.S. aviation. Private planes have been involved in airliner collisions. Preliminary findings suggest grave misunderstandings between private pilots and controllers. But the overriding source of the high accident rate in this sector may be traced to the lack of proper training for private pilots.

A new private pilot with only eighty hours of flight time can legally fly at night into a heavily trafficked control zone of a major airport if his light plane is properly equipped. Flight instructors, it was found, are disgruntled, underpaid, and poorly trained themselves.

Over 10 percent of light-aircraft accidents have been linked to alcohol or drugs; well over 80 percent are due to pilot error.

Recommendation:

It appears vital that all private pilots be trained by FAA-employed flight instructors who are competent and career-oriented. It is also recommended that more stringent licensing procedures for private pilots be initiated by the FAA, and all qualifications for private licenses by *upgraded immediately.*

Air-Traffic Control:

Two present theories exist regarding air-traffic control. Some experts feel that the skies are overcrowded, and others, just as well-informed, indicate that there is air space not being employed. It could not be established at this point whether there are too many planes in the sky or whether their separations are being mismanaged. Further study might indicate a combination of both conditions.

After 340 interviews with controllers, the preliminary digest of results is as follows:

1. 61 percent thought the job was too strenuous for the number of hours required. Controllers complained that they should only have to take short periods on the radarscopes.

2. 81 percent complained that they were oversupervised and undertrained. Often controllers are fired or reprimanded for using the wrong vocabulary. Oversupervision, according to many controllers, makes them more nervous than they should be.

3. 40 percent of controllers felt they were underpaid. Being in civil service, they are compensated according to grade level. A top controller at GS-14 in a Class Five tower might receive as much as $46,000 a year, but the senior pilot he is controlling can make as much as $100,000 a year.

4. 90 percent of controllers felt that the training facilties in Oklahoma City were inadequate.

5. 72 percent of controllers felt that most facilities are understaffed and that trainees should not learn on the job.

Recommendation:

It would have to be asked if air-traffic controllers should be associated with civil service. More controllers working fewer hours at higher pay scales would appear to introduce better candidates to the profession. A longer and much more sophisticated training program for controllers is indicated. Controllers should not be trained almost entirely on the job.

As an example of present trainee procedure, it was found that a "developmental" at age twenty-two with only eleven months in the system was left alone to handle local traffic at a major airport for a period of two hours without supervision. This was referred to as a mistake, but evidence indicates that other similar incidents are not uncommon within the system. The government's answer to the differential between pay scales for pilots and controllers is the statement: "A controller has never been killed in the course of his job, while many pilots have died in fatal air crashes—some caused by ATC-systems errors."

FAA Safety Compliance:

The agency has had a long and negligent history of failure to identify aircraft design problems as well as failure to enforce vigorously required maintenance and/or repair schedules of commercial aircraft. These examples of nonfeasance are best illustrated by the history of the DC-10. The agency was aware of a cargo door problem in the subject aircraft nineteen months before the Turkish crash of a DC-10 outside Paris, France. Yet no efficacious action was taken by the FAA to obviate the design deficiency. In the case of the DC-10 accident at O'Hare Airport on May 25, 1979, the FAA was generally faulted for not identifying the design weakness of the engine pylons and for failure to ground all DC-10 aircraft *immediately* after the accident, thus endangering the lives of air travelers.

Recommendation:

The entire system whereby the FAA certifies aircraft as airworthy should be studied and overhauled. We find that one FAA practice in regard to safety is duplicitous and self-serving. The agency appoints employees of air-frame manufacturers, among others, to be their Designated Engineering Representatives. These engineers, on the payrolls of the manufacturers, assist the agency on safety aspects of aircraft design and production and, thus, their performance cannot be judged as independent.

Internal Operations of the FAA:

It was found that the agency is slow to react. Equipment ordered by control towers is often delayed for months. Often wrong supplies are sent to ATC facilities, and much of the equipment now in service has not been fully tested, nor have the controllers had sufficient experience with highly sophisticated computer radars to make proper use of them.

It was found that near-miss reports and other systems-error reports are often missing from the agency's central files, even though said reports were filed in regional FAA offices.

Recommendation:

The internal compliance practices of the agency should be reviewed in depth.

Airports:

While the management and construction of airports are not presently within the jurisdiction of the FAA, it was found that many facilities are operating beyond capacity and must be termed unsafe. Additional airports are needed immediately, and others must be upgraded without delay. The pressure of air-traffic demands has outstripped 20 percent of the terminals in the United States.

Recommendation:

Federal funding and intervention in the control and construction of airports should be studied as a possible solution to overtaxed terminals.

CORAD:

This computer-assisted radar system presently installed on a test basis at Miami International Airport is too complicated to evaluate properly and it's future in the ATC system cannot be ascertained at this time. However, it was found that the administrator, Mr. Edward Morrison, owns 27,000 shares of common stock and 19,000 shares of preferred stock in Intercom, Inc., designers and manufacturers of the CORAD system.

Recommendation:
Further independent studies of CORAD should be undertaken, plus an investigation by the Justice Department to determine if Mr. Morrison's position with Intercom, Inc., could be tantamount to a conflict of interest.

Respectfully submitted,
Harrison, Rollins, and Smith

The secretary drew in a long, hard breath. From the window of the Lear jet he could see Ed Morrison's car pulling up on the ramp. He placed the report in his attaché case, closed it, and snapped the lock.

Mark Cranston was sickened by what he had just read. But he would not confront the administrator immediately.

Ten minutes later the FAA jet took off for Miami.

7

The seas south of Key Largo are usually patchworked with color—the light green shallows that blend into sparkling azure; the stretches of deep five-fathom water that do not reflect the light of the sun.

On the fourteenth of February all color was robbed from these waters. Churning combers were being hurled along by the forty-knot wind from the southwest, and the ocean was the sullen gray color of the North Atlantic. The wind shrieked and ripped off the wave tops, shredding the water into billions of foaming particles. Nimbus clouds, the scud, were dipping so low they almost nudged the crests of the breaking seas.

The Miami weather station was recording the progress of the low pressure. The system was running according to Jeff's prediction, and he called the station at 11:30, knowing that Lou's Concorde would be nearing the mid-Atlantic island.

Lou would have to make up his mind: land at Bermuda for fuel or press on directly to Miami.

"Jeff Sutton over the tower. What's the central pressure now?" he asked the Miami weather specialist.

"We're reading a drop to nine-ninety millibars."

"How's the line been going...is the drop constant?"

"Yes, the low pressure is now located just south of Miami, off Key Largo."

"Has there been any change of course or deepening?" Jeff asked.

"No," the forecaster said. "It's on its present course and we're looking for a movement out to sea, with clearing skies behind the system."

Jeff had only put down the phone about five minutes when the call came through from Lou Griffis.

"What do you have now, Jeff?" the captain asked, his voice edgy.

"Very bad here," Jeff answered. "Indefinite ceilings, and we're down to partial operations. Departing aircraft only. But the low pressure is running along as predicted, Lou. Key West is reporting scattered clouds at two thousand...this baby is on the go."

"All right, then we'll scratch the Bermuda landing."

"Your fuel okay?"

"We're doing better than I had figured," Lou said. "Picked up a little tailwind."

"How's my daughter? Have you had a chance to talk to her?"

"I'm going back there now."

Lou Griffis snapped off the radio patch to the Miami tower and told his co-pilot to contact London operations indicating that the flight was continuing directly to Miami. A couple of minutes later Lou made his way through the passenger compartment and stopped beside Honey Sutton.

"Just spoke to your dad, Honey. He's expecting us right on time. Enjoying the flight?"

"Yes, I am, Captain Griffis. Can't see very much from way up here, though."

"Well, over the ocean there's not much to see anyhow, but we're just passing Bermuda. Should be coming into the Miami terminal area in about an hour and ten minutes."

Lou looked over at the actress, who had just finished her meal and seemed to be fuzzy-eyed from the wine.

"How are you, Dame Margaret?" Lou asked.

"I'm enjoying my flight, Captain. This flying is really simple and very pleasant," she said.

Lou smiled to himself and wished that he could agree with her.

"Honey talked me out of my fears," Dame Margaret continued. "She's an outstanding girl."

"Takes after her dad," Lou said.

Lou then walked down the aisle and spoke to a few of the passengers, and as he passed by Honey's seat again, he said, "Honey, I know you want to see the cockpit, and though it's against the rules, after we land I'll let you sit in my seat and I'll explain just what we do."

"I know a bit from reading all the books."

"And someday Honey will be flying a plane like this," Dame Margaret declared, "and you'll be sitting back here as old as I am."

Lou thought of what it would be like to fly with someone else responsible for all the decisions. It was a pleasant thought, and this time he was happy to agree with her.

Sean McCafferty's slow-flying Helio float plane was bouncing lightly through the gray skies. At 11:30 that day Sean had been in the air three hours and his airspeed indicator read 120; the crosswind associated with the front to the south had diminished his ground speed to 110.

Sean felt carefree as he flew his plane at an altitude of 6,500 feet, but around him were the forerunners of the weather pushing down on Miami: gray cumulus clouds below him and high above, a stratus layer with sharp, dark gray edges. His flight plan was sandwiched in between, in a layer of clear, pale skies, and the sun— what there was of it—was ringed by haze. The closer Sean got to Miami, the happier he got and the louder he whistled, and he told his children a string of shaggy-dog stories and one-liners.

The Helio was configured differently from most light planes. Originally there had been three rows of double seats and the plane had been certified to carry six passengers, the last two sitting in a double canvas sling seat far in the rear of the aircraft. In a float installation such as Sean's, the center of gravity moved forward because of the weight of the pontoons—678 pounds; therefore the middle seats were removed and the passengers sat in the rear sling seats to offset the center of gravity. There was an empty space of about six feet between the two front seats and the canvas slings.

They had experienced only slight turbulence so far, and Hillary and Katie were sitting on the floor playing Scrabble, having a good time, not in the least aware of the weather south of them.

While the Concorde had been designed to go high and fast, the Helio's criteria were exactly the opposite: she was made for low, slow flying. The big Helio wing was equipped with long trailing edge flaps which slowed the aircraft down to about thirty-five miles an hour for a short-field landing, and a good bush pilot could wiggle this plane into a dirt strip of no more than six hundred feet in length. There were only about six types of planes in the world designed for this purpose, and the Helio was one of the first to handle what was called "off-airport" operations. In the Helio's case, the prototype had taken off from a tennis court at Harvard, where a professor of aerodynamics at MIT had conceived of the strange, outlandish bird that had provided Sean McCafferty with his license.

Sean's plane was not radar-equipped, and he had no way of knowing if he were flying into a thunderstorm in thick weather unless informed by the tower. Sean had to feel the air and his enemies: turbulence, icing, and hail.

Lou Griffis could see these adverseries on his cockpit radar, on whose scope heavy precipitation appeared as a dull white blur. The Concorde also had a large wing to support its powerful engines, but its landing technique was the opposite of the Helio's. The SST could not use flaps to slow itself down for a landing. At supersonic speeds, flaps and leading edge slats would cause unacceptable friction. So another way of slowing down for a landing had had to be discovered.

Basically it was a simple technique. The Concorde landed with its nose very high, and the entire delta wing became, in effect, a huge flap; as the air hit the upturned wing on a landing, it simply slowed the SST down to about 160 miles an hour, the proper landing speed. The problem with such a nose-high landing was that the pilot couldn't see the runway, but the designers solved this by engineering what was called the droop snoot. When the Concorde landed, the nose was depressed by means of a hydraulic motor, thus enabling the pilots to keep visual contact with the runway. And, of course, the inside joke among Concorde pilots was: "What would happen if the bird didn't drop its snoot?"

Somewhere above Lake Okeechobee, ninety-one miles north of MIA, Sean contacted center and was told that the airport was operating at minimums. The children had to go to the bathroom, and Sean's fuel tanks were reading one-half off the full pin, so he pulled out his sectional map, canceled his flight plan, and started his approach toward the nearest field, Okeechobee County Airport. He held some throttle all the way in, trying to crab against the crosswind, and almost up to the touchdown it appeared as if he were going to grease it on.

At the last moment, a gust of wind caught the under edge of the large left wing, pushing it up so the plane stalled, then dropped to the runway with an echoing clank from the big hollow floats. At a landing speed of thirty-five miles an hour, however, the crash sounded bad but damaged nothing.

"Damn...thought I had it right this time," Sean muttered.

"Why does our plane make so much noise, Daddy?" Katie piped.

"I think your father should put a parachute on his plane for landing, girls." Connie smiled at Sean to show she was joking. Scowling, he taxied up to the gas pump and told the amused lineman to top her off.

There was a hazy sun at the small Okeechobee airport, with a light layer of stringy clouds passing overhead. The McCafferty family got out to stretch their legs, and they all went into the terminal for a snack; Sean picked up the phone and called the flight-service station at Vero Beach.

"What's the outlook for Miami?" he asked the specialist.

"Ah...they have heavy frontal activity. Miami is down to indefinite ceilings. You can expect some turbulence, light to moderate. There are scattered thunderstorms in the area, associated with the low-pressure system."

Sean thanked the specialist for the briefing and walked out onto the apron without the slightest doubt that he would push on to Miami. Even if his landings continued to be rough, the Helio float plane was equipped for blind flying, and Sean was cool and skillful at handling the Helio in clouds with reference to instruments alone. The plane itself was extremely safe for instrument flight: in the Helio, nothing happened fast, and with flaps cranked down, the bird could fly all day at forty miles an hour.

"Are we going again?" Hillary asked her father.

"Yes, there's some weather south of us, and it might be a little bumpy, but we only have about a forty-five-mile flight."

"Are you sure we should go, Sean?" his wife asked, looking up at the clouds, beginning to bunch.

"No problem. We have plenty of gas now. If it gets too tight, we'll go to our alternate, Fort Lauderdale. Now, girls, no more sitting on the cabin floor playing. I want you buckled in the back seat," he said.

The four of them climbed back into the amphibious plane, which had never been in the water under Sean's ownership. Five minutes later they were off again after filing a new flight plan for Miami.

Mark Cranston had remained silent for most of the trip, and finally Ed Morrison spoke up, trying to prepare the secretary for the possible conflict with Jeff Sutton.

"I guess you've heard about this fellow Jeff Sutton?"

"Sutton?" the secretary said offhandedly, not implying what he already knew about the facility chief at Miami.

"He's the guy who severely criticized the agency on TV one night."

"Yes, yes, I did hear something about that."

"Mr. Sutton might be showing you our new CORAD system today, but he has resigned from the FAA. The man doesn't believe that the future of ATC will be the computer."

"What do you think, Ed?"

"There's no doubt that we have to use technology to keep the planes apart. It's the only answer."

"What plans does the agency have for computer radars? We can't keep having these midair collisions."

"Of course not," Ed said. Believing that he had a good opening, he took the opportunity of repeating what he had been told by the technical section of the FAA.

Ed's talent in life was for parroting. His memory was keen.

"We are now proceeding full steam on what we call ATARS. That means Automated Traffic Advisory and Resolution Service, and it's the ground-based side of the system."

"What will it do?"

"When two planes are about to collide, it will send out a computerized voice message telling the planes to climb, descend, turn left or right."

"And what's the controller's role in all this?" Mark asked.

"He monitors the talking radar. But that's only half of it. In the cockpit is another part of the collision-avoidance system. For instance, a plane will send out a signal which will echo off the radio signals from a second plane with a cockpit transponder. The cockpit computer records the track of the second plane in relation to the first plane. If a collision is imminent, a warning signal is sent to the pilots. The beauty of these systems is that each of them can operate without the other... meaning that if the ground collision-avoidance system fails to pick up an impending collision, the cockpit computer will take over."

"Why should one fail?" the secretary asked. "In one sense, you're saying that the ground anticollision system is foolproof, and then you say it can fail, but the cockpit computer will save the day."

"The system *is* foolproof, Mark. But we figure it's better to have two systems rather than one. All airliners today have redundant equipment. This jet has two of everything—two pilots... an autopilot for the autopilot."

"And CORAD is the ground end of this anticollision system?"

"Yes. It has three scopes, and when a collision is

132

about to occur, it simply narrows the picture down for a detailed presentation."

"And it talks to planes?" the secretary asked with a doubtful expression.

"Yes. It warns the pilots of a collision, but CORAD can also be programmed to instruct planes for landings and take-offs."

"So what you're saying is that the computer can reason?"

"That's right, and it doesn't forget or become rattled like the human brain. Mark, listen, I know the CORAD system will cost us, maybe, a billion, but we'll get our money back."

"How?"

"Right now we have seventeen thousand controllers in the system. We pay them an average of thirty-eight thousand dollars a year. With the automated radar installed, we could cut our manpower down to, perhaps, five thousand controllers, which would save us about four hundred and fifty million dollars a year. But the biggest advantage will be safety. CORAD cannot make a mistake."

As Mark listened to the administrator's eager voice, he thought back to the Rollins report. The digest had suggested hiring more controllers and giving them better training, rather than discharging men. And Ed owned shares in Intercom, Inc.

To both Mark Cranston and Jeff Sutton, men who understood computers and their limitations, air traffic was at a frightening crossroads. How much responsibility should be handed over to electronic solutions, and where did the human element fit into the gossamer of spinning tapes and solid-state wizardry?

Five weather stations were following the movement of the low pressure that day: the Mexican station on the Yucatán; Key West; Miami; Nassau; and West Palm Beach, located sixty-eight miles north of MIA.

Both the Yucatán and Key West stations were reporting improving conditions, but the weather specialist working the Miami station, located on the campus of the University of Miami, Coral Gables, saw something he didn't like.

The barograph, an instrument which records pressure and displays it with an ink pen along graph paper, had flattened its recording line. Usually as a fast-moving low pressure comes through, the pen will dip down to the lowest pressure reading, and then, like an electrocardiogram's peaks and valleys, the line will start up again, indicating that the system is moving by and the pressure is on the rise, filling in. This had happened at Key West an hour before; the line went up.

At Miami the line went down and stayed there. The forecaster confirmed the local pressure with the flight-service station at New Tamiami Airport, twenty-two miles to the southwest, and with the Miami tower.

There was nothing wrong with the recording barograph at the Coral Gables station. The pressure wasn't coming up. The forecaster then contacted a ship in the synoptic reporting system, an oil tanker heading along the upper Florida Keys toward Port Arthur, Texas.

"This is Miami radio," the specialist said. "Could you give us an update on your central pressure?"

After a pause, the third officer returned to the radio room and reported: "We're reading nine-eighty millibars."

"Has there been a change?"

The ship was also equipped with a recording barograph, and the officer returned to the chart room and looked at the progress of the central pressure. He ran back to the radio room and said, "It's gone down and stayed there for a while, but I just noticed another drop. This thing is going crazy! We're getting torrential rain, and the wind has picked up to thirty-five knots."

The low pressure had stalled.

The weather had changed, and so had the odds againts Lou Griffis.

Jeff and Laura watched the thick weather from the cab of the tower. The airport was allowing planes to depart, but the inbounds were landing on instruments through the heavy rain, and Nick Cozzoli was no longer pinching his traffic. Most of the arrivals were stacked up in the holding pattern, and MIA was taking them in one by one with a good five miles separation between the traffic. Jeff kept eyeing the cab barometer and glancing toward the west. That was where the first portent of the clearing would appear, the movement of the low pressure out to sea.

As often as he looked, the barometer stayed at its low point, and there was no break in the steel-gray clouds. Again he called the Miami weather station for an update.

"This is Sutton up at the tower. What do you have on that low pressure? Our line isn't moving up."

"Mr. Sutton, the front has stalled just south of Miami. We confirmed that with a reading from a tanker only minutes ago."

"Why did it stall?" Jeff bellowed. "It wasn't forecast to hang in here!"

"Obviously, the upper air currents blocked the low. We'll be in for one hell of a time."

"I can see it up here already. We're losing visibility."

"It'll get worse before it gets better."

"How long could it sit there without moving?"

"We've seen the pressure come to a halt for as long as eight hours."

Jeff put down the phone, and his face had turned sallow.

"Bad, Jeff?" Laura asked quickly.

"Christ, yes! The low has stalled. That means we're in for even worse weather. I've given Lou a wrong steer, and he'll be over here fuel-low. We'll have to close the airport if the ceiling drops any further."

Jeff quickly polled the airports in range of Lou's Concorde: Nassau, Fort Lauderdale, West Palm Beach, Melbourne, Tampa, Orlando, and Jacksonville. Each of the towers reported rapidly deteriorating conditions. Tampa was closed to inbounds; Jacksonville was operating, but the scud was coming down on them. The entire state and the Bahamas were affected by the stalled low pressure, and Jeff knew he had to inform Lou Griffis immediately. Pilots would learn of the deteriorating situation as soon as it went out on the wire, but that would take at least twenty minutes, and Jeff wanted Lou to understand what he was up against. Maybe he could pull an alternate airport out of his hat.

Two minutes later Jeff was working the flight through Miami radio.

"Lou, I've got bad news. The low pressure has stalled in the Florida Straits just south of Miami. God, I'm sorry!"

There was a lengthy pause, and finally Lou said, "It's not your fault. You warned me. What's the first open airport in case this weather situation continues?"

"The way it looks now, I'd say Pensacola, Florida. Tampa's about to shut down, along with Jacksonville. Can you possibly return to Bermuda?"

Lou swung his head to the right and asked Cecil Holloway, the flight engineer, if they could reach the Florida Panhandle or return to Bermuda. A minute later Cecil said, "No, sir. We can't reach Bermuda at this point *or* Pensacola. We're committed to Miami or the alternate, Fort Lauderdale."

"Oh, shit!" Lou said out loud, knowing now he should never have taken the flight.

But it was far too late for self-reproach, and he had to get his Concorde down at Miami somehow.

"No, Jeff, we don't have enough fuel to divert at this point. How long is this condition forecast?"

"The chief meteorologist at Miami said it could last as long as eight hours."

"I have no choice. I'll just have to come ahead."

"I'll keep you informed," Jeff said. From the cab he could see that the rain had pulled an ashen gauze over the airport.

"Mr. Sutton," Cozzolli called, "I'm about at the end of my visibility here. We'll have to close down."

Just below them, in the approach-radar room, Hoagy Washington was working the north feeder scope. The room was equipped with ARTS Three—Automatic Radar Terminal Systems. Two scopes handled the traffic from the north and two from the south.

When a flight was handed over to MIA approach control from center, it came up first on a feeder scope. Then, as the flight proceeded closer to the airport, it was handed off to the final scope position, where the traffic was placed in a more detailed separation for landing. And in the last moments of the landing sequence, the final scope handed the traffic off to the cab for landing instructions; usually at that point the controller could make visual contact with the flight, but in marginal weather he would have to rely on a precision-approach scope in the cab.

"We're closing MIA to inbound traffic," came the word from the cab.

A split second later Hoagy Washington received a transmission from the FAA Lear 25.

"Miami approach, this is FAA one-seven-victor... we're with you," the pilot said.

"Miami is now closed," Hoagy responded. "Contact center on 128.75."

"Listen, Miami approach, we have the secretary and the administrator aboard. I'd like to shoot a fast straight in. I'm requesting a precision approach."

"Hold on. I'll check with the cab, but we're below the category-three landing limitations. Our runway visual range is below three hundred feet."

"Get us permission," the voice demanded.

Hoagy picked up his phone and called Jeff.

"The FAA jet wants a precision landing. He's coming in, Mr. Sutton."

"All right," Jeff said. "We'll give it to him."

Jeff took over in the cab, and he notified the Lear 25 that an almost blind landing was approved.

"Okay, here we come," the FAA pilot said.

Jeff walked over to the CORAD platform and looked at the lone target approaching MIA from the northwest. The other targets had been vectored off to their alternatives, and the sky about Miami was relatively free of traffic as each inbound changed direction: the South American international flights went south to the Dominican Republic, the only airport still open; but a few with heavy reserve fuel remained in the holding pattern hoping the soup would lighten and they could sneak through.

"Turn to heading two-seven-zero," Jeff said into his mike.

"Turning right two-seven-zero," came the calm response.

"You're seven miles from the airport...cleared to land on runway two-seven, right."

Jeff gave the pilot his wind and ceiling conditions and continued, "You're high on glide path...over the outer marker..."

"High on glide path...over the outer marker...that's affirmative."

"Left of glide path."

"Left of glide path."

Each time Jeff issued the position, the skilled FAA pilot made his corrections.

"You're two miles from touchdown...on glide path. You're a mile from touchdown...on glide path.... You're over the boundary. Keep descending," Jeff said calmly.

"I don't see a thing!" came the quick retort from the FAA cockpit.

"Keep coming. Keep coming," Jeff said.

"Where am I?"

"Halfway down the runway. We don't see you. Perpare for a missed approach!" Jeff yelled out. "Missed approach!"

"I have the lights. I see the lights. I got it here!" the pilot cried out.

He set the plane down on the runway with less than four thousand feet remaining. The pilot pushed down on his brakes with everything he had and reversed his thrust. Two hundred feet from the end boundary, the FAA jet halted and turned back toward the terminal.

Mark Cranston and Ed Morrison were down safely.

For a moment Jeff was pleased with his own performance, talking the Lear jet down, but almost instantly his thoughts switched far away, to the Concorde now committed to Miami. Jeff glanced over at the barometer. It was still dropping, and now he couldn't even see the runway through the pelting rain.

"Lou...Honey...I'm sorry," he said to himself. "What the hell have I done?"

8

Only minutes before the FAA jet landed, center informed its inbound aircraft that MIA was closed to all operations. Sean McCafferty was then about twenty miles south of West Palm Beach, where the airport was still open and no word about Miami was being broadcast. He flew on, unaware that his destination was buried in fog.

Even so, he felt the effects of the low-pressure system gone wild. The air was rippled with sharp-edged gusts that slammed up and down, and his small plane was taking hard bounces.

"Sean," Connie said, "it's getting rough."

"Just a little turbulence," he answered, looking back at the children. They looked nauseated, as if their stomachs were coming up to meet their throats. "We're almost there," Sean added, "another forty minutes."

Five minutes later Sean heard his call sign.

"Hello five-four-echo...Miami approach. Do you read?" came the crackle from the radio.

"Hello five-four-echo...Miami approach," Sean responded into his mike.

"Miami is closed to all operations."

"How about West Palm Beach?" Sean said quickly, hoping to find an airport where he could calm his passengers down.

"West Palm is just about to close. Squawk ident, please."

Sean pushed the button on his cockpit transponder, and a light came up on the feeder scope in the MIA approach radar room.

"We have radar identification," the controller said. "Confirm remaining fuel aboard."

"Six hours," Sean answered.

The controller could not believe what he had heard. Very few inbounds to MIA ever arrived with that much fuel, but with the Helio's long-range tanks holding one hundred and twenty gallons and at a burn-off rate of sixteen gallons per hour, Sean could outlast the low pressure stall.

"Six hours...is that a confirmation?" the approach controller asked.

"Affirmative...six hours," Sean said rather proudly.

The approach controller vectored Sean to a holding area thirty miles west of Miami, and he was instructed to continue circling at an altitude of six thousand feet while waiting for an improvement in the MIA runway visual range.

Sean headed his awkward-looking float plane south. He was flying through solid gray clouds, and the prop spun off sheets of rain so heavy that the windshield was completely masked, but Sean simply flew on, whistling now and then, watching his instruments, which were now being illuminated by tiny red cockpit lights. The children heard their father's whistling, and they, too, started to hum, and soon all the McCaffertys were singing "Do-Re-Mi" from *The Sound of Music*, their fears evaporated.

The FAA car picked up Ed Morrison and Mark Cranston and they drove out to Thirty-sixth Street, where they were promptly halted by a massive traffic jam because of flooded streets.

Ed Morrison had noticed the sour expression on the secretary's face, and he decided to explain the Harry Boyle situation, so his superior would not encounter any surprises when they finally reached the tower.

"Mark, there's something you might as well know about."

"Really?" Cranston replied, thinking that possibly Ed was going to disclose his sizable interest in CORAD before they tested it at the tower.

"Couple days ago I hired a management consultant through an excellent Chicago firm. You'll see Dr. Montours in the tower this afternoon...a very attractive lady."

"What's her job?"

"We have a lot at stake in this tower, as you know. It's our model facility, and yet the head of the tower, this Sutton, goes and blasts our facility on TV. So I sent Dr. Montours down to check out Sutton...look into his allegations."

"And what did the lady discover? Was Sutton telling the truth?"

"Of course not!" Ed Morrison said. "I've already talked to Dr. Montours. Apparently Sutton is irresponsible. He exaggerates. But something else just happened at Miami. One of the best controllers in the tower, a man named Harry Boyle, was scheduled to demonstrate the CORAD system, but yesterday he had a confrontation with Sutton."

"What kind of confrontation?" the secretary asked, keeping his tone subdued.

"Sutton accused the man of blacking out on the radarscope."

There was a long pause, and the secretary stared ahead. Finally he turned his head toward Ed Morrison. "Did this fellow black out?"

"Not exactly. The whole thing is based upon Sutton's dislike for our new radar. He's pro-union and sees the

141

machine replacing his men, so Sutton cannot be impartial."

"Is Boyle ill?"

"He's a little tired because he takes his job very seriously...a truly loyal and dedicated man. Dr. Striker, the local FAA flight surgeon, says that Mr. Boyle can operate the radar. Sutton disagrees, so they left it up to me."

"You're not a doctor, Ed."

"I know, but I can tell if a man is all right when I talk to him."

The secretary continued to stare at the administrator. How could the man have the audacity to make a statement like that? he asked himself. Or was he just not fit for the responsibility of his job?

"I'd like to speak to this Dr. Montours in private, Ed. There are quite a lot of things going on in that tower that I don't like."

"Nothing to worry about, Mark, but of course, you can discuss anything you want with Dr. Montours. Anything."

Then, with blasts of horns, the lineup of cars began to move, and they drove slowly toward the entrance to the tower.

Jeff called Lou again with the news that the barometer was still dropping, indicating that the low pressure was settling down for a stay south of Miami. The Concorde captain acknowledged the report calmly, as if he knew that a slice of clear sky somehow would open for him.

"Dammit!" Jeff said, putting the phone down. "How the hell can that guy be so cool? My daughter's sitting up there not knowing a damn thing about this weather."

"He's going to do everything possible for himself and your daughter," Laura said, trying to reassure him.

"But how will he get in here? Christ, the ceiling is down on the deck...there's hardly one hundred feet of forward visibility. He hasn't got enough fuel to main-

142

tain a holding pattern, and there's nowhere else to go, short of the Dominican Republic."

Laura could not answer that, and she felt much of the terror streaming through Jeff Sutton.

"Jeff, the Washington group will be here in a minute. Do you know what you're going to say?"

"Oh, to hell with them! Where do I sent the Concorde?"

The phone rang, and Ted announced that the secretary and the administrator had just arrived.

"I'll be right down," Jeff said dully, thinking that it was about the most inappropriate moment for these men to be entering the lopsided world of the tower.

Laura and Jeff both greeted the officials at Ted's security station, and the conversation, although masked in casualness, was guarded. Morrison was plainly cautious, handing out gratuitous compliments to Jeff Sutton as they began a tour in the lower switchgear room of the tower.

When they had returned to the administration level, Mark asked if he could have a private word with Laura Montours. She had not said a thing as they toured endless alleys of computer cabinets and the web of power lines that criss-crossed the bowels of the tower like billions of tiny roots trying to support the long stem of the tulip high above.

During the trip down to Miami, Mark had grown increasingly quiet, as Ed Morrison had noticed. He was despondent because of what he had read in the Rollins report, and his mood was worsened by the weather and the appearance of a stunning woman in the employ of the administrator. He knew that Morrison was a popular Washington bachelor whose sloppy love affairs were tumbled about in the government gossip mill. This Laura Montours was probably another of Ed's girlfriends, a woman who would side with the administrator, slipping in pieces of psychological bridgework to support Ed and his CORAD system.

"Have you worked for Mr. Morrison before?" Mark asked Laura as they sat down in a small vacant office.

"No, sir. I only met him two days ago, when Dr. Barnes, our firm's president, sent me out from Chicago."

"And what is your present assignment?"

"To find out what is going on in this tower... mostly in regard to Mr. Sutton."

"Are you an expert in the area of air-traffic control, Dr. Montours?"

Laura came back quickly, "Not at all. My work is usually concerned with production-line efficiency from the psychological point of view. I told Mr. Morrison that I wasn't being given enough time to come up with any sort of thorough evaluation of the tower, even if I did totally understand ATC."

"Did Mr. Morrison mention anything about CORAD to you?"

"Only that it was extremely important to the agency and to the future of the air-traffic-control system."

"What about Mr. Sutton—how close have you gotten to him?"

Laura eyed the secretary, and for a moment she wanted to laugh. "We've had a series of helpful talks," she said calmly. "He showed me the workings of the tower and the traffic snarl in here. It's very frightening when you think of it. I'm a private pilot myself, and I don't know if I'd land a plane at MIA."

Mark began to feel better about Laura Montours.

"Why do you think Sutton made those statements on TV?"

"He believes them. At least, that's what he told me."

"And what sort of man is Mr. Sutton? He looks rather demure and placid."

Laura smiled again. "He's a fighter, Mr. Secretary. He abhors bureaucracy, especially when it interferes with the protection of human lives."

"No one likes bureaucracy, Dr. Montours. I'm not a politician. I'm a businessman, formerly a computer designer, and I was educated at MIT. But, like you, I'm interested in people... what makes them run."

"Mr. Sutton is a very interesting subject for psycho-

144

logical study. We don't come across many men like him."

"Are you speaking pejoratively?"

"No. Let me explain, sir. In my work, the human emotions that we encounter are usually buried deep. But in Mr. Sutton, we see a man whose basic assumptions about life are very visible. He has unshakable honesty. We don't talk about souls in my business, but Mr. Sutton seems to wage a war against evil, and he's constantly aware that one's destiny is decided day by day...action by action."

The secretary thought for a moment. Quasi-spiritual analyses were not helpful in his business. "He's an impractical moralist...is that what you're saying?"

"Yes. He's a moralist looking for and expecting much more from government and people than can usually be given."

"Very interesting," he said. "We'd have to ask how such a person ever became a public servant."

"I wondered about that, Mr. Secretary. But apparently Mr. Sutton came into air-traffic control with high hopes, thinking it was about the most important job in the world."

"With all these accidents, it might be."

"And Mr. Sutton was disappointed by government action—or perhaps I should call it government inaction."

The secretary folded his hands over his dark gray vest and shook his head up and down.

"So Mr. Sutton gets back at us on TV. He unleashed a verbal barrage and then quit."

"He's bitter, Mr. Secretary," Laura said. "The government...the justice system...the family farm...civil service—all the old institutions have let him down. Jeff Sutton is a holdout and, frankly, I admire the man—though I really can't say if there's room for people like Jeff Sutton."

"I'm going to find out," Mark said. "If this Jeff Sutton is right, then he *has* to be heard. You have to believe

145

in common decency, or else...or else a huge callus forms."

The secretary stumbled as he spoke. He wondered about decency, whether it was still common, or rare.

They left the small office and moved down through the administrative area of the tower, where Ed Morrison and Jeff were talking. Another man had joined them.

"Mr. Secretary," Jeff said as they approached, "this is Harry Boyle, who has spent twenty-seven years in the Miami tower. He knows everything about these airways. And that's Harry's dog, Jimmy."

The secretary smiled and shook hands all around; he leaned down and patted the Labrador, and there was a round of idle talk. Finally they settled down in Jeff's office, and Mark Cranston turned to the business of the day.

"Mr. Sutton, I've studied up on air-traffic control, and I've been to the National and Dulles towers in Washington, so I don't need a briefing on our ATC system as it exists."

"Excellent, Mr. Secretary," Jeff said. "Then we can go right to work."

"I understand that you have some ideas on the improvement of our air-traffic-control system?"

"Yes, sir, I have."

"Well, I'd like to hear them," the secretary said.

The administrator flashed a look toward Laura Montours, who sat straight, her expression totally blank. Morrison, plainly nervous, was searching for some support.

"Mark...ah...we usually go through channels. Today's mission is to evaluate the CORAD, to see it in operation, and we have an opportune day for it, don't we, Mr. Sutton?"

Jeff nodded. "Yes, it's the worst weather we've had here for years. The airport is closed to all traffic at the moment, so our test will be delayed, but I suggest that we move up to our conference room on the radar level and we can discuss the problems connected with this tower."

As they walked out of Jeff's small cubicle, Jimmy began barking, and Harry wiggled his finger at the dog, indicating that he was to stay.

"He wants to accompany us, Mr. Boyle, I take it?" Mark said.

"He follows me everywhere, Mr. Secretary."

"Well, why don't we let the dog come? I used to have a Lab just like you, Jimmy," he said, petting the dog, who was swiping his tail back and forth. "If it's all right with Mr. Sutton, bring him along."

Jeff agreed, and the old Labrador followed the officials out of the administrative section, where they stopped to be introduced to the deputy facility chief. Then Mark went down the line and shook hands with the secretaries, presenting each with a ball-point pen that he lifted from his inner coat pocket. The inscription read: "Good Luck and Appreciation...Mark C. Cranston, Secretary of Transportation."

Once in the conference room on the radar level, the secretary immediately began to question Jeff again.

"Are the skies too crowded?" Mark asked.

"Near terminals, yes!" Jeff answered flatly.

"Ah, that answer had to be qualified," Ed Morrison interrupted.

"It does not need qualification, Mr. Morrison," Jeff said. "We had twenty-one near-misses last year in Miami alone."

"And were these incidents reported?" Mark asked slowly.

"Indeed. They have to be, by law," Jeff said.

"And where did the reports go?"

"They were forwarded to the regional office in Atlanta."

"Curious," Mark said in a musing voice. "When we inspected the central files in Washington, we saw only a few reports of that nature."

"I can explain that," Ed Morrison said, jerking up-

147

right. "Upon investigation, we discarded some of them at the Atlanta office. They shouldn't have been classified as near-misses."

"Did anyone discuss the near-miss reports with you, Mr. Sutton?" the secretary asked.

"They did not."

"Then, Ed," the secretary said, turning to face him, "how do you know the reports were invalid?"

"Based upon the facts, of course."

"But, sir," Jeff said, "the facts were that we had twenty-one near-misses last year. I was here. I saw some of the near-collisions personally on the scopes, and we interviewed nineteen pilots who signed affidavits."

"Just whom do you believe, Mark?" Ed Morrison snapped.

The secretary looked again at Jeff. "Let's forget the near-miss reports for a moment, Mr. Sutton. Do you also have radar failures in this tower?"

"Yes, sir. We file those reports, too."

"And with what results?" the secretary inquired, leaning over the conference table.

"Well, usually nothing happens. Sometimes a unit is replaced; quite often it isn't."

"Then you would say," the secretary went on, "that the air-traffic situation around Miami is in trouble?"

"I did say that on TV, but nothing is done about it, Mr. Secretary."

"What would be your recommendations, Mr. Sutton?"

"Another airport and more experienced controllers working shorter hours."

"Now, now, Mr. Sutton, why don't you explain to the secretary that you're a union sympathizer?"

"Mr. Morrison," Jeff began easily, "the union does not establish hiring practices. It only acts as a collective-bargaining agent making sure that the work rules, such as they are, are upheld on each side. When I say that we need more men, I speak as the head of the tower. I've seen the illnesses here, the nervous break-downs, too few men working too many hours."

"That nervous-breakdown routine is highly exag-gerated," Ed Morrison said, becoming beet red and per-spiring from his brow.

"We can show you our medical records, the missed days, the flight surgeon's reports," Jeff retorted.

"Again, that's interpretation," Morrison said.

"Ed, why is everything interpretation?" the secre-tary asked. "Some facts seem clear. If our air-traffic-control system is working, why do we have so many near-misses and midair collisions? I'm getting heavy pressure from the Hill. Even the President has called me in twice about this ATC crisis."

"It's no crisis," Ed said. "Public hysteria, that's all."

"You know, I don't agree with Mr. Sutton!" Harry spoke up suddenly. "There *are* personnel shortages, but the new radar upstairs which I'm going to demonstrate will go a long way toward solving the problem."

Jeff shot a quick look at Laura. Harry's face seemed drawn and determined once again. He was sliding back. For a moment, Jeff wondered if he should let Harry operate CORAD to avoid an embarrassing confronta-tion; then he realized that it was inconceivable. He could not allow that burnt-out man to operate an un-proved radar on a day when the Miami visibility was down to nothing. Anyhow, at that moment it was ir-relevant; the airport was closed.

Mark glanced at Harry as he said, "Mr. Sutton, I take it you have different views on CORAD?"

"I do."

"Now, wait a minute, Mark," Ed Morrison said. "Mr. Sutton is an ally of the union. They have to protect their jobs."

"Mr. Morrison, I am a little tired of this union com-ment that you keep repeating," Jeff said.

"There's a basis for it," Ed insisted, trying to regain control.

"No basis," the facility chief said firmly. "I've written

hundreds of memos outlining our problems. There has *never* been any action on the agency's part."

"What about the CORAD, Mr. Sutton?" Mark repeated.

"Well, I wrote a sixty-page report listing my recommendations."

"Who asked you to do that?" Mark asked.

"No one."

"Why wasn't I shown the report, Ed?"

The administrator spoke harshly. "It was unauthorized. Furthermore, our technical section didn't believe it was valid. I stopped it on that level."

"Maybe the theory didn't agree with your CORAD theory, Ed," Mark said innocently.

"What is this, some kind of investigation of my central office?"

When the secretary didn't immediately answer, Ed Morrison continued in a strident voice, "Well, I certainly didn't come down to Miami for this!"

"Let's discuss it later," Mark said, then turned back to Jeff. "In simple language, what did the report say?"

"I have a copy, sir, if you're interested, but basically it said that CORAD is merely a more complicated step in a radar system which doesn't solve the problems."

"Of course it does!" Ed said.

"May I interrupt for a moment?" Harry Boyle asked.

He began by straightening his tie. His face was calm and his eyes mirrored none of the inner conflict and madness Jeff had seen the previous day.

"I guess Jeff would agree that I'm the most experienced controller in this tower."

"Yes, Harry came here in 1953," Jeff said. "He has made a fine contribution to the Miami air-control system."

Jeff was trying to pacify Harry, but the controller went on.

"See this pin, Mr. Secretary?" He showed Mark Cranston his small pin with the blue slash.

"Yes, Mr. Boyle."

"Do you know what this is?"

"It's an FAA pin of some sort."

"Not 'some sort,' sir. It's a twenty-year pin. That means they gave me the lunch and I was awarded this service pin. And it stands for something—obligation and duty."

"Yes," the secretary said, smiling and agreeing with a dip of his head.

"We have many men like Harry who have devoted their lives to air-traffic control," Ed Morrison added.

"To go on," Harry said, "I feel that Jeff's suggestion of a new airport is impractical and—"

"Gentlemen, gentlemen," Ed Morrison broke in. "Why can't we stick to the subject? We're here only to evaluate a new radar. Mr. Boyle, what about CORAD?"

"It's the answer, Mr. Morrison. It backs up the controllers. We need this right now. And I'm going to demonstrate how I can control the entire terminal air space with this one radar. Seeing is believing, and you have to take it from me. I have the pin to prove what I have accomplished. Here's the pin."

"Then let's get on with it," Ed Morrison said. "You see how a veteran controller feels about this radar. He's the one we should ask. Show us, Mr. Boyle."

Jeff Sutton came to his feet and turned toward the group. "I'm sorry, gentlemen, but Mr. Boyle is not operating that radar when and if the airport opens."

"Why?" Ed Morrison demanded. "He's the best man you have here. You just said so."

"Harry Boyle is experienced, but he's too ill to handle this radar."

"He doesn't look ill to me," Ed Morrison said. "And our FAA flight surgeon said Harry was okay."

Jeff shook his head. "Mr. Boyle has suffered certain work pressures. He blacked out on his scope yesterday."

"That's a lie, Jeff!" Harry screamed. "You've got a vendetta against me. You're against the new radar and you know I support it."

"Just a minute," the secretary said. "Dr. Montours, what do you know about this?"

"Apparently Mr. Boyle did suffer some sort of blackout. I interviewed another controller who was in the room at the time and saw it happen."

"He doesn't sound or appear ill," Mr. Morrison said. "Are you all right, Mr. Boyle?"

"Of course I'm all right. I wouldn't be in the tower this morning if I were sick."

The secretary rose and stood staring first at Harry and then at the administrator, and finally he said, "I'd like to speak to Mr. Sutton and Dr. Montours in private. I don't like what I'm hearing."

"Why shouldn't I be included?" Ed cried.

"Mr. Morrison," Jeff intervened hastily, "this is my last day in the tower. Now, perhaps I have undermined you in front of the secretary. I didn't mean to do that. Under your agency's direction we have made progress in certain areas, so please do not think I'm the arch-enemy. I disagree with the system, not you."

"I appreciate that, Mr. Sutton, but I still should be in on any discussions. I *am* the FAA administrator, even though you are in command of this tower."

"Well, that's up to the secretary, of course. I don't care if you join the conversation or not."

"Then, Mark...?"

"No." The secretary remained adamant. "May we go outside now? I want to talk to Mr. Sutton and Dr. Montours."

They entered the hall by the radar room.

"Did you submit your resignation because you feared censure from the agency, Mr. Sutton, over that TV program?" The secretary's face was quizzical.

Jeff shook his head. "I cannot put up with things the way they are now, sir. Harry is sick, and other men in here are just as bad off."

"I see. And are there near-miss reports not filed?"

"Yes."

"All right. We're going to look into that. Now, this Harry Boyle situation...there seems to be a difference of opinion as to what happened yesterday."

"What happened, Mr. Secretary," Laura said, "is that Harry went after Mr. Sutton with a fire ax."

"I wasn't aware of that!"

"Well, Hoagy Washington was right there, and you can talk to him about it," Laura said. "The field had to be closed down while Harry calmed down. He's a pathetic case. His file is thick with psychiatric problems and sick-leaves. I just looked at it this morning."

"Well, I certainly understand why you don't trust the man, Mr. Sutton. It's very sad."

Jeff nodded. "It is. I'll show you what CORAD can do, sir, but I'm not letting Harry operate that radar, nor am I planning to close down any other station in the tower on a day like this. We may not even go through with the demonstration if the field remains socked in."

"Yes, yes, I concur with your decision. All right, as the secretary of this department, I can override Mr. Morrison. But are we going to have a bad scene?"

"I think Harry will listen to reason, Mr. Secretary, but I can't guarantee his actions."

The secretary shook his head, and they reentered the conference room.

Mark Cranston came right to the point. "I believe it would be better for the facility chief, Mr. Sutton, to demonstrate CORAD."

Harry stood first, and then Jimmy. Harry took the secretary's hand and shook it.

"If all of you believe that I can't handle the radar, then it's okay with me. I'm not sick. It's Jeff's opinion only, but I'll abide by your decision."

"Well, Mr. Boyle," the secretary said, "I appreciate your understanding."

The phone rang suddenly, and Jeff picked it up. "I'll be right there," he said, and then he turned to the others. "I have to check this weather. While we're all waiting for it to clear, perhaps Mr. Boyle could take you through our radar and approach rooms."

"I'd be glad to show the gentlemen through," Harry agreed.

"All right," Mark said as he got up. "But, Mr. Sutton, even if the airport opens and the test proceeds, I do want to talk to you again. I'm interested in your suggestions."

"I'll be ready when you are, Mr. Secretary."

Laura Montours followed Jeff out into the hall, and he turned to her.

"What's happened, Jeff? You look like a new man all of a sudden."

"The barometer just started up a tiny bit! Hoagy called me from the cab."

"Oh, thank God," she said.

They climbed the metal stairs two at a time, and when they arrived in the cab, everyone was huddled around the barometer. Outside, a deep gray veil had descended about the tower, and the rain slashed off the tinted windows and broke into fast-running rivulets. If the low was beginning to move, there was no portent of it from the tower windows.

All the men were aware of Jeff's concern about his daughter, and they had made a graph indicating the slightest movements of the barometer. They were studying it now as if it had the life-or-death significance of an electrocardiogram.

"See that little move, Mr. Sutton!" Hoagy Washington said excitedly.

"I see it! Have you called the weather station?"

"Not yet, sir. Thought you'd want to do it."

Jeff picked up the phone and dialed the Miami station. "We see a slight movement in the glass up here," he said.

"Yes, we're getting a five- to eight-millibar rise on this end."

"Would you say that the low is on the move?"

"Yes, sir. No doubt about it."

"And what's Key West reporting?"

"Ceilings are lifting...they're reporting fifteen hundred broken."

"Now, listen, this is very important," Jeff said. "When could we get a break in the ceiling here?"

"It's hard to predict, but if the central pressure rises another five millibars within the next twenty minutes, I'd say we're looking at a quick improvement. You should begin to see it with a wind change. It'll go to the northwest. Keep tabs on your wind and glass. The rain will let up, and within, oh, probably an hour, you'll visually see a clearing trend."

Jeff put down the phone and threw his arms around Hoagy and Laura, hugging them as she jumped up and down.

"The low's moving...it's moving out! We have to keep a graph of the wind direction, every five minutes. Call me down in the conference room as soon as you see the shift."

Jeff sat down and quickly worked Lou Griffis through the Nassau radio, and minutes later he had reached the cockpit of the Concorde.

"We're getting a break, Lou. The system is moving out. The glass is beginning to come up."

"Wow...we played this one close, Jeff. How soon will I get a hole?"

"We don't know yet. Should be within half an hour, though. What's your position?"

"We're four hundred and sixty miles from Miami... fifty-one thousand feet."

"How much fuel remaining?"

"About an hour and thirty minutes of flying time left."

"We'll find you some visibility. Be back to you as soon as we see the clearing trend begin to develop. But, for Christ's sake, burn off that fuel slowly."

"We'll try."

Lou clicked off his button, and in the cab Jeff hugged Laura again.

"Best news I've heard in years," he said.

"I thought planes could land in zero conditions these days."

"That may be true in a year or so. Right now we still

155

need about four hundred feet forward visibility. At the very end of the landing, the pilot *has* to see something. He must establish an aiming point on the runway."

They moved down the steps from the cab, and in the vestibule that led to the heavy fire door, Laura stopped Jeff again.

"I'm so happy about the weather." She smiled.

"Yeah, we got a lucky break—first one in a while for me. Laura, by the way, what did the secretary say?"

"He wanted to know about you and Morrison."

"What did you tell him?"

"I told him I was rather shocked by the situation here in Miami."

"Do you think we have a good ear in that man?"

"I'd say so. He's intelligent, and I believe he wants to do the right thing. He doesn't like this air-traffic-control predicament any more than you do. He must be getting one hell of a lot of pressure from the Hill."

"I'm sure he is, and, Laura...thanks...."

She kissed him quickly and said, "Let's tell the secretary the truth."

9

When Jeff and Laura arrived back in the conference room, the officials were still in the approach-radar section, and Jeff went into the storage closet and brought out a mammoth box.

"This is my solution," he said, gleaming with frank boyish pride.

"The ultimate radar?" Laura smiled.

"Hope so," he said.

A minute later the secretary and the administrator reentered the conference room, and Mark Cranston sat down and stared at the box on the table.

"Do you have a surprise for us, Mr. Sutton?"

"It's an idea of mine, sir, for a new radar. Oh, by the way, the weather's improving."

"Good!" Ed Morrison said, wanting to get on to the demonstration.

The secretary pushed to his feet and paced around the room. "Basically, we know the public has lost trust in our ability to safely control aircraft, or separate them. The accident record has been appalling. I believe the solution is more airports, a diversification of traffic, and my findings indicate that the FAA may have to exercise more authority over the nation's airports. There'll be an outcry about big government coming in, but the situation is acute. We cannot have so many accidents and near-misses."

"I agree, Mr. Secretary," Jeff said. "Miami desperately needs a second airport, and so do about twenty other major U.S. terminals."

"But, Mark, we're not here to discuss airports," Ed Morrison insisted. "The agency believes in more terminals, obviously, but the main question right now is technology. New airports will take years to build—what do we do in the meantime?"

"Ed, I'm coming to that," Mark said. "It seems to me that we're putting too much emphasis on the computer, the machine instead of the man."

"It's a combination," Ed Morrison said. "The blend of the human brain with the computer brain."

"Mr. Sutton, you've had experience with ATC and computer technology. Do you believe computers can think?" Mark asked.

"Mr. Secretary, the question is not if they *can* think, but *should* they think?"

"Please continue, Mr. Sutton," Mark said with a smile, realizing that the facility chief had just touched the big raw nerve in the conflict that was ripping the computer community into two separate camps.

"The human brain, as we know, is organized dynamically, and through millions of years of evolution it has become a much more complicated machine than even the most sophisticated computer," Jeff said.

"That's true." Mark nodded. "Even the advocates of artificial intelligence are divided. When I started in the computer business, we told people that the computer would be smarter than human brains. But that was a wild prediction...it never happened."

"In air-traffic control the computer can memorize far more than the human brain," Ed Morrison said. "This is a memory business, isn't it, Mr. Boyle?"

"Yes, it is."

"Well, now," the secretary said, "the computer can memorize the Chicago telephone directory, but the computer cannot make a decision based upon judgment."

"That's programming," Ed Morrison chimed in. "It can make a decision if it knows the input."

"But the output is limited," Jeff said.

"And so is the ability of the human brain," Ed Morrison said.

"Ed, even a baby can distinguish different faces...no computer can do that. No matter how we cut the cake, not even the most optimistic computer specialist will admit that his machine can reason. The computer is limited to what it's been told. Now, my question is this: should we place so much dependence upon a device that can't reason, when we're dealing with so many human lives?"

"No!" Jeff said loudly. "For one thing, the computer has no intelligence or decision-making ability based on reason or judgment. And it can break down. We've had these computer radars go wild in here, and all of a sudden the controllers are frantic. They've depended on this artificial intelligence to the point where many of the men can't separate the traffic without computer tags on the scopes."

"In the CORAD," Ed Morrison said, "you'll see how

the computer automatically knows the position of every plane."

"But it doesn't possess a faculty of judgment," Mark said.

"It's a different kind of judgment," Morrison said.

"Judgment is judgment, Mr. Morrison. It's either right or wrong," Jeff said.

Jeff stood and brought his box toward the center of the table. The secretary meandered around the conference room, shaking his head while eyeing the strange box.

"We won't settle the computer argument today," Mark said. "Okay, Mr. Sutton, it's your turn. What's in there?"

Jeff slowly, dramatically unwrapped the cardboard sides of the box as he spoke. "What you just observed in the radar room, Mr. Secretary, does not represent the sky as it is. You were looking at flat tracking radar, but the sky is hardly flat. The third dimension is now supplied by the tag alongside the target, which says the plane is at ten thousand. So the controller really supplies the missing third dimension. In other words, the most important element is missing from our current radar display—the actual portrayal of the sky as it exists."

There was a general nod of heads. Who could argue against Jeff's basic premise? And then he finally unwrapped his box.

It was a cube of plastic about four feet by three feet, and inside, Jeff had strung out thousands of hairline wires which crisscrossed each other with only a sixteenth of an inch between the lines. And on the base of the plastic cube was painted a runway.

"Here we have a block of air space," Jeff said.

Everyone leaned over the plastic cube, and Laura eyed Jeff closely, wondering just how much this display model had cost him.

"Now, I have rigged this with demonstration lights." Jeff clicked on a series of battery-operated circuits, and two lights came on, representing several aircraft. He pressed a series of other buttons, and the lights moved down toward the runway.

"Fascinating, Mr. Sutton," the secretary said. "Can a display like this be built?"

"Yes, it's already operating on navy ships in the fire-control rooms."

"Third-dimensional radar like this would cost a fortune," Ed Morrison said.

"We might have to spend that fortune," Mark said.

"I see this future for the controller," Jeff continued. "He will sit surrounded by a series of cubes like this. He'll still have the radarscope, but for the first time the controller will see the sky dimensionally, and one plane's actual relationship to another."

"So what you're advocating, Mr. Sutton, is a combination of a new visual display and the computer?" the secretary said.

"Yes. We'll still have altitude tags given to us by the computer and the collision-avoidance system, but I feel the controller will be much more relaxed if he's looking at a correct and total picture. If two targets are coming together, the controller will understand this, because it's right there in front of him, and then his reason and judgment can solve the problem without resorting to computer systems."

"What did it cost you to build this, Mr. Sutton?" Mark asked.

"I spent about eight hundred dollars on it."

"Who asked you to do this?"

"No one."

"I think your effort is very commendable. How do you feel about it, Mr. Boyle?"

"I knew Jeff was working on something like this, but it would take billions of dollars to go to this sort of system, just as Mr. Morrison said."

"Let me worry about the budget. Would it be an easier system to work, from your point of view, Mr. Boyle?"

"I *suppose* we should see the sky as it is, but a trained controller visualizes the same thing now."

"But he doesn't see the planes in relation to each other, as Mr. Sutton pointed out. The altitude intelligence is only a tag."

Harry did not answer, and Ed Morrison moved in front of the block of plastic. "This idea is years away from implementation, and Mr. Boyle is right."

"I thank you, Mr. Sutton, for your effort. We're going to study this very closely. There's good logic here," the secretary said.

As they continued to talk about the block radar, Hoagy Washington, smiling broadly, entered the conference room and placed a note in front of Jeff: "Wind has started to shift to northwest. Ceiling is now lifting. Forward visibility five hundred feet. Suggest we commence operations."

"Celtic 202...Miami radio...stand by for transmission, sir."

Lou Griffis adjusted his earphones.

"Lou, this is Jeff. The low pressure is starting to move out. We have a wind shift...dry air is pushing in. The stuff's breaking up. We still have light rain and a patchy situation, but it'll improve...we made it!"

"We were damn lucky. I'm starting my descent now. See you within forty-five minutes."

Landing the Concorde is almost automatic. Its systems are complex and efficient. When the power is taken off for a descent in any plane, the nose will point down. The Concorde is no different. But an ordinary jet has trim tabs on the tail to deflect the air flow and keep the plane level; the Concorde, for the same reason it has no wing flaps, does not. Instead, to keep the nose relatively level, fuel is pumped aft from the forward trim tank. The weight is shifted and the aircraft's spindle nose comes up. This fuel transfer is automatic, but the procedure is monitored by the flight engineer, who stares at a series of blinking yellow lights indicating the fuel-transfer routine.

Looking out his cockpit window, Lou Griffis could

see towers of dark cumulus clouds, part of the low-pressure system, poking up through the gray stratus layer; the vertical cells ringed his Concorde like enormous ebony buttes rising from a dull gray plain.

It was now 12:20 P.M. as Jeff led the visitors up to the cab for the CORAD demonstration. Outside, it was still angry; the gelid rain was pinging off the canted windows, and the wind crannied through the forest of antennas on top of the tulip. They could now see the blurry edges of the runway lights, but in the chaos, they looked small and seemed to blink on and off as the downpour shrouded them intermittently.

"Okay, start bringing them in, Nick," Jeff called over to Cozzoli. "No departures, just get those guys out of the stack. Use twenty-seven, left and right."

Nick started to undo the holding pattern, and quickly, one by one, the waiting aircraft headed down toward the runways.

"You really impressed the secretary, Jeff," Laura said quietly to him.

Ed Morrison heard it and shot a dour look toward her.

"I'll be talking to Dr. Barnes about you," he said. "You rather took the opposite side, didn't you?"

"I called the situation as I saw it," Laura responded.

"I hope your résumé is typed up," the administrator whispered, trying to shield his anger from the secretary, who was watching the first jet land on runway twenty-seven left.

"What a day!" Mark Cranston exclaimed, turning to Jeff. "Isn't it dangerous to operate in weather like this?"

"Not at this point, sir. We're monitoring all flights via radar, and the pilots have visual runway contact— not the whole runway, but part of it."

Jeff glanced toward Harry as he spoke. The controller was petting his dog and smiling; he seemed to have gained control of himself, and Jeff went on.

"Gentlemen, Mr. Boyle will give you a rundown on the cab operations before we begin the CORAD dem-

162

onstration. I want to check downstairs with the radar men first. Dr. Montours, would you come with me?" Jeff motioned.

Harry had begun to explain the workings of the conventional radar as Jeff and Laura left the cab. Downstairs they paused at the door to the radar room.

"Jeff, what's the matter?" Laura asked, staring up at his pinched face.

"I'm just not sure of Harry. What if he goes a little off again? I don't want to worry about him on top of everything else now."

"Well, why don't you call security? Have that guard come up and stand by in the hall."

"Maybe I should. But I can't let Harry know we're patrolling him."

"He'll be too busy in the cab to notice."

Jeff called the security desk and asked Ted to come up. Then they unlocked the radar door and entered.

"Hoagy," Jeff said, "we'll be starting the CORAD test in a matter of minutes. You'll hear me over the cans. I want you to carefully monitor what I'm doing. Check me out. If you see a conflict, just cut in on my transmission. I'll keep my headset on."

"You don't trust it, do you, Mr. Sutton?" the old black man said quietly.

"Not in this stuff. Actually, not in any weather."

Laura and Jeff left the radar room, and Ted met them outside the elevator.

"Ted, we're going to start the demonstration. What I want you to do is stand just inside the vestibule door to the cab."

"Why is that, Mr. Sutton?"

"Just a precaution. We've had a little dispute with Mr. Boyle over who's to operate CORAD. I'm taking the station, but if there's any further argument, I'll walk over to the top of the stairs and give you a hand signal. But I don't think there'll be any trouble."

"I hope not, Mr. Sutton, not with the secretary and the administrator here."

Laura and Jeff crossed looks and climbed to the cab.

163

Jeff and Laura's fears were allayed.

Harry had calmly and clearly taken Mark Cranston and the administrator through each step of the cab's ATC procedure, detailing the functions of the radar units in understandable terms, and his face bore the color and glow of the old controller Jeff remembered.

"Now, Mr. Sutton will explain how CORAD improves upon the present system," Harry concluded.

"Thank you very much," Jeff said as he mounted the CORAD platform, loosening his tie. "Mr. Boyle has presented a fine digest of the present state of the art." He nodded to Harry in a gesture of appreciation. "The principal advantage of CORAD, gentlemen, is the selective mode of control. These three scopes duplicate the others downstairs, plus the one we see here in the cab. Essentially, CORAD is an overall view of the entire control system, as well as a computer command center. By changing the modes, I can view all the airways adjacent to our South Florida control zone."

Secretary Cranston and the administrator huddled over the CORAD, and Jeff kept changing the modes, scanning various areas of the ATC pattern. The target blips, with their altitude tags, speckled the domed glass of the eighteen-inch scopes.

"Now, in operation," Jeff continued, "the computer simply picks up the number of the flight at the gate. We will demonstrate the action before we move to our full CORAD procedure."

Jeff took a departure strip from one of the controllers. He punched up the number on the creamy-colored computer terminal just below the CORAD scopes.

"I've entered the flight information. The computer data bank has it. When the pilot calls ground control, his voice is translated by the computer into a digital reference that does not conflict with other aircraft on the taxiways. For instance, I'll push the command button, and on the immediate printout we see the taxi instructions for Delta's flight 689."

Up came the words on the terminal printout.

"At that moment," Jeff said, "we know our computer understands the requests. We also have the talking computer, but it's not operational today. For the time being, Mr. Boyle will simply sit beside me and read instructions as they come up on the teleprinter."

"Fascinating, isn't it, Mark?" Ed Morrison boomed, a giant smile spreading across his tanned face.

"Yes, it is. How many manned stations does this machine replace?" the Secretary asked Jeff.

"The two downstairs...two up here," Harry interrupted.

"But I must stress this," Ed Morrison said. "No controller will be fired because of this computer radar. Naturally, the system will probably require less manpower in the future, but we'll reduce manpower mostly by attrition. The main asset of CORAD is its failproof ability."

The men in the tower snapped around, staring at the administrator. He was wrong. The controllers were seeing their jobs evaporate, and Jeff caught their feelings of despair, the agony of having handled a sweaty, thankless job so many years, only to be replaced by a doubtful conglomeration of buttons, semiconductors, and a collection of circuitry which could emulate, supposedly, the human voice.

"Mr. Secretary," Jeff said, "in my opinion we should not cut back on our manpower requirements."

"May I say something, Jeff?"

"Sure, Harry."

"CORAD simply changes the controller's job. At all times one man will be monitoring the system. As soon as the computer sees a traffic conflict, the red light goes on, with a corresponding number. The controller will simply push two buttons: one for the proper scope mode and the other to index the forecasted conflict. At that point the computer, now on conflict-resolution mode, points out instructions like 'Clipper 908, turn left to nine-zero degrees. Threatened conflict! Threatened conflict!' After the pilot effects his corrective action, the red alarm button right here goes amber, meaning that the evasive turn has been completed. When the two conflicting aircraft are directed by the computer to new altitudes and headings, this light, the lower one, goes green. So whether CORAD can think is not the real question. What we have here is the computer monitoring the traffic flow, plus, of course, the eyes of a controller."

"Excellent, Mr. Boyle," Ed Morrison said. "Excellent! You see, Mark, these are our checks and balances. The best of computer technology combined with the human brain of a controller."

"Well, Mr. Sutton, I understand the theory," Mark said. "Let's see how it all works in practice."

"Fine. Harry, would you sit down at the command desk and issue our directive information?"

"But, Jeff," Harry said, "I think we should give it a fair chance. Relieve *all* the control positions."

"We are. As soon as you and I take over, Mr. Cozzoli and his team will cease to control aircraft in the cab."

"What about the radar downstairs?" Harry said.

"Well," Jeff said slowly, "they will simply monitor their positions. Positive control will be up here."

"In my opinion, the radar men should be up here, too. I mean, to prove to the secretary that *complete* control of departure and approach functions are with CORAD."

"I think that's reasonable." Ed Morrison nodded.

"I disagree!" Jeff clipped. "The weather is marginal. Those controllers will back us up."

"Then, what kind of a test is it?" Harry said quickly.

"I'd like the radar stations manned, Harry, as a protection. CORAD is still experimental."

"Gentlemen, gentlemen," Ed spoke up. "If CORAD is to be proved out, we have to test it in the *worst* conditions. I say call the men upstairs."

Jeff stood straighter and sucked in a large breath. He was stony-faced and his long legs were widely spaced.

"I won't do it!" he finally said sharply.

"Then it's not a fair test," Harry answered, swinging his head from side to side.

"Yes! Yes! I agree with Mr. Boyle," the administrator added, becoming visibly frustrated.

"I'm sorry," Jeff said with a smile.

Harry stepped down off the CORAD platform. "I want the approach controllers up here!"

It was, perhaps, the assertive note in Harry's voice, a signal, that started Jimmy barking. The worn-out Labrador was standing at the head of the stairs looking down, his tail extended. Harry moved over and saw Ted leaning against the wall, his hand on his revolver.

"You brought the security guard up, Jeff! Ted, come in here. What the hell is this?"

"I was instructed to stay in the vestibule, Mr. Boyle."

"Who told you that—Mr. Sutton? You're guarding *me!*" Harry whirled. "I'm not going to be patrolled by an armed guard," he said, his face flushed with anger and his hand sweeping past his belt, feeling the knob of the grenade and the tip of his Magnum.

"Of course you shouldn't be harassed, Mr. Boyle," Ed Morrison said. "Mr. Sutton, please, what is going on?"

"This is my tower until five o'clock today. I'll run it the way I see fit."

"As the administrator of this agency, I'm ordering you to release the guard and close down the approach- and departure-radar stations."

"I won't do either," Jeff said slowly.

"Now, look," Harry said, "this test is going on as planned. You promised me that I could operate today. All right, I gave in on that. But closing down just two stations and...and...that armed security guard with his hand on the gun out there! I have pride. I'm a professional!"

"And I'm the facility chief, and in that capacity I am ordering you to leave the cab, Harry."

Harry threw back his shoulders and looked at Jeff with fiery eyes. Harry's face was steeped in light crimson; sweat coursed down his shiny forehead; his eyes were wide, like white marbles, and Jeff recognized Harry's maniacal look, the traces of his craziness creeping back.

Each of the six controllers in the cab glanced at Jeff, then Harry, who was tilting his head to the side in a contorted way, as if his neck had become immobile. There was a lull in the crackle of voices streaming over the speakers.

"Keep your eyes on your stations!" Jeff blasted out, and the men jerked around to attend the traffic.

There were a few transmissions over the speaker, but the hot silence continued, everyone switching glances from Harry to Jeff. The only sounds were heavy breaths and the reverberating rain pinging off the glass panels of the cab, and in the distance the whines of the jets filled the sodden air.

Then Harry uncocked his head. He lowered it into his sunken chest, and when he jerked his head up again, a sickly grin was on his face. His eyes had retreated to their normal position, and the color had left his cheeks. He wiped the sweat from his brow and smiled, looking directly at the administrator.

"I want to be cooperative," Harry said. "Yes, Jeff is the facility chief, and the best one we ever had. I taught him. This man had what I don't—some sort of executive ability. All I ever knew was how to control traffic safely. No one can say that Harry Boyle ever let a mistake go past when he was on the scope. But, gentlemen, I want this test to be a good appraisal of CORAD, not for me, but for all those passengers out there. They deserve the best we have."

Everyone dipped his head in agreement and tried to force a smile in Harry's direction, but the ominous silence continued.

Finally Jeff spoke in a friendly, consoling voice. "Well, Harry, we appreciate what you just said."

"Of course," Ed Morrison added. "Mr. Boyle has his heart in the right place. The man is only trying to do the right thing, Mark. I appreciate his point."

"Fine. I understand the line of authority in the cab," the secretary answered. "Now that we have all this settled, could we please get on with the demonstration?"

"Certainly," Jeff said. "Harry, will you sit down and issue the computer instructions to the traffic?"

"Okay, Jeff. Let's give it a good go."

Harry thumped Jeff on the arm in a good-natured gesture, and Jeff believed that the moment of danger was past. Harry smiled at the others, and once more they returned his grin. Everything appeared resolved. Jeff mounted the CORAD platform once again and sat down in the green plastic chair on roller wheels; he pushed in toward the three scopes, tuned one of them, and with his other hand activated the computer power button. Harry stepped on the platform, and paused just behind Jeff, as if noting the resolutions of the three scopes.

But one hand slid into his coat and snapped out the .38-caliber Magnum, pointing the muzzle directly at the back of Jeff's head.

"Jeff!" Laura screamed. "Look out!"

"Take it easy, everyone," Harry yelled. "Nothing will happen."

"Put that away!" Jeff bellowed as he turned his face into the fat muzzle, smelling the fresh gun grease and oil that Harry had rubbed into the burled walnut of the grip.

"Christ, man, you're mad!" Cozzoli yelled.

"Work your traffic, goddammit!" Jeff cried. "I'll take care of this. Harry, now, come on. This is a sick joke. I'll give you five seconds to lay that pistol on the counter!"

"Mr. Boyle," the administrator said in a halting voice, "you are holding a weapon on a Cabinet member of the United States. Do you realize what you're doing?"

"I'm doing this to prove CORAD. It's what you wanted, isn't it?"

Laura walked toward the CORAD platform, holding out her hand.

"Harry," she said softly, "give me the gun, please. This won't settle anything. You can't kill all of us. There're not enough bullets in the gun.

Harry pulled back the Magnum, keeping it from Laura's reach.

"Stay away, Laura!" Jeff ordered. "The guy's flipped!"

Harry started to laugh. It was a normal laugh for a moment; then they heard the note of almost total derangement. Harry swung his head back and said in a gurgling voice, "Dr. Montours is right. I can't kill all of you with this gun. Don't you people think I considered that? Oh, yes, I considered it. I know that Jeff Sutton is against me...not just now, Mr. Secretary, but all through the years. He even missed my twenty-year lunch, and on purpose. He could have attended and said a word for me."

"Mr. Boyle," Mark said, "I'm pleading with you. Nothing will be accomplished this way. You need help. I'll see to it that this incident is dropped by the Department of Justice, but you must put down the gun."

"The gun is not the only thing, Mr. Secretary. Take a look at this."

Harry pulled out the hand grenade and knotted his hand around the dark gray bulb. There was a muffled cry from Laura.

"This is an antipersonnel grenade. Brought it back all the way from Korea. Ever seen what happens when one of these goes off? Oh, it's terrible. People are ripped apart. Arms and legs come off. No, I can't do what I want with the Magnum, but all I have to do is yank this, and the shrapnel will cut this place up like everyone was tissue paper. They had these grenades during the Inchon landing, but they were outlawed, that's how bad they are."

"Why, Harry, why?" Ed Morrison cried, his eyes darting wildly from one weapon to the other.

"Keep on your fucking traffic!" Jeff yelled out to Cozzoli, "I'll handle this."

"No! *I'll* handle it," Harry said. "We are going to demonstrate CORAD the right way. Now, you watch me, Jeff. I'm going to pull out the pin, and if you cross me again, all I have to do is release the trigger hold.

If it goes off, it will be your responsibility. But you'll be goddamned dead."

"Harry…" Jeff said, watching the pin slowly being eased from its safety tube. "Harry, for Christ's sake. What you'll do is destroy the entire cab. You can kill us, but if the tower goes black, what about all those jets out there ducking through the soup? We'll have a dozen midairs, Harry! It won't be just us, but all those passengers. Think of them."

"I am thinking of them. That's why you're going to do exactly what I say. If you don't, I'm releasing the trigger. I won't be killing the people out there, *you* will."

"For God's sakes, Mr. Sutton, do what he says!" Mark yelled.

"Absolutely!" Ed Morrison cried out.

"Do you hear them, Jeff?"

"What is it that you want, Harry?" Jeff said, lowering his shoulders and keeping an eye on the fused grenade.

"First of all, order Hoagy to place the incoming traffic back into temporary holding patterns, just for a few minutes until we get organized. Then tell him to get the men up from the lounge so they can see the demonstration. Everybody up!"

"Harry," Jeff said slowly, "please! We've been through a hell of a lot together in this tower. Put the pin back in the grenade and let's talk."

"I gave you a chance, Jeff. Now, go ahead and do as I say."

Harry jammed the muzzle of the .38 into the back of Jeff's neck, and the force of it pushed the facility chief's head almost into the face of the scope. Jeff felt a slight tremor deep in his stomach, the first he had felt in the sixty seconds since Harry had pulled out the gun and grenade. He knew he should have terminated the man a year ago. And, too, he realized once again the terrible conflict of trying to be a compassionate human being and the chief of a control tower.

An all-consuming sense of culpability gripped Jeff

Sutton. It was his fault—shared by Dr. Striker, who had said Harry was harmless.

Jeff wished that the FAA flight surgeon could have been there to see the collapse of Harry Boyle, but that, indeed, would not have brought consolation to those whose terror was growing swiftly in the octagonal glass-faced cab.

10

The tower stem, simple from the outside, was actually a complex series of long cavities rising to the cab. The high-speed elevator was placed in the center of the two-hundred-foot spindle. Around it ran a stairwell, and to the sides were two cable trunks carrying the power, phone, and radar lines from the higher levels down to the switchgear room in the subbasement. The tower depended on ninety thousand miles of electrical wires, more than contained in a forty-story office building.

On each side of the cable trunks ran two air-conditioning ducts, one to control the temperature, the other, the humidity. Deep in the tower was a computer that handled the dehumidifiers and cooling compressors for other computers, and these atmospheric-control tapes spun all day, making sure that all the electronic equipment functioned easily.

After the radar blackout reported by Jeff Sutton on the thirteenth, Joe Redmond and his assistant, Leroy Tillis, had started to troubleshoot the cables in the north and south trunks. On the morning of the fourteenth, still unaware that Jeff had been covering for

Harry Boyle, they continued their work, climbing up the metal rungs, pinching the various colored radar lines with their test gear.

At the moment of Harry's spasm, Joe and Leroy were fifteen feet below the cab doing their test procedures by the book. At that moment there were sixteen flights in the MIA approach pattern, including five international arrivals: Belize, Varig, Pan Am, Air France, and Mexicana's flight from Mexico City. The weather had cleared a bit, but the towering cumuli were still stalled, rising like great black cathedrals over the Glades.

At 12:33 P.M. the green phone rang beside Hoagy's radarscope.

"Hoagy, this is Jeff. Ah...we have made a slight change in procedure."

"What's that, sir? Just a minute. Delta 620, turn *immediately* to zero-four-zero degrees. Yes, Mr. Sutton?"

"Well, ah...it's this way," Jeff stumbled on. "The administrator had decided to close down the radar stations, transfer the control position up here to CORAD."

Hoagy held the phone away from his face. He was stunned. The old controller gave an instruction to an inbound 747 and went back to the phone again.

"Are you sure of this, Mr. Sutton?" the black man said in a halting voice.

"Yeah."

"It's kind of risky, isn't it, sir? None of us trust that gadget."

"It'll be all right. Now, Hoagy, in the changeover, place all your inbounds into a holding pattern. When we're operational in the cab, we'll unstack for landing. We're going to hold all departing traffic until we're set. Go to the lounge and ask the relief boys to come up to observe the...this test."

"You sound funny, Mr. Sutton. Are you certain about all this?"

"It's an order...from the administrator. He's the boss."

"But he doesn't know ATC, sir."

"Hoagy, he has agency authority. Now, do what I say."

"All right, but it'll take a few minutes to get things in order."

"Just come up when everything's set."

"Yes, sir."

Hoagy issued another radar instruction and said to the man on his right, "Strangest thing. Mr. Sutton says we're closing down the radar. Get your traffic handed off to center as soon as possible."

"Why is he doing this?"

"Says it's an order from the administrator."

"I wouldn't chance it," the controller said, stuffing a gumdrop in his mouth.

"Well, I don't know. Mr. Sutton always knows what he's doing, and the brass *is* up there."

Harry had monitored Jeff's call, and when they both hung up the green phones, Harry turned to Jeff with a positive shake of his head. "Now, Jeff, that was co-operation. Thank you."

"Then will you please put that pin back in the grenade? It could slip out of your hand."

"All right, Jeff. In it goes."

Mark and the administrator had backed up against the far counter of the cab, trying to keep as far away from the maniac as possible. Laura had remained by CORAD, and Ted leaned against the cinderblock wall of the vestibule, overhearing the conversation above him. First, he thought he should rush Harry and try to kill him, but he discarded that idea as being too dangerous, and besides, the dog had him pinned down; every time he shifted his position, the Labrador, which stood like a sentinel at the top of the stairs, would growl and draw Harry's attention toward him. He knew that Hoagy and the entire radar would be there soon; he would have to try to warn them and hope that one of them could escape and go for assistance. Ted cautiously backed up to the steel door and waited while he took out his .38 revolver and flexed his hand, trying to slide his deformed knuckles through the trigger guard.

"Harry"—Mark Cranston spoke soothingly—"do you know the consequences of kidnapping us? That's what you're doing."

"And do you know, Mr. Secretary, the consequences of continuing this outmoded system of air-traffic control? Look, sir. There's nothing left for me. I was going to be terminated, you know, and my whole life is in this cab. It's the only thing I've ever had besides my family. You've always been a big man, sir...riding in a car with special license plates. I don't have that. I'm a little man, ordinary as hell. But after today, my name will be bigger than yours, Mr. Secretary."

"This is the wrong way to show yourself," Mark said. "Dangerous."

"Well, I would have died anyway if I quit the tower. What's the difference?"

"Now, Harry, stop talking like that," Laura said.

"Oh, it's true. Dr. Montours. Jeff was planning to fire me, and then I would just have sat home with nothing to do but trim the hedge, water the lawn, re-trim the hedge. I would have been dead from boredom and defeat within six months. No one would ever have remembered Harry Boyle at all, but at least this way they'll say there was a controller who pulled out a grenade to prove to the big shots that a new computer radar would make a difference. Right now, I'm a criminal, I guess. I'll go to jail, but someday I'm sure people will remember what I tried to do—not for myself, but for air-traffic control. You'll never know, Mr. Secretary, how I loved this job. Keeping those planes apart was maybe the reason I was born. It gave me something important to do in life. Not as big as your job, sir, but it was very important."

"So you think this is a heroic act?" Mark said.

"Yes." Harry nodded vigorously. "The point has to be made, and Jeff Sutton wouldn't do it."

"Harry," Ed Morrison said, "I understand how you feel, but let's be reasonable. You can accomplish your goal in other ways."

"And, Harry," Laura added, "you're not going to die.

What if they promise you a good job with responsibility and your own secretary—wouldn't you like that?"

Ed Morrison, seeing the smile begin on Harry's face, stepped forward.

"Of course, Harry," he said. "I'll make sure you get a good job with more salary. Much more salary. But I can't do it if you continue to hold that gun on us."

"I don't believe you, Mr. Morrison. You *already* promised me a job. If I give you the gun, I'll be taken out of here in handcuffs and you won't have a fair demonstration of CORAD to see how ATC can really work."

Mark Cranston, who had shot a quick look at the administrator when Harry mentioned his previous offer of a job, now turned back to the disturbed man.

"Harry," Mark said, "I'll back up that promise. There'll be no handcuffs. Just trust us, please."

"Gentlemen..." Jeff said, standing up.

"Sit down, Jeff! I have the gun pointed at your back. If you don't sit down this minute, the pin will come out again."

"Okay, Harry, all right, I'm down. Now, can I say something?"

"Anything you want," Harry said, as he stepped off the CORAD platform and glanced over at Jimmy, who was staring at Ted.

Harry walked over to the top of the stairs and pointed his gun directly at the guard.

"Ted, toss down that gun. Your hand is so crippled anyhow that you can't fire it."

Ted looked up at Harry, straight into the big hole at the end of the muzzle. He slowly threw the .38 on the floor; it bounced along the concrete and slid over to the first rise of black metal stairs.

"That's good, Ted. Now, don't get ambitious."

"Don't worry, Mr. Boyle, it's not worth it to me."

"Fine. Now, Jeff, what were you going to say?" Harry asked, his attention drifting away from Ted.

"Gentlemen, this demonstration of air-traffic control is *over*. You've seen what's wrong here. Harry Boyle is out of his mind. I should have fired him long ago, but if I terminated every man here with Harry Boyle's syndrome, all those with ulcers and headaches and back pains and colitis, I'd be down to a few inexperienced developmentals. What's wrong with air-traffic control is not just the radar; the pressure on the men is too much. He's an acute case, sure, but there are others working up to Harry's state. The answer is not in that machine, but in more men, more airports and third-dimensional radar. Harry Boyle just proved my point. You heard him. He's got this pathetic idea of heroism...the ATC martyr."

"This is no time for one of your speeches, Mr. Sutton," the administrator said. "The responsibility for this man's actions rests upon your shoulders. Look what you've let us in for."

"I accept that. But if we get out of here alive, I want you gentlemen to remember this. All my memos, my talks in Washington, didn't do a damn bit of good. But Harry is driving the point home, not for himself...for *me*!"

"Don't worry, Mr. Sutton, I'll never forget this," Mark Cranston said.

Harry started slapping with his gun in one hand, and again a demented laugh spewed from his mouth.

"It's Jeff Sutton who's sick," Harry cackled. "That's why he's bailing out. *He* can't stand the pressure. I'm perfectly all right. You'll see how I can handle every single situation in the tower today. All the planes will be handled safely."

Down in the vestibule, Ted heard footsteps outside the gray fire door. He eased it open for Hoagy and the other controllers who had left the lounge for the cab on Hoagy's orders. Now everyone in the tower, except for those in the administration section, was directly under the eye of Harry Boyle.

"Mr. Washington," Ted whispered, "Harry Boyle's up there with a gun. He's got a grenade, too. The guy is crazy."

Hoagy was already backing through the half-open

door when Harry suddenly appeared at the head of the stairs waving both the Magnum and the grenade.

"Stay where you are, Hoagy! Get back in here."

Hoagy paused, thinking that he could slip out the bulletproof door before Harry punched off a shot. The controller was so out of control, Hoagy figured that the shot would probably go wild.

"Come in and close the door!" Harry screamed. "Hurry up!"

Just as the men crowded into the vestibule, letting the door swing behind them, Ted dropped to the gray concrete floor. He grabbed his gun, pointed it upward, and fired.

The shot missed.

The sound rang off the hard surfaces in ear-shattering reverberations. Even before the echo was soaked up, Harry fired back at Ted, and the copper-filled slug hit Ted in the chin with such force that it splintered his whole lower face. The projectile exited under the chin and tore through the guard's grizzled neck with so much power that Ted was heaved up and back.

He opened what was left of his mouth and started to say, "No...no..." but his mouth closed immediately.

The man was dead.

Only the battering rain could be heard, mixed with the bellowing wind. The controllers in the cab walked over behind Harry to stare down at the bloody rivers beginning to stream from Ted's neck.

Hoagy leaned down, then looked up at Harry Boyle.

"My God, what have you done?" Hoagy cried, tears coming to his eyes.

"I didn't mean to," Harry said in a high, shrill voice. "I didn't want to do that, but he fired at me first."

"He was only doing his job," Jeff said.

"And I'm doing mine," Harry replied, turning around to those behind him. "You see now...*see*...I'm not kidding...am I? Now, get back there! All of you. Don't reach for the phone, because I'm taking out the grenade pin. It'll be worse next time!"

Harry descended the stairs. He looked down at the

crumbled body of the guard ringed by the horrified group of men.

"Ted, I'm sorry. You shouldn't have done that."

The he turned to the rest. "All of you, empty your pockets. The door keys...hurry up! Come on!"

One by one, they gave their color-coded keys over to Harry. Satisfied, Harry Boyle locked the door to the tower cab and stuffed the bulk of the keys in his pocket. He climbed the stairs, and Hoagy stared at the deep red footprints he left on the shiny black metal stairs.

"I made a horrible mistake," Jeff whispered to Laura. "I should have known. It's my fault that Ted died."

"No, Jeff. You had no idea it was going this far."

"Shut the hell up over there," Harry snarled. "Let's get started."

"Mr. Boyle, you still have time to give up that gun. If you don't I'll personally make sure that you're executed for first-degree murder," Mark said.

"Do you know something, Mr. Secretary? I don't give a damn. It really doesn't matter. But notice how I laid in my shot. I'm good at this, so just keep that in mind, all of you."

The phone rang. Harry picked it up.

"Tower."

"This is Redmond. I'm in the cable trunk, checking out that radar failure yesterday. Thought I heard some shots...everything all right?"

"Of course. It was just a backfire from one of the ground service vehicles."

"Ah...is Mr. Sutton there?"

"Yes."

"Would you put him on, please?"

Harry clamped his hand over the phone and signaled Jeff.

"Now, you just tell him there's not a goddamn thing wrong."

"Yes, Joe?" Jeff said, taking the phone.

"I was saying I heard a shot, Mr. Sutton. Two shots, I think."

"They were just backfires."

179

"Didn't sound like backfires, Mr. Sutton. Too close."

"You know how sound travels through rain."

"Suppose that was it, then. Also, Mr. Sutton, I've been pinching the lines. There's no pulses—are we operating the tower?"

"Not at the moment, Joe. We've closed down for transition into the CORAD mode. All the planes are in the holding pattern."

"I see. Well, I'm almost finished, and I still don't see no problem."

"All right, Joe. Just...ah...keep it up."

Desperately, Jeff wanted to signal Joe, but he couldn't do it over the phone, and Joe Redmond went back to work. Jeff knew their only hope was to get word out that the tower was under seige, and the only person who could do that was Joe Redmond, hanging off the clammy steel ladder in the trunk. But the radar technician had almost worked his way to the top. Jeff tried to figure some way to signal him by tapping out a code on the linoleum floor; he would have to position himself far to the side of the octagonal cab, right over the cable trunk.

"Harry, I have a request."

"Yeah, what, Jeff?"

"My daughter is coming in on the Concorde very shortly. I'd like to contact the flight via Miami radio."

"What for?"

"Well, they had a fuel-low problem, and with this weather and working CORAD, I just feel uneasy."

"I'll handle the flight with special care, Jeff," Harry said, his voice returning to normal, as if nothing had happened.

"Do you mind if I call them?"

Harry motioned with his gun. "Go ahead."

Jeff picked up the phone and dialed the number of Miami radio and requested a patch-through to the enroute Concorde flight. Miami center instructed Lou Griffis to come up on local frequency, and within fifteen seconds there was radio contact with the rapidly descending Concorde.

180

"Lou...Jeff."

"How's the weather?" the Australian asked.

"Actually, it's improving. We have one-thousand-foot visibility with a ceiling of eleven hundred."

"Sounds good."

"How are you doing on fuel?"

"Well, better than we thought. Much better. We're estimating the control zone in, oh, about twenty minutes, maybe a little less."

"We'll be looking for you," Jeff said. "The airport is closed for a couple of minutes while we demonstrate a new radar, but we'll be taking you in."

He put down the phone, wanting more than anything to give a warning message to his friend. Neither he nor anyone else thought of checking the weather radar, up above CORAD. None of them saw the huge, towering cells begin to move toward the airport. Pumping heat and violent up- and downdrafts were slowly closing in on the runways. If there had not been much frenzy in the cab that afternoon, one of the controllers might have noticed the buildup in the atmospheric electricity.

"Now, we'll begin," Harry announced. "Jeff, you and Dr. Montours get over by the far side of the cab. Mr. Morrison...Mr. Secretary...you stand near the platform. And, Nick, you read out the terminal."

Harry spoke with perfect businesslike dispatch. He displayed no after effects from having just killed a helpless old man.

"Would you listen to reason...please?" Jeff said desperately, in one last attempt to bring Harry to his senses.

"I have listened to reason, and it never got me anywhere."

The CORAD test was on.

11

February 14, 12:42 P.M., the skinny Concorde was descending out of its high, icy world.

Her long needle nose—the beak, they called it—was spearing through cumulus clouds, pale gray at their whiskerlike ends, darker toward their guts. Far off to the sides could be seen big hollows of sparkling blue skies girded by clouds, some majestic cumulus, and then the nimbus family, the true indicators of highly unstable air.

Lou had a sense of elation. The flight was almost over, and he smiled as he punched the microphone button for a cabin P.A.

"Ladies and gentlemen, this is Captain Griffis. We are now just east of Nassau, the Bahamas, and descending through thirty thousand feet for our approach into Miami International Airport. We'll be over the terminal in about fifteen minutes. The temperature in Miami today is seventy-one degrees and, unfortunately, it is raining. We do not anticipate any air-traffic delays; however, there is an area around Miami of slightly choppy weather, and I am going to turn on the seat-belt sign for your comfort and safety and ask those in the aisle to return to their seats. Thank you."

Honey Sutton, hearing Lou's P.A., reached over and lightly touched Dame Margaret's arm.

"Dame Margaret...Dame Margaret."

The old woman cocked one eye open, closed it again, and then raised her head from the seat pillow.

"What...what?"

"Oh, I didn't mean to scare you. But the captain just said that we're beginning our descent. We'll be over Miami in about fifteen minutes."

"Already? Seems I just closed my eyes, and we're there."

"You've been asleep for an hour, Dame Margaret."

"Thanks to you, dear. As a matter of fact, I rather like flying. It's like sitting in a theater with no stage."

Honey Sutton didn't quite understand the meaning of the old actress's analogy, but she smiled and agreed.

Sean McCafferty's Helio Courier was circling through light rain and moderate turbulence, portents of the thunderstorms edging upon the Miami runways. At 12:46 Sean was at five thousand feet, cutting through steely gray clouds with almost zero forward visibility, but MIA center saw the small plane as merely a sluggish speck on the radarscope. His engine sounded content, and like Lou Griffis, Sean felt satisfied and happy that he was nearing Miami.

"Sean, it's getting bumpy again," Connie said.

"I know, dear, but nothing to worry about. Do you feel sick?"

"Just a little."

"How are you girls doing back there?" Sean asked, swinging his head around.

"We like it!" his daughters enthused.

As soon as Sean swiveled his eyes toward the instruments, he realized it had been a mistake to take his attention off the panel: the Helio dipped one wing, and the unstable air sent the plane on its own way.

"Sean," Connie yelled. "Something's happening."

"I know, I know," he answered back.

Sean, adroit and steady when it came to flying by instruments alone, lowered the wing, brought the nose up gently, and in a matter of seconds the plane was flying straight and level once again. Then they took a particularly hard bounce, and Connie grabbed her husband's knee.

"Sean, we'd better land," she cried out.

"It's not necessary. We're doing fine. Miami's expecting better weather."

He looked over at her for a split second. Her mouth was wide open, and her normally placid blue eyes seemed panicky. She really was frightened, he realized.

"We'll slow the bird up a bit, and you'll see how it smooths out," Sean said comfortingly.

He cranked in one-quarter flaps, came back on the manifold pressure, retrimmed the aircraft for sixty miles an hour, and true to his prediction, the bumps and jiggles almost disappeared. Unlike almost any other private plane, the Helio could maintain a safe air speed of about thirty-five miles an hour with no danger of stalling.

The advantage of the Helio over all other aircraft was the antistall, antispin protection, and if the engine suddenly quit, Sean could simply crank in full flaps, point the nose into the wind, and the bush plane would settle with the speed of a parachute, about thirty-five miles per hour, and the ground contact, while teeth-shattering, would be survivable.

According to some, these safety features of the Helio created an odd risk. Flying at a diminished speed of fifty or even forty miles an hour, a pilot could enter an avalanche of vertical wind shear, either clear air turbulence or the violent downdrafts of thunderstorms, without even knowing what was happening if he did not monitor his vertical-air-speed indicator.

The entry movement was just too slow for a traumatic upset.

On the other hand, if the Concorde, or any other big jet, entered the same meteorological phenomenon at two hundred miles an hour, the aircraft could be yanked completely out of control.

Thirty miles southeast of Sean's Helio, the MIA tower was smelling like a musty locker room at halftime. Harry Boyle had ordered the field opened once more; the flights were commanded off the stack, and the CORAD test began. Morrison and the secretary were no longer interested in an evaluation of CORAD. Their thoughts were pinned on one hope only: getting out of the cab, not ending up like Ted.

Joe Redmond had finished his long day's work. He could find nothing wrong with the radar cables, and he climbed down the clammy trunk, exiting through the steel door to the switchgear room. Leroy Tillis was already there.

"Find anything, Leroy?"

"No, sir," the black man answered. "Not a thing."

"Leroy, did you hear two backfires a while ago?"

"Sounded like shotgun blasts, Joe. I used to shoot turkeys over western Georgia with my uncle, and those didn't sound like no backfires to me."

"I didn't think so either. In fact, I called the cab about it."

"Oh, what did they say?"

"Mr. Sutton told me it was noise from ground-service vehicles."

"Ain't none of those around. Outside the tower there's nothing but grass. The hard surface is five hundred yards away."

"I was thinking that, and, you know, Mr. Sutton didn't sound right."

Leroy laughed. "Well, he would be nervous with the administrator up there and all."

Joe shook his head. "Mr. Sutton's a calm guy. Doesn't get riled up much. We'll ask Ted if he heard the sounds."

Wiping the hot dampness from their faces, the two men shuffled up the stairs to the security station. When they unlocked the door, Vic Sloan, a very fat former transit policeman from New York City, was sitting at the desk yawning over an old copy of *Penthouse*.

"Where's Ted?" Joe asked.

"In the cab. They said Boyle was actin' up."

"Who said that?"

"Mr. Sutton, I guess. I got called over to relieve Ted.

Wish he'd come on back here, too. It's time for my break."

"Did you hear some gunshots before?"

"Naw."

"We did," Joe said.

Vic threw his magazine down. "Well, let's see if Ted knows anything about it."

The guard pushed the buzzer to the cab, and after abour five rings, Harry Boyle answered.

"This is Vic down in security. Can I speak to Ted?"

"He's busy," Harry yelled into the phone.

"It's important...ah...his wife is sick. *Have* to speak to him."

"Well, you can't!" Harry snapped, clicking down the phone.

Vic stared at the two maintenance men as he put the phone down. Then Joe said, "Let's get up there!"

They ran down the linoleum hall to the administration section and asked one of the secretaries to sit at the security desk.

Less than a minute later the three men emerged from the elevator at the upper level and trotted through each of the sections: the radar room, the lavatories, the lounge, and the conference room.

"Why would they empty out the whole place?" Joe asked.

No one could answer. They walked along the corridor, turned left into the vestibule leading to the cab.

Joe Redmond stopped short.

Under the glare of the fluorescent lights he noticed a small rivulet of red streaming beneath the door, just where the rubber seal joined the metal doorjamb. Joe knelt down, pushed his finger through the crimson liquid, and brought it to his tongue. The briny, warm taste told him what it was.

"Is that what I think it is, Joe?" Leroy asked.

"Blood."

Vic put his ear to the cold gray metal and came away with his shoulders hunched in a shrug.

"Don't hear nothin'," he whispered.

186

"Try the door," Joe said.

Slowly Vic clamped his meaty hand around the knob and tried to turn it.

"Locked."

"How about knocking?" Leroy whispered.

"You don't knock with a situation like this. Who the hell knows what's happenin' in there?"

Vic knelt and poked his index finger in the widening stream. He smelled it, tasted the smudge of red on his finger, and turned to face Joe and Leroy.

"You're sure as hell right. Christ, I wonder who got it?"

Leaning against the other side of the steel door, Hoagy Washington heard the muffled sounds outside.

"Somebody's out there," he said to the controllers herded together just inside the door.

"What do you hear, Hoagy?" one of them asked.

"Can't make it out. They realize something's wrong, I think," he said after a long pause. "Better not move though, or we'll end up like Ted."

As they whispered, Vic and the other two men moved away from the cab door.

"I'll tell you how to handle this. We can't risk a damn thing up here," Vic said. "Let's get our asses downstairs and call up field security."

Two minutes later the phone rang at the chief security office at the main terminal.

Clint Adkins, the fifty-year-old sergeant on duty, picked up the phone and listened while Vic Sloan described what they had seen and heard.

"Are you guys bullshitting me?" he said gruffly.

"No, sir!"

"I'll call over there and talk to Sutton."

"Won't do any good."

"You leave it to me. Stay right by the security desk."

Clint, a cherry-faced ex-cop from the Dade County Department of Public Safety, dialed the number of the cab.

"Tower," Harry clipped.

"This is the security desk at the terminal. Put Mr. Sutton on, please."

"He's busy."

"I don't give a shit! Put him on," Clint ordered.

Harry placed his hand over the phone.

"It's security," Harry yelled over to Jeff. "Get on the other phone, and remember—this little pin is about to come out again."

Jeff picked up the phone on the far side of the cab, and with one eye he watched Harry Boyle.

"Mr. Sutton, is that you?" Clint asked.

"Yes. What's the problem?"

"Vic Sloan just phoned over here with a wild story. Said they heard gunshots, and then there was a stream of blood coming out from under the door to the cab."

Harry, hearing this, shook his head violently at Jeff and raised the Magnum, pointing the muzzle directly at Jeff's midsection.

"Ah...I don't know what the hell they're talking about. No one's injured here. Those shots were back-fires."

"Well, I'm embarrassed I called. I think Sloan's kind of cracked. Sorry to bother you, Mr. Sutton. Just wanted to check things out. Thanks."

Clint slammed down the phone and punched the security-section button.

"I just spoke to Mr. Sutton. He says there's nothing wrong. What the hell are you pulling with the administrator up here? Shit, man, this ain't no time for practical jokes."

"Call again and ask to speak to Ted," Vic said.

"I'm not calling anybody. Makes us look like idiots. Maybe we are."

"Listen, Clint, I'll put Joe Redmond on the phone. He's the radar-maintenance man who heard the shots. It's not just me that's actin' up."

"Okay, put him on...what is this, Redmond?" Clint said in a deep, sharp voice.

"Leroy—he's my technician—and I heard shots ...two of them, coming from the cab. Then we went up there to the door and saw blood coming from underneath."

"How do you know it was blood?"

"I tasted it. Listen, sergeant, I know blood and I know gunshots. Those weren't backfires from ground-service trucks. Anyhow, there ain't no ground-service trucks around the tower, 'cause they don't drive on soggy grass. And why should they drive near the tower? We've got an underground parking lot."

It might have been the assertive way Joe Redmond spoke, or the logic behind his conclusion, but Clint Adkins told them to stay put while he checked.

He walked out of his office to the FAA district unit three doors down. He explained what had happened to the duty officer.

"You were assured by Mr. Sutton personally?"

"But I think we'd better take a look," Clint said.

"We could get a pair of powerful glasses and go up in the old tower...get a good view from there."

Clint sighed. "With all I've got to do, now I'm spying on the tower. You make me sound like a creep...but, okay...." They started to search for the binoculars.

In the cab, Jeff was whispering to Laura. "I *have* to do something. The Concorde is approaching the pattern, and that weather scope looks cluttered as hell."

"We can't yank the gun away from Harry. He'll only pull the grenade pin. Let me try again to persuade him...the woman's touch."

"No, I can't let you risk it."

"But look what else we're risking," Laura said, her dark eyes sweeping the room.

Even though no one was paying attention to the demonstration, it was, nevertheless, going quite well: the computer was tapping out the clearances; Nick Cozzoli was reading them into his boom mike; the traffic was well separated, and ostensibly there were just two men and a busy computer handling the fifty-seven flights in the Miami control zone.

"See how well we're running, Mr. Secretary?" Harry said brightly. "I have everything under perfect control."

Mark Cranston did not respond either by a change in his stare or a movement of his body. He was too shocked to react.

"Yes, Harry, this proves that CORAD is part of the answer," Ed Morrison said patronizingly.

At that point Laura moved forward. "Harry, I agree with the administrator. You've proved your point. You *can* handle the tower alone, and CORAD does its job. Now, I am going to stand right here and you are going to hand me that gun, grip-first. Either you're going to blast my head off or give me the gun."

"Harry," Ed Morrison said, "we don't want any more people killed. Here's my proposition. CORAD works, right, Mark?"

"I'm convinced," the secretary answered, half under his breath.

"Give up those weapons and you can still operate the radar," Ed continued. "We can't evaluate it properly like this. My nerves are jumpy."

"That's right, Harry," the secretary said. "If you surrender the gun and the grenade, there will be no prosecution."

Jeff could see the white blurs of the approaching cells of the weather radarscope, which was canted slightly in his direction. With his trained eye, the facility chief suddenly realized that the real danger clawing at them was not a midair; the computer conflict mode would probably handle that. Nor was it Harry, for Jeff was certain that the man had enough sense left not to fire his gun again or detonate the hand grenade.

The adversaries now were the boiling thunderstorms.

The computer identified and monitored the moving targets, but machines, as sophisticated as they were, could not deal with the violent downdrafts associated with the cresting storm cells creeping toward the MIA approach path.

"Harry," Jeff said, "please look at the weather scope. Those cells are piling up."

"I see them. I'm planning to vector traffic around them. Just get Dr. Montours back. Let me handle this. I've vectored traffic around thunderstorms for twenty-seven years. I know what I'm doing."

"Do you mind if I look over your shoulder? Four eyes are better than two."

"All right, Jeff, that's fair, but one wrong move by you, and this whole place goes up," Harry said, and he pulled the pin from the grenade.

Six hundred yards across the field, Clint Adkins and the duty officer entered the deserted old tower and pointed the ten-power binoculars toward the cab of the tulip.

"What do you see?" Clint asked.

"With all this rain, things aren't clear. But…ah…I don't know. They seem to be standing around watching the CORAD scope. Nothing unusual. Take a look."

Clint brought the glasses up to his eyes and studied the soft-edged objects across the field. "Doesn't seem out of line to me."

"You people were seeing things," the duty officer said, laughing.

"I'm calling that Sloan on the carpet."

"Think you should," the deputy said, starting toward the stairs. "He's on my shit list. Blood…gunshots….God!"

12

"Harry, I'd vector that inbound Air France wide of this cell," Jeff said, pointing to the hotdog-shaped white blur on the weather scope.

"He's got cockpit radar," Harry answered, quickly gazing at the sweep. "Well, I'll check with Nick. Give them all a wide clearance."

"Already have, Harry," Nick answered back.

"But look at the Delta 876. He's close in there," Jeff said, pitching his voice.

"Shit, Jeff, let me run this," Harry said. "Nick, get Delta 876 on the horn. Get a pilot report."

"Right away. Delta 876, MIA tower. You gettin' bumped around up there?"

"Negative. A few nips in the air, that's all," the captain said.

"Stay wide of that stuff," Nick responded.

"Tower, we have it, huh? You take care of the control; we'll thread our way around up here. Got it?"

"Affirmative," Nick said. "You've got it."

"See, Jeff, no sweat," Harry said. "Get the hell over to the side with Dr. Montours."

"If you put the pin back in," Jeff said, looking at the grenade, wondering if he could grab it with one hand and take Harry's gun with the other.

Jeff abandoned the idea and went to sit on the worktable next to Laura. Harry pushed the pin back into the grenade, returning his attention to the CORAD scope.

"My God, if something happens to Honey, I'll never forgive myself," Jeff whispered to Laura. "And the Concorde is almost in the flight pattern."

"Where?" she asked.

"About thirty miles east."

"This could go on all day if we don't think of something," Laura said.

"I'll try to plead with him once more."

"It'll be a waste of time, Jeff. The guy's over the edge."

Jeff shrugged his shoulders and moved to the center of the cab just in front of the CORAD.

"Harry..." he started.

"I'm busy, Jeff, can't you see?"

"Do you remember the time we had the softball game with the Delta and Eastern gate attendants?"

"Yeah."

"We had a good time that afternoon, didn't we?"

"Sure."

"Well, Harry...I mean, just for the sake of our friendship...maybe the good times we've had together...couldn't we handle this differently? Please, I'm begging you...give me the gun."

"It's too late, Jeff. Get the hell back there!"

Mark signaled Jeff away from Harry, and the facility chief returned to the far side of the cab.

"He's too far gone," he whispered to Laura.

"I have an idea," she said. "I'll ask him if we can cook up some tea or soup. If you divert his attention, we'll let him have it with a splash of boiling water, and then you dive for the ordnance."

"He'll see you coming."

"I can move damn fast, my dear boy. I'm half Indian, remember?"

"Yeah, and what if he throws the grenade?"

"The pin's in."

"He'll go crazy, Laura, and start firing off shots."

"No, his eyes will be poached by then. We can duck...the slugs might go wild."

"What are you talking about over there?" Harry asked over the chatter of the radio.

"We were just saying how we need something to settle our nerves," Laura said. "Harry, do you mind if I make some soup or tea for everybody?"

"That's a good idea, Dr. Montours," Ed Morrison said. "How about it, Mark?"

The secretary nodded.

"All right," Harry answered.

Laura moved to the built-in two-burner electric heater on the other side of the cab. She reached underneath and pulled out a packet of dehydrated soup.

"Harry, what kind do you like, split pea, chicken, or onion?" Laura asked.

"Oh...onion."

She took the packet out, filled the saucepan to the top from the faucet beside the burners, and clicked on the electric button to high heat.

The phone rang, and Harry picked it up.

"It's the Concorde flight, Jeff. You can take it over there, but I'll be listening."

"Hello, Lou," Jeff said.

"We've intercepted the ILS for two-seven-right, Jeff. What about the stuff in here?"

"It's just to the north of the approach path. Let's confirm your altitude and heading. Squawk ident," Jeff said.

A white slash came up on Harry's local scope.

"Do you have them, Harry?" Jeff asked.

"Sure. We have positive radar ident."

"Lou, are you getting much turbulence?"

"Some."

"And how's your fuel?"

"Not bad. Forty-three thousand pounds remaining."

"Let's check your altitude again."

"I'm just out of six thousand."

"Is that what you get, Harry?"

"Exactly. What the hell do you think?"

"It's all confirmed, Lou."

Lou Griffis' mind was eased. He looked at the white

clutter on his cockpit weather scope. The dangerous blurs representing the high thunder cells were north of him, and he started his final approach descent, going through the prelanding checklist. He ordered gear down, and Charles Moran, sitting to Lou's right, pulled the actuating knob in front of him. The lights switched from amber to deep green, indicating that the main and nose gear were down and in the locked position.

Shafts of light amber pierced the thick clouds that were engulfing Sean's float plane, but the shearing wind had not let up and the Helio was bouncing violently on the waves of pumping vertical air.

"Sean, I think I'm going to be sick," Connie said.

"This stuff is breaking up. Hold on."

"I don't know if I can," she said, clamping a hand over her mouth.

"Okay. I'll call Miami approach control."

Sean picked up his mike and contacted approach control, and Nick Cozzoli's voice crackled through.

"Miami approach. Go ahead, Helio."

"We're experiencing heavy turbulence up here. Can I get slotted in?"

"We'll take you. Turn to heading three-zero-zero. Descend to three thousand feet."

Sean repeated the instruction back to the tower; he turned into the wind and cranked in more flaps to the point where his ground speed was down to no more than twenty-five miles an hour.

"That's better, Sean," Connie said. "Thanks."

"They'll bring us right in. We'll be on the runway in a matter of minutes."

"Katie...Hillary...are you all right?" Connie asked, turning around.

They did not answer. Their faces were sugar-white as the two girls held on to each other.

Twenty-four miles east of the MIA two-seven-right threshold, the SST flight had gone through five thousand feet in its routine nose-high descent. The snoot was down, the speed and rate of descent on the numbers.

According to the CORAD computer, supported by the instrument flight plan, Sean McCafferty's float plane was to cut into the glide path two miles short of runway two-seven-right and land in front of the Concorde, thus maintaining horizontal separation and eliminating the possibility of the SST overtaking the small aircraft. The theory was sound. Nick Cozzoli tapped the vector information into the computer; a new conflict point was established on the twirling data banks.

But Harry Boyle and CORAD were unaware of one irregularity.

It was assumed by the computer program that light aircraft proceeded at a pattern speed between sixty-five and one hundred miles per hour, while heavy aircraft were programmed in an envelope between 155 and 195 miles per hour. The computer did not understand that there existed one aircraft in the world that could fly at thirty-five miles per hour under perfect control: the Helio Courier.

After the new vector and landing instructions were transmitted to Sean by Nick Cozzoli, the small plane hit a wild draft of air.

"It's all right," Sean said calmly.

He cranked in full flaps, pitched the nose high. His air speed fell off once more, and just as the white airspeed needle slipped onto the zero pin against the press of the wind, Sean fed in power to hold him in the air.

"Isn't that better?" Sean said, smiling to his wife and children. "We'll be on the ground soon."

The progress of Sean's flight was visually blipped on Harry's local scope, but he had nineteen other targets on the glass and did not notice the Helio's speed change.

The Concorde continued its descent for runway two-seven-right. Sean cut across the Concorde's path at thirty miles per hour indicated speed, but the ground speed was no more than fifteen.

The inevitable happened.

Lou's SST got there first because of its accelerated approach speed.

At exactly that moment, 12:57 P.M., the Concorde was still at two thousand feet, and the Helio was five hundred feet below Lou's plane. Even though the small aircraft was in the wrong position, the two planes were flying at different altitudes, so the conflict alarm did not sound on the CORAD panel. Had an experienced, well-trained controller such as Cozzoli been monitoring the local scope, using the precision-approach radar, he would have instantly recognized that the Helio was out of sequence.

Lou Griffis was handling his aircraft easily. There were a few bumps, but his glide path and rate of descent through the clouds continued to go by the book.

Suddenly Lou screamed, "Oh, shit!"

His eyes glanced at the vertical-air-speed indicator. It was unwinding rapidly.

The altimeter needle spun.

Lou, an intuitive pilot, didn't need these gauges to tell him what was happening: his stomach pushed against his rib cage as the Concorde was suddenly hurled down, caught in the vise of hurricane wind.

"Take off thrust! Take off thrust!" he yelled, pushing the levers forward.

It was too late.

Lou understood aerodynamics and design regime from his months with Bristol working on the Concorde's early engineering. But like most pilots, he had little understanding of the intricacies of wild air.

All pilots had experience with two general categories of turbulence: CAT, or clear air turbulence, which was predictable to some extent; and vertical shear, associated with towering thunder cells. But there was a third, little-known adversary, the "downburst." This avalanche of rapidly descending air, associated with lower thunderstorms, consisted of cascades of wind rushing to the earth at velocities of about two hundred miles per hour. These freak storms were localized, covering a limited area. In rare instances, they would occur near runway thresholds.

A typical killer downburst was recorded on June 24, 1975, at JFK airport over the threshold to runway 22. Several airliners making the landing that day reported heavy concentrations of downward-moving air. Eastern's flight 902, a Lockheed TriStar, was about to land when the pilot realized he was being hurled into the ground short of the runway. He applied thrust and abandoned the approach, continuing to Newark for his landing.

The flight behind him, Eastern's number 66, was caught in a second downburst cell, but the pilot did not recognize his dilemma soon enough. He applied takeoff thrust, but the turbines did not spool up in time. His 727 was dashed to the ground so violently that it disintegrated, killing 113 people.

Those who studied these downbursts found that they usually occurred during freak storms, and only at low levels. But now one had grabbed Lou's Concorde at a much higher level, 1,900 feet. As he brought the thrust levers forward, the flight was east of MIA over a thickly packed urban area, just west of Interstate I-95.

The Concorde's turbines screamed. The flight engineer quickly started to transfer his fuel aft again, the droop nose eased up. It would take five seconds for the turbines to react; until then the Concorde was caught unmercifully in the tornado-wind funnel. Unless Lou could create enough thrust, the SST would be smashed into the cluster of cinderblock houses below him.

The noise in the cabin was unbearable: plates and pillows were flying about wildly; the passengers began to shout; the Concorde shuddered, and if the passengers and crew had not been buckled in for landing, they would have flown about in a weightless condition.

"Come on, you son of a bitch, get hold!" Lou screamed.

"We're going through one thousand, Lou!" Charles yelled.

"Don't tell me! I can feel my stomach meshed in my tonsils."

Lou said an instant prayer that his turbines would catch hold in time so he could climb out of this hell. Why hadn't this been forecast? He felt he should have been told, but all his fuming was useless. It was now a matter of survival.

13

The small alphanumeric altitude readout beside the radar target on the CORAD scope began to change rapidly, reflecting the insidious fall of the struggling Concorde, but the alarm light and warning signal did *not* click. Technically, there was no conflict between the SST and any of the other traffic. The computer was not recognizing the unauthorized descent, and it could not visualize or discern the downburst that was gripping the SST. The CORAD display was so jammed with white dashes and precipitation clutter that Harry did not notice the fast-flipped numbers.

Four hundred feet below the Concorde, Sean, too, had sensed with a lump in his throat that he was tripping out of the sky. He hastily applied the throttle and eased back on his control yoke, aiming the nose of the small plane upward at an angle of twenty-five degrees. The air was now so saturated with rain that Sean could hardly see out his windshield; the only way he knew that the prop was functioning was the steady hum of the 295-horsepower Lycoming engine.

"Something's happening, Sean," Connie yelled.

"We're in bad air, but we'll be all right. Trust me, huh? There's no danger. None. I'm just poking along...."

Those were the last words the quiet accountant from Tallahassee uttered for some time.

The Helio float plane, weight 3,600 pounds, was plummeting toward the ground.

The weight and pressure of the downburst had created high velocities, and once they combined with the forces of mass and inertia, the Concorde was no longer an airfoil; it descended like a diesel locomotive falling off a cliff. And any heavy plane would have reacted in much the same way.

Sean merely heard a strange guttural roar from above. Then a black mass passed over his windshield. In the deafening turmoil, there was a dull explosion. For an instant Sean thought his engine had thrown a rod. Black chunks of litter dashed against his windshield, but Sean had no time to figure out what they were, for suddenly a round metal cylinder ripped through the windshield and control panel at a point almost in the center.

The Helio's sharp prop tips had ground up the Concorde's nose tires. After they exploded off their rims, the Helio's three-bladed propeller shredded the rubber as easily as a kitchen appliance grinds up tenderloin.

So powerful was the weight and thrust of the Concorde plowing down upon the light plane that the nose-gear strut entered the Helio cabin and exited in one continuous uninterrupted assault. After demolishing the panel, the nose gear ripped aft and down until the wheel hubs of the SST's nose tires were entangled in the bottom tubing of the bush plane.

Only the Helio Courier could have withstood it. Any other light plane would have been reduced to a thousand pieces of metal. But the Helio had been designed to withstand forces of fifteen G's positive, in case of a crash landing on a mountain or in the jungle—home country for this extraordinarily tough little plane.

Technically, it was not a midair collision.

It was more of an impaling, perhaps the first in the history of aviation. When it was over, the Helio was stuck on the nose of the Concorde like a piece of lamb on a skewer.

The speed of the Concorde, its weight of 240,000 pounds, and the vicious downburst all combined to set up an accident so rare that no one had ever thought about it. But computer studies later indicated that there was enough velocity and downward pressure for the Concorde to stick its nose gear through the Helio. Still, it was contrary to all odds, just as the barrel roll and dive of the TWA 727 near Detroit on April 4, 1979, had defied the most pessimistic speculations of those who write the flight manuals. To everyone who studied the Miami impaling and the Detroit nose dive, it reinforced the contention that flying was still an art and not yet an exact science. Those who respected this truth survived; many of those who denied it perished.

Connie screamed. She had no idea what had happened.

Sean was yanked from his seat and the side of his skull was grazed. He lost consciousness. Thrust sideways by the impact, Connie was untouched by the strut. As the giant spear entered the Helio, it tore the skin and tubular frame on top and cut a line into the aircraft much the same way a fish hook enters the mouth of a hungry lake bass, slicing back the flesh of the jaw until it meets the bone and stops. As the Concorde nose gear came to the end of its travel, the Helio's bottom tubing and the Concorde's wheel hubs became one mélange of metal. The McCafferty children were knocked back against the aft section and their legs were crushed, pinned against the unyielding frame.

Screaming in pain, both Katie and Hillary thought the small plane had crashed. In the horrifying pandemonium, they lost all sense of time and place.

Lou knew that something was wrong; his SST was out of trim and he assumed the problem had something to do with the downburst. There was so much clamor, the howling wind and pings of hailstones, plus the screams of the turbines spooling up to fight the descent, that the detonation and collision below were muffled. Honey, who was sitting directly over the nose wheel, felt the bump. She thought she heard a crash, but when she looked from the window, she saw nothing but the blanket of water-soaked air, which had diminished visibility to about five feet.

"I'm getting it back! I'm getting it!" Lou yelled in delight to his crew.

The turbines had taken hold. They sucked in great quantities of wet air, compressed it, heated it, and belted the vital thrust from the afterburners. The flight leveled out at 400 feet. They had been hurled down almost 1,500 feet by the furious wind, but now the great Olympus engines of the Concorde were taking them up—but not without a price. Huge amounts of precious fuel were being consumed by the hungry turbines.

"Gear up," Lou commanded.

Charles pushed the handle to the retracted position. Two of the green lights went amber, indicating that the main gear had withdrawn into the wheel wells, and the big bay doors were hydraulically closed and locked. But the nose-gear light continued to blink amber. When Charles pulled his cockpit lever, the hydraulic jacks began to whirl and the gear started up; then the jack gears spun free and halted as the wings of the impaled Helio were thrust against the Concorde's opened bay doors. The gear travel halted abruptly. The indicator light flickered.

"Must be the bulb," Lou said.

"I'll put the gear down again," Charles answered as he pushed the handle down.

The nose gear lowered the Helio nine feet. There was a grinding of metal as the tubes refastened their grip, and the small plane continued to be an integrated part of the SST nose strut as it was lowered and locked into the full down position for landing.

"That's it. The gear is okay. The circuit probably got banged up in the turbulence," the copilot commented.

"Bloody air," Lou said. "I'm not getting my air speed.

The trim seems strange. Pumps working forward, Cecil?"

"Yes," the engineer said. "No panel problems. Pressure on all pumps, sir. Turbines in the green."

The Concorde continued to climb through the thick rain. Her speed was sluggish and there was a slight pull against the control yoke, but no one in the cockpit could possibly have known the cause.

Three seconds before the CORAD alarm signal in the MIA tower beeped quietly, the conflict light went red. Jeff jumped toward the scope.

"Don't try anything, Jeff!" Harry shouted.

"What the hell's the matter?" Nick said.

"We just lost a flight...a small light plane. It was on approach to two-seven-right," Harry answered.

"Lost it? Where, for Christ's sakes!"

Harry looked at the computer printout. The message read: "Celtic 202, turn right to heading three-two-zero. Conflicting target! Conflicting target!"

Nick Cozzoli hastily transmitted the corrective action to the Concorde. The buzzer went off at the same instant the printout spewed from the computer terminal.

"I'll handle this," Harry said.

"Contact the Concorde!" Jeff said sharply. "We've got a midair! God damn that CORAD."

Jeff's mind unwound a series of terrifying pictures: the crash of the small plane against a control surface of the SST, a repeat of the San Diego midair when a Cessna brought down a huge airliner many times its weight and size. Jeff's mind was jammed with the screams he could imagine were reverberating about the Concorde's cabin. He heard his daughter, then saw her eyes, stark, wide, and locked open in panic. He imagined flames beginning to spit out of the Concorde's wing; the spindle of the struggling Concorde headed downward as Lou Griffis fought to save himself and all those aboard.

The pictures went blurry for a moment, and Jeff

Sutton moved over to the CORAD platform, with Laura holding his arm.

"Get the hell out of here, Jeff!" Harry screamed.

"Listen, you bastard, my daughter's aboard that flight!"

Nick was ahead of them, and he yelled into his mike. "Helio Courier...five...four...echo...Miami tower."

He repeated the message. "Helio Courier...five ...four...echo...."

Silence.

"We've lost them, Jeff," Nick said. "No response."

"Celtic 202...Celtic 202..." Harry chanted into his microphone. Jeff grabbed the mike out of Harry's hand.

"Be careful!" Mark yelled.

"Lou," Jeff cried into the radio. "We dropped a flight off the scope...a light plane. We think you had a midair. Lou..."

The Australian's voice came back remarkably clear. "A midair? We were tossed about...fell over a thousand feet. Then I got a new vector, which I executed. Now what?"

"Celtic 202," Nick interrupted. "We show you at two thousand feet...heading three-two-zero degrees."

"Affirmative," Lou replied.

"Turn left to heading one-eight-zero," Nick instructed.

"Turning left to heading one-eight-zero," Lou said.

"Get those other flights out of there. Put them in the stack, Nick!" Jeff ordered, his voice bristling with emotion and authority.

"*I'm* handling this," Harry said.

"Like shit you are!" Jeff bellowed back, his hot breath hitting Harry's moist, sallow face.

"Lou, are you sure there wasn't a midair?" Jeff said into the hand mike.

"I'm positive. My controls are working on the button. No warning signals except a blinking nose-gear light, and my trim is a little off. Nothing serious. Just got bumped about. Wait a minute..."

The intercom rang in the SST cockpit, and one of the stewardesses asked, "Are we okay, Captain?"

"Yes, we're out of the turbulence and I'll make a P.A. Did you girls hear anything back there that could have been a collision?"

"What...a collision? No, sir."

"Everything's all right?"

"Well, the passengers were very scared, but it's settling down. A few people were airsick."

Lou made a short P.A. explaining the turbulence and indicating there would be a short landing delay. Then he came back on the mike to the tower.

"Jeff, no midair. Even a light plane striking us would have been felt at this pattern speed. There would have been some damage, or some indication."

"I guess so," Jeff said. "That's right...well ...ah...what's your fuel remaining?"

"We have fifty-nine minutes. Plenty," Lou answered.

"Okay. We'll wait until these thunder cells pass, then vector you right in. We've cleared the incoming traffic out. The sky will be all yours, Lou."

Jeff turned to Cozzoli. "Now, where the hell is the small plane?"

"It just disappeared, Mr. Sutton. We don't have it no more."

"We don't have it no more," the facility chief said, mimicking Nick. "Planes don't disappear!"

"The computer says the Concorde was conflicting with light aircraft," Harry concluded. "They must have hit."

"Fuck CORAD. You *can't* have a high-speed collision with no damage. Shit, that Concorde was coming over the fence at 170 miles an hour.

"Would have to be damage at that velocity," Nick agreed. "Yes, sir."

Jeff walked over and spotted the supposed conflict point on the ground map. He quickly called the Dade County police, figuring that if the small plane disintegrated in the air, it would have sprayed debris all over the thickly populated housing development east of the airport. There would be police reports.

"Sergeant Harrison," came the answer from the station.

"This is Sutton over at the Miami control tower," Jeff said. "We just lost a plane off the radarscope. It must have gone down just east of the airport. Any calls?

"No, sir."

"Are you sure?"

"Rain's pretty bad. We've had a bunch of car crashes, but that's all."

"We figure you have a plane crash, too."

"I'll put it out on the radio, but when one comes down, we always get a lot of calls, and fast. I know—it's happened a few times already."

"I'll contact the sheriff's helicopter division and the civil air patrol," Jeff said, "but I'm almost positive the plane is down somewhere around northwest Thirtieth and Twelfth Avenue. *Has* to be."

"Maybe. But if it went in, how come nobody reported it?" the sergeant said.

"I don't know. I'm out of answers at the moment."

"Let me see...think we got four cars up in that area now..."

The dispatch sergeant turned to his communications officer, and priority calls were put out to the patrol cars in the area of the presumed midair collision.

"Hold on there, Mr. Sutton...we're getting word back in a minute or so."

Jeff eyed Laura who was now on the far side of the cab by the electric hot plate. Mark Cranston had crossed to stand by her, and he whispered, "Are you all right, Dr. Montours? This is a very frightening situation."

Laura nodded. "I'm going to get that crazy guy," she said with cold determination, in a voice she had never known she possessed.

"How?" Mark saw her glance at the pan of hot water, and he exclaimed, "You'll be killed!"

"I'm going to risk it," she said. "I have to."

Laura's mind sprang back to her conversation with

Jeff Sutton. She *was* cautious and self-protective, not a risk taker, but Jeff's unyielding resolution to barge forward against great odds for what had to be done had made a mark on her.

Harry had to be stopped or they would all die. Laura was certain of that.

Throwing a pail of boiling water into the face of a maniac who held a grenade and a powerful handgun, still warm from a point-blank killing, was about the last thing Laura Montours had ever expected to do in life. She remembered the night before, when she had panicked in the open-cockpit plane, something she still did not understand; whatever the reason, she had made up her mind to get Harry, even if she had to suffer, even die.

"Let me do that," Mark Cranston whispered to Laura.

"No, I have to handle it."

"Cut out that goddamn whispering over there!" Harry yelled.

The police sergeant came back on the phone and said to Jeff, "There's no report of a plane crash. None of my men heard or saw anything. No calls to Metro dispatch."

"Look," Jeff blurted out, "a plane disappeared off our scope. It had to come down. Now, how can it fall in a crowded area of Miami without anybody knowing?"

"Well, what do you want me to do? We don't have a crash report. Am I supposed to make one up for you, Sutton?"

"Of course not. Call me back immediately at this number if you get any information."

Jeff gave the police the private tower number and put down the phone.

"Where the hell is that plane?" Jeff yelled. "Where?"

Thinking that Harry had handed the control of the tower back to Jeff Sutton, Mark walked over to the CORAD platform.

"Are you sure there was a collision?" he asked.

"I think so, but something's crazy here."

"I thought CORAD was supposed to prevent this. Why didn't the alarm sound?" the secretary asked.

"It did," Harry said.

"But the plane disappeared," Mark added quickly.

"Here's the way I see it," Harry said calmly, as if his madness had totally evaporated. "There *was* a conflict upcoming. The computer saw it. But in the meantime, the light aircraft was disintegrated before the collision. The computer only said that the conflict was coming...it didn't say it happened. It wasn't CORAD's fault, Mr. Secretary."

"I still don't quite understand," Mark said.

"Well, I think Mr. Boyle's evaluation is reasonable; at least, from what we know," Ed Morrison spoke up. "But, Mr. Boyle, we've had too much drama here. Would you please give up the gun and the grenade? We'll agree that this demonstration is over."

Harry's eyes widened again. The madness filled his eyes and Laura felt a chill as she brought her pan of water to a boil.

"Let's not argue," she said in a soothing tone. "Have some soup, everybody."

She handed the cups to Mark and Ed. After a pause, Harry took one.

"I'm still controlling," Harry said. "Still controlling...it wasn't because of CORAD's incapability that we lost the light plane."

Cozzoli had vectored his traffic away from the threshold, and Frank Bolton, a young controller, contacted the Civil Air Patrol and Miami center, indicating that a plane was "off the scope."

Laura moved over to fill the secretary's cup with the steaming water, and he shook his head slightly. She looked away and signaled Jeff what she was about to do. Harry's eyes were riveted on the scope; he held the plastic cup in one hand, the Magnum in the other, and the grenade with the pin replaced was resting on the CORAD work counter. Jeff nodded to Laura that he was ready to spring for the handgun.

Laura bit her lip and suddenly slung the boiling water in Harry's face.

Screaming in pain, the deranged controller reflexively fired a shot. The slug tore through the roof. Howling with pain and anger, he dropped his cup, picked up the grenade, and yanked out the pin. The guard handle flipped free as he held it up in his hand.

"You bastards!" he shrieked, firing wildly.

One blast grazed Laura's upper arm. The bullet cut a clean, small flesh wound; the slug didn't expand, and as the projectile continued its trajectory, it tore into Ed Morrison's stomach. There the lead-sheathed copper finally fragmented, and Ed crumpled to the linoleum floor. He rolled over and coiled up like a snake, belching with pain.

Hoagy rushed up the steps.

"Hold it! Get down!" Jeff shouted.

Harry was blinded; the rest of his shots went wild. Jeff wrestled the grenade from Harry's knotted fist and tossed it through the window of the cab with a great side-arm pitch. Just as the mango-shaped lump careened through the glass, it burst with an orange flash of light.

The cracking explosion hurled the glass inward.

Slivers of spearlike crystal mixed with razor-edged shrapnel turned the cab into a blur of flying objects. One caught Nick Cozzoli in the neck, and he stiffened, trying to yank the ragged glass out of his gullet but his hands fumbled and grew weaker, and the controller slipped to his knees, his head slumped down on the CORAD computer terminal.

Another piece of the tinted window lodged in Harry's stomach, and Jeff's forearm took three daggerlike splinters, but his wounds were superficial, nothing more than stings. A tiny shrapnel hunk tore into the fleshy part of Mark Cranston's shoulder, but this, too, was only a slight wound. Harry fell over his CORAD, and the blood cascading out of his stomach tinted the greenish scopes crimson.

For the second time in two days, Jeff Sutton pushed the security "goose button."

Vic Sloan and the others sped up into the cab. The alarm also sounded at Miami center, in the terminal security office, and in the fire house. The trucks rolled.

There was silence in the cab, broken only by the chatter from the flight transmissions and the continuing howl of the wind through the broken glass. It swept the cab like a small tornado and whirled the papers in the air.

Jeff's mind also whirled with a terrible sense of guilt. His entire career, what he thought was his kindness to so many controllers, including Harry Boyle, had collapsed in this one appalling moment. Then, as his head cleared, he tried to calm down by saying to himself: No one could have known Harry would do this...*No one*. Then another thought slid into his mind: Maybe I don't know what this job has done to any of my men, or myself.

Finally Jeff looked around at the bloody wreckage of his cab. Almost everything was gone: Ted was a corpse, and probably the madman who had so violently flung them all into the nightmare was dead as well; the cab of the "ultimate" tower was destroyed, all its safety devices meaningless in the end. A Cabinet member was wounded, and the FAA administrator lay on the floor quivering with shock and a torn-up gut; in the corner Nick Cozzoli struggled to live, and then there was the beautiful, brave woman with a wound in her shoulder.

It all added up to a terrible defeat. Jeff gently wrapped his arm around Laura's waist and turned her pale face upward, seeing the tears glisten in her eyes.

"I'm sorry," he cried in choking breaths. "Are you all right?"

"Yes...hurts a little...not serious," she murmured.

He pressed his lips to her forehead and then turned to the others.

"Medical help is on the way. Let's get this place

functioning again. Hoagy, all you guys, start cleaning up. And get the downstairs radar positions going."

Kneeling next to Mark Cranston, Jeff asked, "Are you all right, Mr. Secretary?"

Mark had his coat off and had pushed up the sleeve of his blue-striped Brooks Brothers shirt.

"Doesn't look bad. I was lucky."

Mark rubbed his hand over the shrapnel wound and gazed down at the snow-white face of Ed Morrison, who was gulping air, his eyes closed. The administrator tried to say something, but his tongue was clamped against his teeth, and from the side of his mouth there began a small trickle of blood.

Jeff walked over to Harry and pulled him from his slumped position. In Jeff's mind the controller's death was a blessing. His life, his sensibilities, had ended years ago, but he had very cleverly concealed the depths of his delusions.

"Good-bye, Harry," Jeff whispered. "I still think it was the system's fault, not yours."

The Labrador padded over and stood by Harry, and then the dog lay down with his head on the controller's feet.

Jeff stepped over to Cozzoli. The brazen, black-haired Italian smiled up at him.

"I'm not going to make it, boss."

"Sure you are, Nick. Takes more than a gun and a grenade to stop you."

Nick started to grin. "No, I feel it going out of me. But, Mr. Sutton, you'll never have another guy like me. I knew that fucking traffic...I knew."

He coughed, and the blood gurgled in his throat.

Jeff put his hand on Cozzoli's shoulder. "Don't try to talk any more."

Nick gasped. "Never could stop talking, could I, Mr. Sutton? Don't blame yourself..."

"That's enough," Jeff said. "Take it easy. The medics are on their way."

Jeff's eyes filled with tears as he turned away, and Laura crossed the cab and put her arm around him.

Jeff reached up and clasped her hand. "You pulled us out of this, Laura."

"And so did you, Jeff," she said, trying to smile, but still shaking.

"How's your arm?"

"Doesn't hurt much."

The secretary shuffled toward them through the mounds of broken glass. The rain pouring into the opened cab coursed down his face.

"Thank you, both of you," he said. "I didn't think any of us were going to make it."

"I had my doubts, too, Mr. Secretary," Jeff said. "I knew he was sick...but not this crazy. I should never have let him near the tower."

Just then a radio transmission crackled above the peal of the wind.

"MIA tower...Jeff...Jeff." They recognized the voice of Lou Griffis.

"Yeah, Lou?"

"Just heard from the center that the field is closed. What's wrong?"

"We had an explosion in here."

"Say again."

"An explosion...."

"Is your equipment still functioning?"

Jeff looked around the conglomerate of radarscopes; the sweep lines continued to make their way; there was a slight crack in the precision radarscope's glass, but the damage seemed to be negligible.

"Luckily, the equipment is all right. Lou, squawk ident...let me see how you come up on my local scope."

The bright light flashed on the green glass as Lou touched his ident button on the cockpit transponder.

"Perfect identification," Jeff said.

"I think we have a problem up here," Lou answered. "Maybe there *was* a midair. Perhaps the light plane took part of our vertical stabilizer off."

"Are you still in positive control?" Jeff asked.

"That's the strange part. There are no warning lights, and the controls are fine, but we can't seem to trim the bird. We're requiring about ten thousand pounds of additional thrust just to hold altitude."

"Anything wrong with the turbines?"

"No, my flight engineer is satisfied."

"Lou, there have been no reports of a plane down. It just disappeared, but I don't know where. Listen carefully. The weather is easing up. I'm looking at the weather scope now; the big thunder cells are moving out to sea."

"We saw that, too."

"Let me vector you right past the tower. I'll take a look at your surfaces."

"Ah...you said there was an explosion in the cab?"

"Affirmative."

"Christ. Well, aren't you diverting traffic, then?"

"No, we'll be open in just a minute. Not for everybody—just you. The other traffic will be held in the stack."

"Okay, but whatever we're going to do, let's make it quick. I'm burning off a bloody lot of fuel."

"Do you think you want to try for a landing?"

"Not until I know what's wrong. Damn thing has got us puzzled. All right, we'll start the fly-by."

Jeff identified the flight once more on the scope. He told Lou to make a right turn and descend to fifteen hundred feet.

The Concorde started around, and Lou said to his copilot, "Doesn't feel right, Charles. Just out-of-whack someplace, but here we go."

14

When Sean McCafferty regained consciousness after a few moments, he thought he had been transported into some extraplanetary universe, plunked down into a segment snipped from *Star Wars*. The world in which he found himself was convulsed, entirely foreign to the accountant whose life so far had been completely ordinary and very rational.

Being accustomed to figures, he had always known where he was at all times. He saw life in hard-edged numbers: his address, postal zone, telephone, his account with the local bank. Flying was an adventure, but still orderly: the runway had a digit, his small plane had a radio frequency, and altitude, air speed, and the other coordinates formed a collection of exactitudes.

Now, suddenly, he was out of numbers.

For the first time in his life he did not know where he was or what was happening to him. As his eyes and head cleared, he looked up and saw the bent, shredded frame of his beloved plane. The windshield and panel before him were a spaghetti of interlacing wires, tubes, and dials, a completely mulched mess. Nothing was recognizable.

For a second he thought they had crashed. But how could they have, at eight hundred feet? That was where they had been when some massive cylindrical object shot through the windshield. He glanced up again and saw a dark grayness and gradually became aware of the rain slinging into the peeled-away plane, criss-crossed by bent alloy tubes.

The noise was unbearable.

The air pressure created by being hurled through the dense clouds at nearly 200 miles per hour was squashing his nose and lips and his eyes watered as he fought for consciousness.

He could not hear the high-pitched Concorde turbines, for they were located far behind him, but the wind careening about the wreckage whistled at such a stinging pitch that it pained his ears and threw off his orientation.

Sean looked around and saw the grease-streaked strut jammed right through the center of his plane. His mind was befuddled, his eyes emulsified in tears, partly from fright, partly from the lash of the wind pressure. The man did not know what he was looking at. It was not apparent that the tube was part of a landing gear. Whipped around in the moist air, he could see nothing above him but the blackness of the Concorde's open bay doors.

His senses sharpened. Sean unloosened his seat belt, and over the cry of the wind he heard his wife and daughters screaming. He could glimpse the girl's arms, and he edged himself toward them, holding onto the slippery gear strut. Sean knew they were still flying—but how could they be? he kept asking himself. Then the clouds opened a bit, and he realized he was looking up into the underbelly of a fuselage. It was then he realized that the strut was part of a landing gear. Slowly the idea formed that they were being carried along by another plane. He knew it was much larger than the Helio, but still couldn't guess it was a Concorde.

"Sean!" Connie cried. Her face was bruised and her drenched hair was flying about. "Darling, what happened?"

"I'm not sure...I think we hit another plane. Are Katie and Hillary all right?"

"No, they're both hurt...their legs."

Sean looked down and saw a confusion of torn seats and blood. His daughter's shins and kneecaps were open and bleeding. It was almost impossible to distinguish between the litter and the arms and legs sprawled at grotesque angles as if they were Raggedy Ann dolls. Katie was unconscious, and her sister was whimpering half in bewilderment, half in shock.

"Oh, my poor sweethearts...maybe I can move them," Sean said.

"No, I tried that," Connie cried. "Their legs are broken. Katie has a bone sticking out."

"My God!"

"Sean, I'm so frightened. Are we going to crash?"

"I don't know. We're stuck to a nose gear...must have collided with a big plane."

Sean looked down through the openings in the bottom of the Helio's fuselage, and he noticed one of the landing-gear hubs.

"That's a landing gear, all right. Must have happened in the downdraft."

"Sean, we have to *do* something. The girls are losing a lot of blood."

"I can't do a damn thing," Sean yelled over the pitch of the wind. "They *have* to know about us up there!" he said, pointing above.

"Oh, why in God's name did you ever take up flying?"

Way above the Helio, Lou and his flight-deck crew had no inkling of what had occurred. Such a phenomenon was not included in the syllabus of possible aviation mishaps.

Yet, it had happened.

Lou knew there was a problem, though. As he guided his SST down toward the tower for the fly-by, his needle nose wanted to duck, even with all the trim fuel pumped aft to lower the tail. He felt the increasing pressure against the yoke, as if the Concorde had made up its mind to be mischievous.

"Jeff, there's a real drag and trim problem here," Lou said into his microphone.

"All right, stay with it, Lou. You're at one thousand feet...two miles from visual contact...one-half mile from visual contact...you're doing nicely," Jeff said as he watched his precision radar.

"Breakout time!" Jeff yelled into the mike.

Jeff and the others stood at the shattered cab window and saw the beak of the white SST appear out of the low drifting clouds.

"Christ...look at that!" Jeff screamed, his eyes pinned to binoculars.

"Am I seein' things, Mr. Sutton?" Hoagy called.

"What is it?" Mark asked.

"There was a collision," Jeff said. "That's a float plane hanging off the Concorde's nose strut. Goddammit!"

The Concorde and its partner were swiftly enveloped in the low-racing clouds.

"Lou...Lou..." Jeff yelled into his mike.

"Yeah, Jeff. See anything?"

"You won't believe this...you have another plane with you."

"What do you mean? What other plane?"

"Your nose gear is stuck through the center of a small float plane. That's causing your drag and trim problems. The air pressure hitting that damn thing is forcing your nose down."

"Are you joking?"

"No, no! There is a plane hanging off your nose gear."

Things began to clear in Lou Griffis' mind.

It explained why the nose gear could not retract. The drag of the small plane upset the trim and was forcing them to use an added ten percent power just to maintain altitude.

At that moment a captain from the Dade County Police Department entered the cab, along with the other officers and firemen who were milling about.

"Mr. Sutton, I need you for a report."

"Get the hell out of this cab!" Jeff yelled. "I've got a Concorde in trouble up there. Empty the cab. Everyone except Hoagy...Bolton...the secretary and Dr.

Montours...*out!* Joe, you stay here with Leroy in case we have radar problems. Get your spares and tools up here fast."

"Mr. Sutton, I've got the press calling, and the commissioner is on the phone," the police captain insisted.

"I don't give a damn!" Jeff cracked out. "Where the hell are the medics? I want some doctors. Don't tell the press a goddamn thing."

Mark Cranston moved forward. "I'm the Secretary of Transportation, Captain. I'll back Mr. Sutton up. Please do what he says."

The police captain and the others stepped over the carpet of splintered glass, and Jeff returned to the radio.

"We're going to get you down safely, Lou. Is everything okay except your trim?"

"Nothing wrong, but it will be a miracle if we can drop that small plane off my nose strut."

"What if we foam the runway?"

"Well, I like that for openers."

"No, wait a minute, there's a problem," Jeff said. "The light plane is canted down at an angle of maybe twenty degrees. Those float tips would hit the concrete and flip the plane back up under your fuselage. There has to be fuel in that guy's wings, and you'd have a primary explosion."

"Yeah, and that would detonate my fuel tanks just aft of the landing-gear bay. We'd go up like a rocket. Jeff, can you get us a vector out to sea? I'll climb to ten thousand; that way I can conserve a little fuel until we figure something out."

"I'll give you a holding-pattern vector off Miami Beach. What's your fuel remaining?"

"Just a minute...ah...about forty-five minutes at this rate of burn-off. I'm going back there and pull open the nose-gear inspection hatch. I've got to see this for myself. If we can get that plane unhooked somehow, we might have a chance. Do you suppose anyone's alive in there?"

"You came by so fast, I couldn't see. One thing in

218

our favor—the front is passing quickly now. We should have clear visibility very soon."

"Yep, at least we can see what we're doing," Lou said in his slow Australian drawl. "Jeff, I'd appreciate it if I could get a direct hookup with George Hornsby...he's Celtic's chief pilot. Tell him to contact a fellow named Ralph Caldwell with the BAC Filton division. The chap knows more about the structural design of these Concordes than anyone else. We'll have to establish a four- or five-way telephone hookup. And, Jeff...move fast, huh? Keep this frequency open. I'll call you back."

"You got it, Lou...everything."

Charles Moran had heard the transmission to the tower, and even though he had been a combat pilot during the Korean War, his face went powder-white during the exchange. He shook his head, his eyes filled with alarm.

"Skipper, we're not getting out of this one, and you know it." He spoke in a cultured accent heard more often in the halls of Parliament than in airplane cockpits.

Lou unbuckled his seat belt and grabbed the handsome copilot by his dark blue tie.

"Never say that, lad. I need your help! You can't give up."

"Captain Griffis, he's right," Cecil Holloway said. "How do you think we'll land?"

"How the bloody hell do I know? Maybe a water landing. Maybe we can cut the small plane away. Don't ask me yet!"

"Well, it had better be soon, because we're sucking up the kerosene," Cecil said.

"It will be soon. Both of you...stick with me."

"What else can we do?" Charles Moran said.

Lou sat down again and quickly pressed his P.A. button.

"Ladies and gentlemen, this is Captain Griffis. We are currently over Miami Beach headed toward a holding pattern at ten thousand feet. About eight minutes ago we experienced a collision with a light plane, or I should say, the light plane was hit by our nose landing gear. The control tower tells us that the small plane is hanging off our nose gear. We will try to extrude the plane and make our landing. There is no present danger of fire or explosion. Our engines and controls are not affected. However, I am going to ask for your cooperation. If there is a doctor aboard, or anyone with mechanical experience, or anyone who can handle tools, I am asking those persons to come forward. I will enter the cabin in a few moments and personally inspect the damage to our nose gear by pulling up the carpet and dropping down into the nose-gear well. I want to assure everyone that our engines and flight controls are operating to full capacity. The problem is only connected with the nose-gear landing wheel. All the other wheels are in perfect working order. Thank you for your cooperation. Please remain calm and follow the instructions of your cabin attendants."

"What did he say, Honey?" Dame Margaret asked, rousing.

"We hit a plane...and it's still with us," Honey said, looking from the window. "But I can't see anything. The rain is too thick."

"Are we going to crash?" Dame Margaret asked fearfully.

"No, no. Captain Griffis will get us down."

"Before, you told me why I might be afraid to fly, but you never mentioned anything like this."

"I know. I never thought of anything like this. But listen to me—my dad is in that tower. He's a very sharp man, and Captain Griffis up in the cockpit is one of the best Concorde pilots there is. He helped design this plane. I have faith in them."

"I'm praying, just in case."

"So am I," Honey said.

In the cockpit Lou clicked off the intercom and climbed out of his seat. Charles glanced up at him.

"Why didn't you tell them the truth?" he said.

"I did."

220

There was a pause, and then Charles said, "You know we can't land without the nose gear, and the petrol is running low."

"I asked for your help, not your criticism."

"It's not criticism...just cold, hard facts, sir."

"You concentrate on keeping this plane in the holding pattern."

Lou shot a fierce look at his copilot and moved aft to the locker; taking a rope and safety belt, he left the flight deck.

"Captain Griffis," the senior stewardess said as he entered the cabin, "how serious is it?"

"Damn serious," Lou said, half under his breath so that the people in the first few rows could not hear him.

"Several people have volunteered."

Lou looked up and saw five men and a woman between the ages of eighteen and about sixty. A white-haired man stepped forward and presented Lou with a card.

"I am a doctor, sir. Dr. Hugh Collins," he said in a crisp Harley Street accent. "A general practitioner. But I don't see anyone hurt."

"I was thinking of the people trapped in the light plane. They might be injured."

"Oh, yes, of course. Unfortunately, there would be very little I could do for them without supplies."

"Captain, my name's Hank Brandt. Used to teach welding but like the doc here says, I don't have tools or nothin'."

The others shouted out their credentials: a structural engineer, a mechanical engineer, and a young girl who had helped her brother overhaul an engine.

"Fine...fine...just help me open the inspection hatch, and I'll appraise the situation," Lou said.

He walked toward the rear, and in the center of the aisle he showed his helpers how to pull up the carpet beside seats 14 A and B.

"All of you people from here back, take seats in the rear of the aircraft. There's going to be a lot of wind through here in a minute. Things will fly about."

221

"Oh, Honey, I wish this were over," Dame Margaret cried, clamping her hand again around the young girl's arm.

Honey patted her hand and glanced up, to see Lou approaching them.

"Everything's going to be all right, Honey," he said, pausing by their seat. "Now, you take Dame Margaret aft and do exactly what the cabin attendants tell you."

Her eyes searched his face for a moment; then she nodded quietly and unbuckled her seat belt, then reached over and helped the old actress with hers.

There was a quick movement aft, and in the cockpit Charles Moran noticed that the pressure lightened on his control yoke. The redistribution of thirty passengers was helping to equalize the balance of the Concorde.

Lou's volunteer team quickly peeled back the carpet, and in a matter of seconds the aluminum inspection hatch was exposed. Lou unscrewed the caps, and a swoosh of air shot up as the cabin pressure was equalized with that of the outside atmosphere. When the geyser of incoming air stopped, Lou fastened the safety belt around his midsection, tossed the toggle end to one of the men, who wrapped it around the frame of a seat.

"Be very careful now. When I open the hatch, air will rush around the cabin. Buckle yourselves into those seats."

When the passengers were secured, Lou pulled open the inspection hatch and felt the circulating air within the wheel walls hauling him down, but he shortened up on the safety line and stuck his head through the opening.

At almost the exact moment that he looked down into the bay, the Concorde came through a lacing of lighter clouds, and suddenly the darkness below was washed with brilliant sunlight.

The captain had secretly doubted that he would find a plane attached to the nose strut. Even if they had collided, the other plane would have to have been ripped away by the tons of air pressure. But Lou was

222

looking down on the mangled fuselage of an aircraft, and he could see people kneeling inside.

From the Helio, Sean looked up with wide, expectant eyes. He waved at Lou and then began to signal violently with his arms for help, as if Lou were about to climb down and grab him.

"How many of you are in there?"

Lou's words were gobbled up by the screaming wind. So were Sean's cries for help. Lou notched his hands together like a victorious prizefighter, trying to indicate to the man below that they would be rescued. He then slammed down the hatch and ran forward to the cockpit telephone.

"Charles, the tower is right! There *is* a plane hanging off our gear."

"My God, what does it look like?"

"It's banged up, and there is a man down there alive. I can't find out anything unless he can hear me. Bring the gear to the up position."

"If the wings hit the bay doors, we might get a detonation. There has to be fuel in his wing tanks, Captain Griffis."

"I know, but I think the tanks are outboard of the bay doors. Nothing happened the last time we retracted. Bring up the gear. Get his wing against the bay door; then maybe I can speak to him."

Charles Moran lifted the extended gear into the retract position. The jack motor hummed, but again the light only blinked amber, since the travel was halted halfway.

The aluminum on the outer skin of Sean's upper wing surface bent and crunched against the stiffer nose-gear bay doors. Lou was right. The gas tanks were still eleven inches outboard of where the Concorde's gear doors punched the wing skin.

Lou heard the whirl of the hydraulic jacks. Making certain that his safety belt was secure, he opened the inspection door again and ducked his head into the well. Sean McCafferty was about six feet closer now.

"Can you hear me?" Lou yelled.

"Yes, sir," Sean yelled back, cupping his hands.

"What happened? Oh, forget about that. How many people do you have in there?"

"Three besides myself. My two daughters are pinned in the wreckage. They're bleeding badly. Please, can you do something?"

"We'll try. I've got trouble, too."

"Are we going in?"

"I hope not. Now, tell me the condition of my wheels. Below you... *below* you!"

Sean nodded and knelt down and looked out through the crisscrossed holes of his lower fuselage.

"They're no tires on the wheel hubs," he yelled back. "One of them is sort of bent."

"Inward or outward?"

"Inward, it looks like."

"Okay. What kind of a plane is that?"

"A Helio Courier."

"What?"

"Helio Courier.... it's a bush plane."

"Do you have any tools aboard, like a hacksaw?"

"Negative," Sean yelled up.

"All right. We have to pull your people up here and then cut the plane away somehow. There's a doctor aboard here, and I'm going to call for cutting equipment."

"Call who?"

"Might try a midair transfer. Just tell your family to hang on."

"They don't have much choice."

"Neither do we."

"Please!" Connie screamed as she crawled forward and looked up at Lou. "My children are bleeding to death!"

Lou nodded, made the same gesture with his fists as before, smiled, and slammed the inspection hatch shut.

Lou Griffis was reporting his airborne condition to Jeff Sutton as the paramedics ran up into the cab.

"Christ!" one of them exclaimed, looking around.

"Don't just stand there. Get these people out of here!" Jeff shouted above the rush of wind curling into the cab, still bringing torrents of rain.

The paramedics quickly went to work on Harry Boyle, trying to find a sign of life. Nick Cozzoli was given a blood transfusion, while another team knelt beside Ed Morrison.

"This man is gone," one of the paramedics said a minute later, pointing to Harry.

They took Harry, Nick, and Ed Morrison from the cab, and then two medics came back.

"I think you people ought to come with us, too," one of them said, looking at the blood around Laura's arm and inspecting the secretary's wounded shoulder.

"We want to stay," the secretary said, looking at Laura. "Don't we, Dr. Montours?"

She smiled and nodded.

"All right, but let us clean these wounds up and give you some antibiotics."

As the two paramedics dug into their supplies, Jeff called over to Hoagy, "Do you have that telephone patch-in yet?"

"Almost."

"Tell them it's an emergency."

"They know that."

Jeff picked up the phone and punched the main switchboard number, which flashed in the administration section of the tower.

"This is Sutton. Get me Homestead Air Force Base. Say that the Secretary of Transportation, Mark Cranston, wants to speak to the base commander. It's an emergency!"

"Yes, sir."

Jeff turned to Mark. "I have some ideas, sir. They may work...may not."

"Good," Mark said. "I trust you to handle this."

Jeff forced a smile for the secretary. With the specter of Harry Boyle before him, he wished he could be as sure of his own judgment as Cranston was.

225

15

The unprecedented welding of the Concorde and Helio took place at 12:59 P.M. Miami time, 5:59 London time, and eight minutes passed before the phone rang in the London home of Celtic's chief pilot.

He was watching the BBC Home Service when his wife entered the room and told him there was an urgent call from the United States.

"Hornsby here," he said crisply into the phone.

"Captain Hornsby, my name is Jeff Sutton. I'm the facility chief at Miami tower...a friend of Lou Griffis'. Your Concorde hit a light plane about ten minutes ago." Jeff spoke somewhat mechanically, smothering his own sense of dread.

"My God, how did it happen? Was anybody killed?"

"No fatalities yet that we know of. Flight 202 was on final when it got caught in a freak downdraft, and apparently the SST collided with a Helio Courier."

"A helicopter?"

"No, it's an American bush plane."

"What are the damages?"

"We believe the small plane's prop slashed the Concorde's nose-wheel tires. The downward accelerations drove the nose strut right through the Helio."

"Ah, so the Concorde is trying to land without nose tires?"

"It's worse than that, Captain Hornsby. I'm afraid the Helio is stuck on the nose-gear axle, and the nose-gear steering unit is clamped in a bunch of metal."

For an incredulous moment George Hornsby jerked the phone away from his face, then said, "Would you repeat that, sir?"

"The Helio is hanging off the strut at about a twenty-degree down angle. The plane is just riding around with the Concorde."

"I can't believe this!"

"It happened. Apparently the Helio is built of tough alloy tubing and it's strong as hell. The collision munched the tubes together, forming a web around the strut. That's all we know at the moment, sir."

"Is Captain Griffis having control problems?"

"Not exactly, sir. He's out of trim somewhat, and they're burning kerosene like hell."

"Yes, yes, of course."

"Lou suggested that we immediately get onto a man named Ralph Caldwell at the Filton Division of BAC."

"Excellent suggestion. Ralph is old but he's a brilliant structural man. I don't know if we can reach him, actually—the chap is semiretired. What emergency procedures have you initiated, Mr. Sutton?"

"I'm trying to get through now to Homestead Air Force Base. We'll attempt a midair transfer of tools. Obviously, we have to cut the light plane off, if that's possible."

"Could I put you on hold for a moment, Mr. Sutton? I'm going to ring Caldwell."

In a small suburb of Bristol, Ralph Caldwell was reading in the upstairs room of his tarnished brick row house about eleven blocks from the engineering building of the Filton Division. The phone rang, and George Hornsby quickly relayed his information to the elderly designer. Then he asked, "Does that American know what he's talking about, Ralph? Could this really happen?"

"Yes, it could happen under the right circumstances. I know that Helio. It's a bloody tough little bird. They used them in Vietnam for insurgent work. All right, enough chatter. I'll get onto the engineering section. You tell Lou Griffis not to do anything until I talk to

227

him. Should take me about six minutes to reach the plant. We'll establish a conference call directly with the computer terminal room."

After hanging up, the perplexed designer contacted the engineering department and ordered the Concorde data banks hooked to the outsized computer. Ralph Caldwell pulled on his raincoat and ran out into the backyard. The clear British skies of that day had given way to winter slush; rain was falling, mixed with light sleet and ice. The old designer jumped into his Austin and pushed the gas pedal, only then realizing that he had run out with only his slippers on.

"Blasted thing!" Ralph yelled out as the starting motor whined without sparking the plugs.

The turning and cranking of the small engine went on, and finally it caught. Ralph gunned the four-cylinder motor, backed the car out, and saw his wife at the curbside with a pair of socks and shoes.

"You forgot these, love."

"Hell with them. Haven't time!" Ralph said as he waved her off and drove furiously down the cobbles of the street.

The complexities of the problem were already tumbling through his head. How would they detach the small plane? It would require cutting materials, skillfully operated. The Bristol designer knew the Concorde fuel situation, the trickiness of trimming up the tanks for a landing. Ralph's usually fertile mind came up with no solution. Some brilliant idea *had* to come to him, but it was absent as he spun his small car through the narrow streets of Bristol toward the engineering building.

Suddenly Ralph became aware of the blue turning lights of a constable's cruiser behind him. He stopped and yanked down the window.

"Going a little fast there, sir," the constable said, coming up to his window.

"I have to get to the Bristol factory, officer. There's a Concorde in trouble over Miami, Florida. I'm a consulting engineer with BAC."

For a moment the constable looked at him oddly; then he touched his cap and said, "Well, if that's it, I'll get you there in a jiff. Climb into my motorcar."

In matter of a few minutes, with the bell ringing, they were at the oval entrance to the Bristol factory, building 19, the engineering department.

In Miami, time seemed to freeze, but the hands of the tower clock continued to nibble away at the precious minutes. Jeff stood at the far end of the cab, peering up through his binoculars and cradling the phone in his other hand.

"Mr. Hornsby, why haven't we heard from Caldwell yet?" he asked.

"It would take him a while to reach the factory."

"But why couldn't he give us advice from his house?" Jeff asked.

"He doesn't have the engineering data there, Mr. Sutton. Oh, just a moment, the other phone is ringing. I expect that will be the president. Keep on the line, please."

As they waited in Miami, Mark Cranston looked at Laura and smiled. "Dr. Montours, I wonder if anyone besides me needs a drink."

She laughed. "Yes, about ten."

"There's some whiskey in the pantry off the conference room," Jeff called over. "Against the law, of course."

"Do you want a drink, Jeff?" Laura asked.

"No, not now."

She noticed the grim expression on his face and moved toward him.

"Jeff, don't worry. We'll get her down."

"How?"

"There are a lot of people working on it now. They'll come up with something."

"Better come up with a miracle. Why? Why? Of *all* the flights..."

She paused uncertainly, shook her head, and then

229

walked toward the stairs. Mark crossed over to Jeff and patted him on the back.

"Jeff, I'm praying for you."

"Thank you, sir." He turned. "How is your shoulder?"

"Not bad at all. The pain has stopped, and they'll dig that shrapnel out later."

The other line rang suddenly, and Jeff snatched it up.

"I have a Colonel Brady on the phone," the operator announced.

Jeff explained the situation to the air-force officer, who had a difficult time understanding how it had happened. He seemed skeptical.

"Can you help us?" Jeff yelled.

"Well...ah...I don't know."

"You don't know!" Jeff blasted.

"Give me that phone," Mark Cranston said.

"This is Secretary Cranston speaking."

"Yes, sir!" came the fast reply.

"Are you going to mobilize that base immediately for us up here, or do I call the Joint Chiefs of Staff? I know General Hopewell very well, Colonel Brady...and I play golf with the Secretary of Defense."

The colonel's tone changed instantly and he said, "Mr. Secretary, the entire base is at your disposal. I'll get out an alert, and we'll mobilize at once. It's just that I couldn't believe what Mr. Sutton was saying."

"None of us could, but I saw the situation with my own eyes. The Concorde made a pass by the tower. Here's Jeff Sutton again."

"We'll be right back." Laura gestured from across the room, as Jeff nodded and took the phone.

"Colonel Brady," Jeff said, "we have a patch line in to an engineer at the Filton division of BAC. They were co-builders of the Concorde."

"I see."

"There's an engineer there who knows more about the Concorde than anyone else. Hopefully, he'll give us some answers. In the meantime, I have a couple of ideas of my own. Do you have those attack choppers?"

230

"Yes, fourteen of them."

"And what is their top speed?"

"They're jet powered, and I'd say if we fire-walled them, we'd be looking at one-seventy, maybe a little better."

"Could you effect an air drop to the Concorde?"

"Do you mean a personnel drop?"

"No, just a bundle of cutting tools and other equipment."

"If the Concorde slowed down to about one-sixty, we could stay with them. But, sir, I have a better suggestion. We have a turbo-prop cargo plane here, the Hercules. She's highly maneuverable. That airplane *can* keep up with the Concorde, and she has reel winches aboard and a cargo door, of course."

"Great! Colonel, would you get all your cutting equipment and oxygen tanks out to the aircraft, along with ropes and toggles? And I'll tell you what to load after I speak to the British engineer. One other thing..."

"Yes, sir?"

"Do you have flatbed trucks down there, those big semis?"

"Sure do. About twenty of 'em in the motor pool."

"How fast can they go?"

"Loaded?"

"Unloaded."

"They're turbo diesels...about seventeen hundred horses. If you had distance to wind them up, maybe one-twenty to one-thirty miles per hour."

"And do you also have those air bags used to put under planes when they go in?"

"Sure. We inflate them, and they lift the wreck up so we can slide the jacks and dollies under."

"I want you to get ten of those diesel tractors up here with all the air bags you can find, Colonel. Plus tanks to inflate them. We'll also need shackles and chains to hook them up to the back of the flatbed semis. Also, I want ten men on each flatbed with CO_2 tanks... plenty of portable CO_2."

"May I ask what this is for, Mr. Sutton?"

"Well, I have a plan," Jeff said. "Keep on this line, Colonel Brady. We'll talk again just as soon as the call comes in from England, but, Colonel, the Concorde is running out of fuel, so can you fill my shopping list right away?"

"You'll have it all. The base is already on alert. But, sir, what are the flatbeds for?"

"I'll answer that later."

The hall outside the conference room was crowded with police and newsmen as Mark and Laura entered.

"Mr. Secretary," a reporter called.

"How did you get in here?" Mark shot back.

"Police allowed us in."

"What police?"

"Metro."

Mark went up to the lieutenant who was leaning against the radar-room door.

"Lieutenant, I'm Mark Cranston, Secretary of Transportation. You have absolutely no jurisdiction in here. This is federal property. You cannot authorize newsmen in this tower. Now, empty this place immediately. Leave two guards here and the paramedic team. That's it! Do you understand?"

"Yes, Mr. Secretary!"

"Burke, here, from the Miami *Post*," a small man with a peach-fuzz beard yelled. "Could you give us a statement, sir?"

"No statement."

"We already know quite a bit."

"Oh, what do you know?"

The reporter started flipping his notebook pages. "Let's see...there was an experiment going on in the tower when the collision took place. You didn't see the small plane hit the Concorde because you were using a new kind of radar. *And* one of the controllers went crazy and killed some people with a handgun and a live grenade. Have I got it right?"

"Who told you that?"

"Mr. Alcorn, Celtic station manager. He also said that this was a tragic failure on the part of the Federal Aviation Administration and that Celtic is going to sue for damages."

"That's absurd," Mark said.

"Can I quote you on—?"

"That's enough," Vic Sloan said as he ushered the group of Dade County police officers and the newsmen toward the elevator door. "FAA security will take care of things here. Out, gentlemen, please."

"I'll be back later for the whole story, Mr. Secretary," the reporter yelled with a smirk on his hungry young face.

Laura and Mark padded across to the conference room and closed the door. He leaned against it for a moment, then let out a big sigh.

"This is going to be worse than I thought."

Laura said, "Well, I think a drink would help at this point."

She went to the pantry bar and found whiskey and ice, and Mark poured two drinks for them.

"Here's to...well, getting those planes down," Laura said, lifting her glass.

"Yes, certainly," the secretary responded; and after a pause he said, "Guess I didn't pick the best day for a visit."

"No, I'll go along with that."

They drank, and then Laura said, "The press sure picked up the bad news fast. I can't imagine the Celtic station manager making a statement like that."

Mark shook his head. "Irresponsible...but what *will* we tell them?"

"About the Concorde or Harry?"

"Both," the secretary said.

Mark noticed a quick change of mood come over Laura. She sat on the couch shaking her head and looking at the royal-blue rug with the American eagle embroidered in the center.

"What's the matter?" he asked.

"I wonder if Harry Boyle would have let that grenade go? I mean, if I hadn't tossed the boiling water at him?"

"He was out of his mind, Laura. He killed that helpless security guard in cold blood. You mustn't blame yourself. You did the right thing. And how could we have gotten that Concorde down if Harry were in charge of the cab? He wasn't going to yield."

"No, he wasn't. Pathetic man."

"Now, I keep asking myself: are there others in the ATC system like Harry Boyle?"

"Jeff says there are."

"That's really a frightening thought."

The secretary poured himself another drink and sat down next to Laura.

"I still can't believe all this happened," Mark said. "My heart was pounding up there like I'd just finished five fast sets of squash."

"Mine, too."

"You had a lot of guts, Laura."

"Funny thing...I never did anything that physical in my life. But I keep wondering about this tower. It's almost inhuman to have to work in a place like this—the pressure, the claustrophobic feeling. Do you have to be mad to take on the job of air-traffic controller, or does the job make you mad?"

"Maybe it's both."

"Mark, I'll tell you something. Your department had better get a handle on this situation, and right now."

"I knew things were wrong, but not this critical." He paused again, and his eyes settled on the luminous panels in the ceiling. "Laura, I'm going to tell you something in confidence. Six months ago I initiated an investigation of air-traffic control at the request of the Executive Department. The management firm hired a private outfit, which discovered that Ed Morrison has a substantial interest in CORAD."

Laura stared at him, and then things began to click into place.

"I wondered why he was so protective of that radar."

"We don't know how deep the criminality goes—the

report was just handed to me this morning—but Ed is involved."

"My God, wait till Jeff hears this! Or...is he to know?"

Mark nodded. "I wouldn't be telling you this, except...well, I feel I owe you both an explanation. I think you've earned the right to my confidence, and a lot of the problems with ATC can be attributed to my executive staff. I had the wrong people. Of course, I inherited them all, including Ed Morrison. But that doesn't make me feel any better right now."

"Well, Morrison might never be investigated, you know. A paramedic told me he lost a lot of blood." She paused for a moment. "It was probably inevitable anyway that something like this would occur someday in another tower, with another controller as burnt-out as poor Harry."

Mark Cranston heaved himself to his feet. "Perhaps you're right, Laura. Come on, let's go see what's happening with the Concorde."

Ten thousand feet over the lazy ocean swells, the Concorde swung in oblong loops. The front had moved through and vanished eastward, and a pure pink light flashed out from the west. A swarm of small planes accompanied the SST in its pattern, diving at her, coming up under her so dozens of photographers could click off tight shots of the hanging Helio with their long lenses.

"Jeff," Lou said into his mike, "we've got too many sightseers up here. Could you clear them out? I want the whole sky to myself."

"Sure, Lou. We'll call Miami center and vector them away from there."

"And, Jeff, there's only about thirty-seven minutes of fuel remaining. What about the conference call to England? Is Caldwell available?"

"Yes, we were just informed by the overseas operator."

"I think you'd better get that chopper loaded with

whole blood. The doctor on board is yelling down to McCafferty—that's the pilot of the small plane—about his two daughters. They're in shock and losing blood rapidly. They're pinned in the wreckage."

"Yes, yes, we'll do that."

"He needs syringes and morphine, plus IV equipment."

"Got it."

"Do you think we can make a transfer, Jeff? I mean, at one seventy? I can't slow it up any more than that."

"We'll have to try it, Lou. They've got a turbo-prop plane standing by, besides the attack choppers. Homestead is giving us their full support."

"I'd also alert the Coast Guard for a water landing. I think that's what will happen."

"Then you'll drown the people in the Helio."

There was a pause, and then Lou said, "That's right. I can't understand how they lived through the accident to begin with. We'll try to save them, but I don't know... God, I feel so helpless."

"So do I," Jeff answered. "Totally helpless. How is Honey...she okay?"

"Fine. She's a brave little girl. Ah, just a minute, Jeff."

"Skipper..." Charles was saying in the Concorde. "The fuel flow rate is increasing."

"All right. Let's prepare for a water landing, then. Have the stewardesses pull the rafts down and give the passengers instructions."

Lou returned to the mike. "Jeff, I don't see any way out now except ditching."

"Lou, you'll flip it! With that plane hanging on to you, the goddamn bird will explode before the nose hits the water. It's too dangerous."

"But I'm running out of time, Jeff! I have to make a decision."

"How about a midair fuel transfer?"

"No good. We're not set up for that. I can hack a hole through the cabin floor to tanks nine and eleven, but we'd have a cabin full of kerosene if the hose broke."

"Christ, yes. You'd be blown up from the inside!"

Even as the two men talked, a stewardess had already appeared in the cockpit in answer to the call bell. Lou turned to the girl.

"Maggie, it looks like a water landing offshore. Please prepare the passengers."

The tall, slender cabin attendant spoke in a flat British accent. "Very good, Captain Griffis," she said calmly. She displayed no emotion whatsoever as she turned to exit the cockpit; Lou Griffis might have been asking for a ginger ale and a cracker.

16

The Concorde structural data was "spun in" to the terminal printout in the third-floor engineering office of BAC. In front of Ralph Caldwell, who was already sneezing from wet, cold feet, was a pile of weight and performance data, and his agile, bony fingers were poised, ready to tap the smudged buttons of the well-worn computer terminal.

The phone rang, and the international operator said that the conference call and radio patch-in to the Concorde was ready.

"Hello...this is Ralph Caldwell on the Bristol end."

"Jeff Sutton...MIA tower."

"Lou Griffis...how are you, Ralph?"

"Fine, Lou."

"George Hornsby here."

A brisk voice cut in, "Roger Smith speaking. We

want that bird down with no loss to lives or the plane, if possible. My prayers are with you, gentlemen."

"Thank you, Mr. Smith," Ralph said. "Now, let's talk slowly. Let me size up the situation. You have a Helio bush plane stuck on the nose-gear strut."

"That's affirmative, Ralph," Lou said.

"From what you could see, how securely is the small plane on there?"

"*Very* securely," Lou replied. "If it wasn't, the wind pressure would have yanked it off. All I could see was twisted tubes when I looked down from the nose-bay inspection hatch."

Ralph's hands raced over the computer. He fed in the wind pressure per inch acting against the bulk of the Helio.

"She's taking about seven hundred pounds per square inch...maybe eight hundred. What a tough little bastard. Okay, we'll assume," Ralph continued, "that it's really hung in there. How much fuel is remaining?"

Lou looked over inquiringly at the flight engineer who was monitoring their conversation on his headset. The numbers were passed: "21,789 pounds."

"And what's your thrust setting?"

"About eighty percent."

"That's a lot," Ralph said.

Again he clacked the buttons, letting out a giant sneeze.

"That gives you thirty-one minutes' flying time with a two-minute reserve. Give me a confirm on that, Lou."

Once more, Cecil Holloway nodded.

"That's a confirmation, Ralph."

Laura and Mark entered the MIA cab. She carried a small glass half full of vodka and attempted to pass it to Jeff, but he waved it away.

"Now," continued Ralph, "we have to buy time. Time is the prime element. But first, here's what you can't do: no pancaking the Concorde into the sea. The approach speed would be too high for control. With your new drag element, the fuselage would probably break up into a hundred pieces, as if you'd hit a brick wall. You can't land on a runway with that light plane hanging off there.

"As soon as the nose wheel settled, even if you held it off as long as possible, the small plane would flip aft and explode. That would kick off a major detonation in your tanks, directly under the passenger compartments. Agreed, Lou?"

"Yes. The fuel in the Helio would act like a detonator. Okay, that's what we *can't* do.... Now, how do I land this bird, Ralph?"

Ralph eyed his engineering team, which was listening to the conversation. Each of them concurred in Ralph's analysis.

"We *have* to remove that light aircraft and try for a landing on bare rims, hoping you can slide over a well-foamed runway."

"We have plenty of foam," Jeff interrupted.

"Proceed with the foaming job straightaway," Ralph ordered.

"But how do we get the light plane off our strut, Ralph? It's really meshed in there!" Lou yelled into his mike, watching the fuel needles edge toward the white pins that indicated "empty."

"We'll have to attempt a midair transfer," Ralph said. "Write this down and do just what I say. We could cut through the Helio's alloy tubes with an acetylene torch very quickly, but the sparks might ignite the draining petrol."

"I didn't smell any petrol," Lou interrupted.

"You couldn't smell a fuel-line puncture at that air speed, but the light plane's gas cock and valve must be open. There are fumes, even though the main tanks aren't punctured."

"If we can't cut the plane away with the torch, how the devil do we do it?" Lou asked.

"Mr. Sutton, do you have an open line to Homestead Air Force Base?"

"That's affirmative, Mr. Caldwell," Jeff said. "And

we have chase helicopters waiting, plus a Hercules turbo-prop."

"That's splendid," the engineer said. "May I have a word with the air-force officers?"

"Sure. They're standing by," Jeff answered.

Jeff punched the phone button on the second line into the cab, and a voice responded promptly: "Colonel Brady, base operations."

"Homestead, we have an engineer from England on the line now," Jeff said.

"Good. The airborne equipment and crews are ready, but we don't know what we're supposed to load."

"This man will tell you. Is your maintenance chief there?"

"Yes, sir...Captain Betzig."

"Ralph," Jeff said, "you now have Colonel Brady and Captain Betzig on the line from Homestead Air Force Base."

"Gentlemen," Ralph said, "we're going to attempt a tool transfer between the Hercules and the Concorde. Are you listening, Lou?"

"I'm reading."

"We will open the left-side-aft galley-service door. It's the plug type, Colonel Brady. Did you hear that, Lou?"

"Yes, sir."

"The door is located just forward of the trailing edge of the delta wing. That means, Colonel, you can slide your bundle along the wing, and Captain Griffis and his men can haul it in through the opened door while the Concorde maintains a fifteen-degree nose-up attitude. Fifteen degrees, Lou...no more!"

"Got it," Lou answered.

"But, sir," Captain Betzig said, "what are we transferring?"

"Here's the order," Ralph said. "They'll need three air-powered hacksaws with spade handles, the reciprocating kind. The compressors will have to generate about ninety pounds air pressure. Are those pumps on hand, sir?"

"Yes, sir," Captain Betzig said. "But why three units?"

"Because, gentlemen, we not only have to cut the small plane away, if possible, but also reduce the weight of the Concorde. We're gutting the Concorde's cabin. Now, besides the pumps, they'll need five lengths of three-wire extension line to be jacked into the Concorde's main electrical panel. They will require safety belts and fifty-foot lines with toggle snatches, also a chain jack hoist with metal stretcher clamps, plus a shearing jack capable of two hundred pounds pressure. I also want walkie-talkies and two remote extensions to the standby VHF radio. Do you have these supplies, Homestead?"

"Yes, sir, all of that is fairly standard for us. Everything's in the shop," Captain Betzig replied.

"Load them up straightaway. Pack the material in soft transfer bags so you don't puncture the wing skin."

"Yes, sir," Captain Betzig said. "We can put a hundred men on it if necessary. I'll get off now and start rounding these things up."

"I'm still here," Colonel Brady said. "We discussed medical supplies. They're loaded in the Hercules."

"Fine," Jeff said. "Get that one in the air immediately. That will be the first transfer."

"Will do."

"Ralph," Lou broke in quickly, "why the hell are we establishing a workshop in here? We don't have time for all this!"

"But we are going to purchase a little time, Lou. First of all, read me your payload figures."

The flight engineer handed Lou the Concorde's weight and balance sheet.

"We have forty-two passengers. Figuring them on an average of one hundred seventy pounds each ... ah ... that's a payload of 7,140 pounds. We have baggage rated at 2,184 pounds, and the rest of it is air cargo ... 18,676 pounds."

"What is the air cargo?" Ralph asked.

"Medical-analyzation parts, machine parts, and general cargo bound for Brazil."

"So, you're at gross?"

"That's affirmative," Lou said.

"Okay, here's what we're going to do. As you know, Lou, we have two cargo compartments: one under the lower forward fuselage, the second one aft of the galley just before the tail pressure bulkhead. Go to seat number eleven. Pull up the carpet and get someone down into that cargo compartment. Start fetching up the luggage. Repeat the procedure aft. After you pull the service door open, start chucking everything out while in a fifteen-degree inward bank. No more than fifteen…that will discharge the load almost automatically. Ropes and belts around everyone. There will be an outward pressure of air as soon as the door is swung open, but that will stabilize. Still, you will experience a heavy rush of ram air, so everyone will have to be tied in. No moving around the open door without a toggle belt. We should be able to reduce the weight by some 18,000 pounds by jettisoning the cargo, according to my figures. Now, do you have that?"

"Affirmative," Lou said. "Is that before the transfer?"

"Get right onto it. You have five belts with ropes in the starboard locker."

"I just had one on," Lou answered.

"Excellent. Now hold it a second…." Ralph flipped through his weight data and raced his hands over the desk calculator.

"You have forty vacant seats. Each one weighs sixty-seven pounds. I want those removed from their tracks. You know how, Lou. They will fit through the aft door. Over the side. That will save 2,680 pounds. Then, I want all the hand luggage jettisoned, everything removable from the galleys. When the pressure tools are in, we'll start cutting out the galleys and lavatories and finally most of the radio racks and navigation equipment. We should be able to clear out another 10,000 pounds."

"Yes, I understand," Lou said.

"I've just calculated the following," Ralph continued. "With a reduction in weight, we can come back on the turbines by twenty percent and...let's see...maybe your flight engineer can follow me through. With that fuel flow, you'll have an extra twenty minutes of flying time. Confirm that."

Cecil worked his own computer and nodded to Lou.

"We're confirming that," Lou said. "As of this minute, we should have fifty-one minutes of flying. That's not much time to hack the light plane away and get the kids out—if we can."

"I know...I know," Ralph said. "But there's no other choice."

"What if the crash trucks followed alongside and got their CO-2 nozzles on the Helio?" Lou suggested. "Wouldn't that prevent an explosion?"

"Your nose wheel with that plane hanging on there will come down at about one-fifteen knots, and no crash truck can reach that speed hauling a full load of foam and light water."

"That's right," Jeff said. "They can hit maybe sixty."

"So that won't work, Lou," Ralph said. "No, the only solution, as I see it from the engineering point of view, is to get that plane off the nose strut and lighten up the Concorde."

When the conversation ended, Lou went aft and assembled the passengers into several work groups: seven men entered the forward baggage bay, handing up the luggage after the hatch was opened, and the bags were passed aft one by one.

Some of the passengers were shaking, others crying, but Dame Margaret stood, and in her most clarion stage voice, with both hands wrapped around her handbag, said, "We must all help out. Everyone. There is no time for fear or self-pity."

She said this as she began handing over the cases, one of which was hers.

"Good-bye, Dior dress. I never liked you anyhow."

Honey stood right beside Dame Margaret, and as activity hastened, the crying and the outward panic seemed to evaporate, for a while at least.

Homestead Air Force Base was turned into a whirl of activity. Men ran from one area to another; the jets on the pads were spooled up and the cargo plane was loaded, her turbo-props spinning in the afternoon light, which had turned to a buttery yellow as the storm clouds moved out.

The large deep-blue semitrailer trucks whined their way onto the pad, and men in helmets were ready to make the twenty-mile trip up to MIA.

Captain Betzig, a career air-force man with a protruding lower jaw and rugged no-nonsense face, picked up the phone in a cab of one of the semitrailers and called Jeff Sutton in the tower.

"Mr. Sutton...Betzig. We're ready to roll with the trucks, and the Hercules is about to take off."

"Good."

"We contacted the Dade County sheriff's office and both the Miami and Coral Gables police. LeJeune Road is being blocked off now so we can roll at top speed. But, sir, what are the trucks *for?*"

"A standby idea."

"Well, there's plenty of CO-2 bottles aboard, and more than a hundred guys."

"Good. One more thing, Captain. Get plenty of ropes for your men. They might have to discharge the CO-2 on the runway while the tractors roll down there."

"All right. We're moving out now."

"Go to the Thirty-sixth Street gate. It'll be open. Bring them right onto runway two-seven-left...to the threshold."

"Got it."

"How long will it take?" Jeff asked.

"About fifteen minutes."

"And that's about all the time we have, so tell 'em to floor those accelerators!"

* * *

Lou started his work immediately. He belted himself to a back seat, having opened the aft galley-service door, and the cabin air swooshed out as the pressure equalized; and then the arms of ram air curled back into the cabin. But just as Caldwell said, he found the door would open and stay there, held by the bounding air sliding along the fuselage. Behind Lou, eight volunteers opened the aft cargo section; luggage and boxes of air-freight equipment were quickly pushed out, while Charles Moran hand-flew the Concorde in a series of fifteen-degree turns.

Then, with a box of socket wrenches, Lou showed them how to unfasten the seats from the tracks. One by one, the leather seats costing four hundred and ten dollars each were pushed back and dumped.

The SST started to gain altitude, and Charles, the only one left in the cockpit, came back on his thrust levers to stabilize the plane at ten thousand feet.

"It's working! It's working! I have already reduced thrust by six percent," he yelled into the mike.

"Excellent," Caldwell answered. "There was no doubt in my mind it would help."

Suddenly there were brighter faces in the tower. Hoagy came over to Jeff and placed his arm around him.

"We have a good chance now, Mr. Sutton."

Jeff did not react one way or another, but simply stood there, his binoculars fixed on the sky over Miami Beach as he waited to see the Hercules appear over the horizon and begin its drop. He had punched his stopwatch, and already fourteen minutes of the Concorde's flying time had been used up.

"The man in England sure knows his stuff, doesn't he, Jeff?" Mark said with a bright face.

Laura, who was standing next to Jeff, noticed his tight lips.

"Jeff, don't you agree with what they're doing?" she asked.

He turned to her and Mark. "Let's go down to the

conference room for a minute. Maybe I do need that drink."

"Sure," Mark said.

Jeff left the cab in charge of Hoagy, and the three descended to the lower level.

Joe Redmond was standing outside the radar room.

"Mr. Sutton, how are the scopes and radios working? Notice anything after that blast?"

"Everything's still working fine, Joe. I don't know why."

"Yeah, that was some explosion up there."

"Joe, I'd appreciate it if you'd go up and stand by. Is the runway foamed yet?"

"Yes, sir, and they even got trucks coming down from Lauderdale."

"Good."

Jeff, Mark, and Laura entered the conference room, and Jeff went directly to the bar and poured himself a drink.

"Guess I was more shook-up than I realized," he said, downing the liquor.

"Did you get hurt?" Mark asked.

"No. The glass flew around me somehow."

"Jeff, you're not convinced this suggestion of Caldwell's will work, are you?" Laura asked.

He sat down at the conference table and pulled a pad of yellow paper toward him.

"No. It's all right for Caldwell to sit over in England and tell us what to do. Theoretically, he may be right, and if we had three hours to take the Concorde apart, I'd say fine. But look at my watch. It says we're down to thirty-eight minutes. Those people up there aren't skilled mechanics. They won't know which tube in the Helio to cut, and they all have to be on ropes. What happens if the small plane lets go suddenly and takes everyone with it?"

"But, Jeff," Mark said, "even if there are a thousand ifs to this, Caldwell said they couldn't land on water

246

without breaking up, and they can't hit the runway with the small plane. So what is the choice?"

Jeff started drawing a helicopter with a Concorde below it on the yellow pad.

"I've got an idea. I know it will sound crazy, but what if the chopper could hang out a stainless-steel cable off its reel winch in a big hoop, a lasso, and if Lou could guide his needle nose through this loop. Then we'd have the nose of the Concorde through the loop and the chopper following the SST on final about fifty yards above. Now, what happens is this: the loop is held slack all the way until the Concorde touches down. The chopper remains just overhead, keeping up with the SST. As the Concorde decelerates, they take up on the winch. When the Concorde's nose comes down on the runway, the cable is pulled tight and the chopper begins to gain altitude, putting upward pressure on the nose. In effect, it holds the Concorde's nose off the concrete until the SST slows up. If there is a fire or explosion upon impact, it will occur when the Concorde has slowed up to a very moderate speed, and the crash trucks can catch up in time to handle it. They can lay out a foam blanket under way...if the speed isn't too high."

Jeff slipped back into his seat and blew out a long breath. "I know it's wild. I *know* it. I also know that there isn't enough time to make Caldwell's plan work."

Silence.

Finally Laura said, "I'm afraid you're selling this to the wrong people."

"She's right, Jeff," Mark answered slowly. "Mine is a desk job. Maybe it can be done, maybe not, but I couldn't begin to evaluate your proposal."

"Oh, shit!" Jeff said, pounding his fist into the shiny conference table. "I wanted your support."

"Well...how?" Laura asked.

"Anything, Jeff," Mark added. "But what can we do?"

"I can't get on the horn as a glorified controller and suggest these things to a senior engineer. Frankly, I don't have the credentials to propose such an idea, but

247

I feel it might work. My daughter is up there. Honey's trapped on that flying bomb, and that's my fault, too!"

Mark glanced at Jeff and said, "Of course, I'll back you up. For whatever it's worth, you have my complete support."

Laura crossed the room and placed her hand gently on Jeff's shoulder.

"Come on, let's get started."

They left for the cab.

17

Jeff climbed the steel stairs with all juices going and recited his solution to those on the conference line.

Colonel Brady drawled slowly after hearing Jeff's idea, "Well, of course, we do have fast turbine helicopters equipped with reel winches and plenty of cable, Mr. Sutton. Our pilots could maneuver those whirlies into position for a loop pass. Also, sir, we have a clutch on the reel winch to let it run wild if something should go wrong."

And for a moment a satisfied smile and a nod of exultation came from Jeff. He thought he had delivered the answer, the only one.

"Caldwell, here, Mr. Sutton. I appreciate your thinking, but let me tell you what's wrong with your idea. I'll assume that this cable could be swung around the Concorde by skilled piloting, but, sir, you must understand our Concorde design."

"Design? What's that got to do with it?" Jeff said sharply.

"Everything," the engineer responded positively. "Behind the nose of the Concorde, the fuselage is constant until it flares in toward the tail assembly just beyond the aft pressure bulkhead. Our construction is of the double-bubble type, blended at the floor level rather than truly circular. We have hoop frames set at a twenty-one-inch pitch. The stringers are closely spaced to support the skin, which is three-mm in thickness. The forward frames have a single skin attachment, but the others toward the rear have a double flange design. Each frame is in two pieces, and at some points we use cleat brackets."

"Mr. Caldwell," Jeff interrupted. "Please, sir, I don't need a voyage through aircraft design. Just tell me in plain words if my idea will work or not."

"Negative. The nose section will not withstand the pressure of a taut cable. The only section of the fuselage which can take the tensile load is at frame thirty-one— that's just aft of the forward passenger door, where the fuselage takes on its uniformity. I'm worrying about the end take-up position of the cable. How do you tighten it up at the exact point where the Concorde's tensile strength can handle the bending moment? And let's say that the cable rode off; then you'd have the strand entangled with the light plane. In that case it would be too far aft of the Concorde's datum point for the chopper to hold the nose off the ground, assuming that the reel winch could be taken up at just the right moment. Also, if the cable swung back, it would conflict with the wings of the light plane, causing static electricity. At that speed you're risking a fuel ignition from the small plane that would certainly trigger a major fuel fire or explosion from the Concorde's petrol tanks. I'm sorry, Mr. Sutton, I could not approve this."

"Well, Mr. Caldwell, I'll tell you something. Maybe my idea isn't practical from the engineering point of view, but they're going to run out of fuel up there, and they'll be *dead* sticking that big plane down here.

"We've already lightened her up about eighteen

thousand pounds. The fuel *is* being conserved, Mr. Sutton."

"Okay, okay. But we don't have experienced personnel to handle the tools except for Lou, maybe, and the flight engineer. You have amateurs hanging into the fuselage of a light plane trying to use power equipment they've never seen, much less handled. My daughter happens to be aboard that plane today, Mr. Caldwell! I think your solution is nothing but goddamn wishful thinking. There isn't time! Can't you understand that? There isn't time!" Jeff yelled into the phone.

"Mr. Sutton, I'm sorry about your daughter and I do understand. But we *are* jettisoning the load."

"Not enough can be pushed out, goddammit! We are down to thirty...no...twenty-seven minutes' flying time, and the tools aren't even aboard yet," Jeff yelled.

"Try to be calm, Mr. Sutton."

"I am calm. But if this doesn't work, tell me, Mr. Caldwell—which is worse, a ditching at sea or landing on a foamed runway?"

"Ditching would be far more dangerous."

"I agree with that," Lou cut in.

"What's the worst thing that could happen if we put it down on the runway with the small plane still hanging on?"

"As I said, Mr. Sutton, the nose of the Concorde will contact the runway at about one-ten knots. The Helio will flip back, hit our tanks. You'll most likely experience a primary explosion plus a secondary detonation when the flash point of the fuel in the Concorde's tanks is reached."

"How survivable?"

"All those left in the small plane will be killed instantly. It's unlikely that the flight-deck crew will survive. The nose will be immediately ground up in the runway. Beyond that...the science of kerosene detonation is hard to predict, Mr. Sutton. Some planes can impact a hard surface at ninety knots and there'll be no explosion. Others can make contact at fifty knots and their fuselage will blow sky-high. But I would say that smacking the belly at about one-ten knots with gas in the small plane and at least some jet fuel left in the Concorde's tanks...you're going to see one devil of an explosion. It'll be almost the same as the Canary Islands disaster. When you have two moving objects, both loaded with inflammables impacting at high G forces, you're looking at what we call a compound detonation. The results are devastating. Very quick, I might add. What's remarkable, also, is that you don't need a lot of kerosene for a high-impact explosion. Even if Lou lands with tanks almost dry, the fumes will remain. That causes detonation."

Jeff Sutton was an imaginative man, and he had always prided himself on his ability to make quick decisions. He was not one to give up, and even though his first solution was, apparently, unfeasible, he was still ready to offer another solution.

"Would you listen to something else, then, Mr. Caldwell?"

"Of course, I'll listen."

"Here's plan number two," Jeff said in short bursts. "I've already ordered ten big semitrailer flatbed trucks from Homestead Air Force Base. They're on the way now. This might sound as crazy as the last idea, but here it is. These trucks are damn powerful. They're used to cart around missiles and big turbines. They can do over a hundred miles per hour, I'm told. So, the Concorde is on final approach with the small plane still hanging off there. The trucks are wound up, and they roll down the runway dragging those big crash bags, the kind they inflate when a plane goes off the runway. Hopefully, the Concorde's nose settles down into the bags, and that way we soften the impact. We prevent the explosion."

"How did you get onto that idea?" Caldwell asked.

"The first model of the U-2 spy plane was designed that way. Trucks with bags followed along under each wing, cushioning the runway impact."

"There's one thing wrong," Caldwell said. "If you did time it right—and the whole job is timing—the bags would burst while being dragged up the runway. Heat friction. You can't foam down the runway, because the trucks need grip for traction."

"I thought of that. We'll run a quick practice on two-seven-left, get our timing, and see if this brainstorm will work. After we mess up that runway with the foam, we'll switch to two-seven-right for the real event."

"But how do you propose to foam the runway?"

"By hand. Air Force men will be positioned on the flatbed trailers with hand-operated CO_2. We just have to lay down enough to keep heat friction from exploding the air bags."

"I've never heard of anything like that." Caldwell sighed.

"I haven't either. Maybe it will work," Jeff said.

"Sounds very improbable."

"They have plenty of bottles coming up here. The men will be tied down. It's only a hope, but, my God—that's all we have at this point!"

"Ah, Mr. Sutton...Roger Smith here," an unctuous voice cut in. "I've been listening very carefully to everything, and I'm greatly concerned, of course...but your idea of dragging bags along the runway or lassoing our Concorde seems a bit extraordinary. Surely, a more scientific approach is called for. What do you think, Mr. Caldwell?"

Again there was a lengthy pause, punctuated by loud breathing.

"Well, I don't know what to say," the old engineer stammered. "I can't give you an opinion on lorries racing down a runway dragging air bags, but controlling the SST in that situation would be difficult. The speed of the Concorde's nose gear coming down on the runway would have to be timed perfectly with the vehicles, as I said. There's no danger in what you have just suggested, if we get that far. But I don't think we will."

"Mr. Caldwell, this is Charles Moran, the copilot. We're lightening up considerably now. The controls feel better. We might just have enough fuel to make it down safely, sir."

"All right," Jeff interrupted. "But do I have permission to prepare the runway for the air bags?"

"Why not?" George Hornsby chimed in. "It can't do a bit of harm."

Upon receiving Captain Betzig's emergency signal, the police had cut off the main north-south street feeding into MIA from Homestead to the south. Now the turbo-charged tractors rolled, followed by mobile command centers and two-and-a-half-ton personnel carriers piled high with chains, air bags, and compressors.

The four-lane highway was vacant, and the drivers of the twenty-ton tractors slipped from one gear to another as the diesels wound up and their speedometers were wiggling at ninety in their low gear; and still the accelerators hadn't touched the steel floors.

"Is this going to be the drag race of all time!" cried Lonnie Wooten, a 250-pound black air-force sergeant driving the lead tractor up the deserted highway. "Is this gonna be somethin'. I'll talk about it all my life! Look at this baby go."

Above them and six miles out to sea, the Concorde's thrust levers were gradually being eased back. And they were holding altitude. Everything was happening exactly the way Caldwell had forecast. They *were* buying time.

Lou stood near the open galley-service door to the rear of the Concorde, a safety belt snugging his midsection and a lanyard line snapped around the empty seat tracks. The wind cut in and blew about the cabin. Three men, belted and roped, stood with Lou, waiting to receive the drop of cutting tools.

The intercom in the galley rang, and Charles said, "Lou, I'm going to lift the nose now for the pass. The Hercules is a hundred feet over us. The pilot says he's about to let the reel winch go."

"We're ready back here."

Charles applied a bit more thrust and then radioed, "We're in position, Air Force. I'll hold the nose high.

You just drop it along the wing and it'll slide back to the open galley door. Can you see it from your position?"

"That's affirmative, Concorde. We're letting the reel winch down now."

From the Hercules door, the first of six bundles of tools, ropes, slings, plus medical supplies, was lowered to the Concorde. Again, just as Ralph Caldwell had predicted, the bundle touched the wing lightly, and with the nose-high altitude being held by Charles Moran, the soft-packed load merely slid along the inner wing root; it slipped aft and was halted by the plug hinges of the open service door. Lou reached over and secured a line around the flopping canvas bundle. He passed the rope behind him, and three men hauled the 200-pound load inside.

"We've got it! We've got it!" Lou yelled into the galley. "Tell Air Force to reel up for the next one."

Within nine minutes they had passed 690 pounds of equipment onto the Concorde without incident. Caldwell continued to be right.

Almost every passenger, including Dame Margaret, took on the task of unpacking the bundles. With the electrical lines stretched from the main panel, the air compressors whirled into action; the reciprocating hacksaws were quickly moving their sharpened teeth back and forth. Lou showed two men how to operate the equipment, and they went to work on the aft galley and lavatories. Contrary to what Jeff had feared, the tools were not that difficult to operate. The spring blades sliced through the aft bulkheads, and in a matter of minutes the galley was a pile of metal ready to be jettisoned.

Lou fastened another belt around his waist, the sort used by telephone linemen. Shinnying down the Concorde's nose strut to the Helio would be no more difficult, he hoped, than sliding down a slippery telephone pole. He hooked on his walkie-talkie and power saw and descended through the hatch as five men let off his safety line.

Lou placed his foot on the retract struts, wound the

254

safety belt about the nose strut, and signaled for the men to let off the block and tackle. Slowly, then, with a 180-mile-an-hour ram air pulling at his gut, he was lowered through the bay to the top of the twisted Helio.

Clamping both hands about the power hacksaw, he squeezed the trigger, and the small teeth, pumped by ninety pounds of compressed air, whipped back and forth faster than the eye could see. The blade sliced through two extruding alloy tubes of the Helio as if they were links of sausage meat.

After three tubes fell away, Lou signaled up; the block and tackle were let off, and he slid into what was left of the small plane.

Connie crawled forward and clutched him.

"Thank God you're here!" she yelled over the whistling squall of the air.

"We have medical supplies," Lou bellowed. "Are you people all right?"

Sean grabbed his arm and pointed to his two daughters pinned in the aft end of the cabin.

"Please get them out!" Connie cried, crawling back over the wreckage toward her children.

Lou looked at their pierced legs and the small faces contorted with shock and pain, and he was almost sick. Then he happened to notice the bare wheel hubs of the Concorde. They did not appear flattened or crushed by the travel through the network of steel tubes.

How the fuck could this happen? Lou thought as he pushed the button on his walkie-talkie.

"Charles, I'm in the Helio looking down at the wheel bogie. Go over to the left seat and give me a turn on the nose-wheel steering."

After a second the electrical motor took the hubs from side to side, and the bare rims turned thirty degrees in each direction.

"We have some steering!" Lou yelled back. "I don't know how, but we have steering control. I think we can get these people out in a hurry and this damn little plane off here."

Lou signaled up to his men, and they started hauling him back out of the Helio.

"Hey, wait, where are you going?" Sean cried.

"I'm fetching the doctor for you."

18

Charles Moran, who had been grimly pessimistic since the ordeal began, suddenly brightened.

"We're doing splendidly! Captain Griffis has entered the light plane," he said in a cheery voice over the VHF. "Also, apparently, we still have nose-wheel steering. The strut damage might be superficial."

Hearing the transmission, Mark clapped his hands. "It's going to work!"

"That's grand," Ralph Caldwell said. "Let off your thrust just a bit, Mr. Moran. I want you to descend in ten-degree circles at two hundred feet per minute. Make sure it's two hundred. That should conserve your burn-off and set up your approach nicely."

"I have it. And, sir, they've dumped the rear galley. Should we start on the forward galley and radio panels?" Charles asked.

"Yes, straightaway. But do not touch the forward equipment rack. You'll need communication with the tower. The second unit holds your inertial guidance, air-conditioning circuits, and the rest. You can tear into that, but don't go near the main breaker panel."

"I understand," Charles said.

"Jeff, things are going all right!" Laura exclaimed, pointing to the clear skies over Miami Beach.

Jeff smiled, his first in almost an hour. He glanced toward runway two-seven-left as the convoy of flatbeds and the air-force personnel carriers rolled onto the apron.

"I'm still going to get those trucks ready to roll."

"Yeah, I'd do it, Mr. Sutton." Hoagy nodded. "You never know."

The phone rang and Jeff took it. He listened to the terse statement, and when he put the phone down, he turned to Mark Cranston. "Morrison just died. Nick Cozzoli is on the critical list but looks like he's going to make it."

"What a tragedy this whole business has been," Mark exclaimed.

His voice was properly somber and he felt guilty, but underneath, the secretary was somewhat relieved. Now the disclosure that Ed Morrison was a holder in the computer company could be dropped and an embarrassing Justice Department investigation might not have to proceed.

Jeff established radio communication with the air-force command unit, and Captain Betzig said, "What do you think of that for speed, Mr. Sutton? Got my men and ten tractors here in fourteen minutes. Is that not a record?"

"You bet it is," Jeff replied.

"And we were monitoring the VHF frequency. I heard our plane dropped the gear aboard the Concorde and they're doing okay."

"That's our information," Jeff said.

"We'd better get the peacetime Distinguished Service Cross for this," Betzig said.

"The medals later, Captain Betzig, when it's all over. We may not need all ten tractors but for now, take two of the units and start at the threshold of two-seven-left. Blow up the air bags, shackle them on, and lay down the CO_2."

"Practicing, Mr. Sutton?" the captain asked.

"I want to know if your rigs can actually hit one-ten

and at what point they reach top speed. Also, we need to see if the air bags can be dragged along."

"Got it, sir."

There was a flurry of orders which seemed to create disorder as men scampered about hauling gear off the personnel carriers; the heavy-duty air compressors were cranked into action; ropes were twisted about the stakes of two flatbeds, and heavy CO_2 cartridges were tossed aboard. In a couple of minutes the partly inflated bags were shackled to the drag bolts and bridle chains were run up and secured to mountings on the rear of the low trailers. The men climbed aboard the flatbeds, dropped to their bellies, and fastened the safety hooks to the one-inch Dacron lines crisscrossing the forty-two-foot trailers like the web of a giant spider.

There were two air-force personnel in each cab: one to drive, the other to read out the speedometer over the two-way radio tuned to the tower frequency.

Captain Betzig, a second-generation German-American with a mass of pure blond hair, climbed up to one cab and clicked his transmit button.

"We're set, Mr. Sutton. Ah..."—there was a giggle in his voice—"can I tell the gentlemen to start their engines?"

"I'll give you a start and punch my stopwatch," Jeff replied.

"This ought to be interesting," Mark said to Laura.

Laura smiled as Jeff ordered, "Hit it, gentlemen!"

The massive turbo-diesels roared. The slack came up on the cables and the air bags slid along the macadam surface already hosed down and glistening in the afternoon sun that bathed the hushed airport in brassy light. The CO_2 was sprayed from the black nozzles by a group of twelve men laid out and tied onto each flatbed truck. They worked the CO_2 systematically, some shooting out the liquid, others behind them hauling back the empties like a well-trained motor brigade.

The tractors started off like drugged turtles.

One gear slid to the next; there were grinds and puffs

258

of ash-black diesel exhaust popping up in round little belches:

"What the hell is the matter!" Jeff yelled, seeing the two tractors barely under way during the first five hundred feet of runway.

"Hang on, Mr. Sutton. There's gears to go through; we can't skip any of them on this sort of transmission."

Slowly the tractors gained speed. One thousand feet and they were crossing the thirty-mile-an-hour range. It had taken them twenty seconds, Jeff noted on his stopwatch.

"They ain't gonna make it," Hoagy commented. "Like mules."

But the puffing tractors began to gain speed as one gear led to another and the drivers flipped their hands over the forest of handles rising in the center of the cabs.

The tractors took two minutes and nine seconds to attain one hundred miles an hour, which disappointed Jeff. They used up almost a mile and a half of runway, but after reaching one hundred, with the flatbeds shaking and swaying and the tractors barely in control, the speed accelerated quickly as the mass effect of their ground weight took over.

"One-fifteen...shit!" Captain Betzig yelled out victoriously. "What did I tell you?"

"Take a visual on the spot," Jeff said.

"Got it. Got it. Are we shaking the guts out of these tractors...we're going to blow something. They weren't made for this crazy service."

The tractors slowed down toward the end of the fourteen-thousand-foot runway.

"Well, we didn't lose a man, and the bags didn't pop, thanks to the CO-2 covering," Betzig exclaimed.

"But it took a hell of a long time to wind them up," Jeff said.

"Mr. Sutton, these rigs are supposed to haul missiles around. They're not formula racing cars."

"I know, I know. We'll just have to back 'em up and

start the tractors while the Concorde is way out on final."

"We now have thirteen minutes' flying time, with two minutes' reserve," Charles Moran said into his mike.

"Read you," Jeff said. "The runway bag test just worked, in case we need it."

"Don't think we will, Mr. Sutton. We're putting the doctor down inside the small plane right now. We should be able to cut her away and get everyone aboard very soon."

Just over the nose-gear inspection hatch, Dr. Collins, a flabby, soft man in his middle fifties, was belted up, and he looked down into the cavity of the nose-gear bay, hearing the rush of spinning air.

"I don't like this, Captain Griffis!"

"Neither do I."

The doctor was lowered slowly into the cabin of the Helio with his bag of medical supplies and a portable walkie-talkie hanging off his safety belt, which was pinching the rolls of fat girding his waist. When he had boarded the Concorde flight for a holiday with his sister in Palm Beach, the doctor never imagined he would find himself swinging down the nose gear of the supersonic.

As soon as he entered the Helio, he saw the two young girls, gray and lifeless. He took their pulses and immediately jabbered into his radio, "Captain Griffis, these two girls are in deep shock. Very little pulse. I'm starting IV's and a blood transfusion."

"Can they be cut out of there?" Lou asked.

"I can't tell."

With Connie and Sean helping, the plastic IV's were ripped open and the needles set while Connie held the bags. The doctor took out plastic pouches of blood and started each girl on a transfusion. After about a minute he called for oxygen, and two swinging bottles were lowered into the Helio, clanking back and forth on the ripped tubular frames.

"We're getting some improvement down here, Captain Griffis," the doctor reported, seeing a hint of color return to the girl's faces.

"Good. What about extracting them? Time is getting short."

Dr. Collins began to pull away the shredded seats and litter of the aftercabin. He noticed that one metal tube was thrust through Katie's upper thigh, and her sister's shinbones were locked into a twisted series of aluminum tubing.

"It's a mess," Dr. Collins called into his walkie-talkie.

"But...can we cut them away?" Lou asked quickly.

"I can't seem to find where one piece of metal ends and the next starts. One girl has a jagged tube twisted about her leg. If we start cutting into that, we'll cut her leg off, too."

"Can't we cut short of her leg?" Lou called.

"No. The piece seems to come out of the other end. It's twisted through the back of the plane. How do I reach it?"

"I'm coming down," Lou said.

"Wouldn't advise that; there isn't enough room in here."

"Tell the parents to come up. I'll sling a line down with belts."

Dr. Collins turned to the McCaffertys. "The captain says that you two should leave. We need work space to free the girls."

"No," Sean screamed.

Connie shook her head. "I'm not leaving my children."

"But there isn't enough room to work. For God's sake, don't you want your daughters out of here?"

"Okay, I'll go up," Sean said, "but let my wife stay with them."

"There's nothing she can do here, sir."

"The girls need to know Connie is with them."

"Captain Griffis," Dr. Collins radioed, "the wife wants to stay."

"Tell her it's an order."

"I already did. She won't go."

"All right, here comes the line. Attach it to the pilot, and I'll be down with the hacksaw."

"Ten minutes' flying time," Charles Moran announced. "I'm out of sixty-five hundred and descending."

"Well, we have a problem back here, Charles. Keep me closely monitored."

Sean was hauled up, and Lou quickly descended into the Helio.

"You see that tube?" the doctor said to Lou. "I can't get it out of her leg from this position."

Dr. Collins signaled Lou to the front of the small cabin and yelled into his ear, "We're both thinking the same thing, aren't we? There's *no* way to get these youngsters free. We'll have to hack the plane away from the bottom and let them go. Nothing else to do. It's those three or *all* of us."

Lou did not answer. He started the power tool and began going through the bottom tubes, those clamping the Helio to the nose-gear strut, thinking, perhaps, that if the tubes were free, the weight distribution might change and the children could be pulled off their anchors.

"You'd better get out of here and take the woman with you," Lou screamed, the contours of his optimism changing rapidly. "This thing might drop off at any time."

The doctor hesitated for a moment. Then, evidently feeling justified in wanting to live, he nodded and called up for another belt. It was lowered, and he asked Connie to wrap the belt around her midsection.

"Captain says there's too much weight in here. We could make the plane drop off."

"I'm not going!"

"Yes, you are!" the doctor said.

He tried to snap the belt around Connie's waist, but she flailed out at him, connecting her knotted fist to his lower jaw, and Dr. Collins reeled backward and fell on top of Lou.

"Come on, get the hell out of here, will you?" Lou bellowed, trying to be heard over the curtains of wind walloping in and out of the tubes.

Lou struggled to his knees; they both fought with Connie.

At that moment they were below four thousand feet, and Charles had to apply more and more thrust to hold his slow rate of descent.

"These turbines are gulping kerosene at a much higher rate now," the copilot yelled into his mike.

"Of course, the fuel burn-off rate goes up markedly at lower altitudes," Ralph Caldwell replied, unperturbed. "How much time remaining?" he asked, working his own computer.

"I show six minutes."

"What's the problem with the cutting?" Ralph asked. It was the first time his slow and sanguine voice had been threaded with slight hesitation and doubt.

"Ah...I think the kids in there are mixed up with the tubes. I really don't know."

"For Christ's sake, send the flight engineer back to find out!" Ralph ordered crisply.

Cecil weaved his way from the flight deck to the inspection hatch and jammed his radio to his lips.

"Captain Griffis, we have six minutes before decision time. Can we cut them away or not, sir?"

"Problem is, I can't reach two of the tubes with the saw. Ah...I'm through one of 'em, but...oh, shit...when I poke the saw out, the windage tears away."

"Sir, they want to know if we can do it," Cecil said urgently.

Lou did not have time to answer; Sean McCafferty, who was still in his safety belt, suddenly appeared through the hatch. His body clanged and bounced against the bulkheads of the gear bay.

"Goddamn fool!" Cecil cried into his radio. "The pilot's swinging back down there!"

"Pull him up! Pull him up!" Lou screamed.

It was too late. Sean had already entered the cabin of his wrecked plane.

"I told you to stay the hell up there! It was an order!" Lou shouted.

"I'm not leaving my family!"

The flight engineer ran back up to the cockpit.

"Captain Griffis can't get his saw outside to cut away the rest of the tubes!" Cecil said.

"Dammit! We're going through two thousand now. I'm increasing thrust all the time," the copilot said.

"Only four minutes left," Ralph intoned. "Can you dump any more?"

"We don't have time, sir," the copilot blurted out. "Mr. Caldwell, I'm sucking it dry. We'll have to go for the runway, and right now! Our calculations were off slightly on the lower-altitude fuel rate."

Ralph looked at the men in his engineering office and shook his head.

"It's all figured out on paper," he said with a large sneeze. "What happened?"

"We'll have to use the air bags!" George Hornsby broke in.

"Yes, I'm afraid so," Ralph agreed. "It might have been the air density. I was off by only three minutes."

Jeff Sutton felt no victory in the sudden switch to his plan. In fact, he had no idea if it would succeed, despite the rehearsal.

There were too many variables and contingencies. Like Ralph Caldwell, he too might be proved wrong in the end.

During the time that the doctor and Lou were inside the Helio, Jeff had backtracked the path of the Concorde on final approach to runway two-seven-right. He calculated how long it would take the tractors to reach 110 miles an hour and at what point along the runway they should be when the Concorde finally let its nose gear settle. By plotting the time and speed of both the SST and the tractors, Jeff figured that five trucks should roll just at the moment the supersonic crossed over the outer marker, an electronic beacon six miles west of the runway threshold.

Jeff knew the problem: getting the tractors up to speed in time. He could always slow them down if they were too far ahead of the Concorde, but to grab speed quickly would be impossible.

The sun was now peering from behind the layers of magnificent light-rimmed clouds, as if all the best scenery had been hauled out for the bizarre third act. To Jeff it seemed like a tragic opera, for none of them knew how it would end.

Jeff continued to call out the orders over the ground frequency. He had originally planned to command the operation from the runway, but upon further thought, the facility chief felt he would be able to oversee the entire performance better from the tower cab.

"Are your trucks ready, Captain Betzig?"

"Yes, sir. Men, foam.... Engines ready. Prayers all around."

"We're saying 'em, too. We'll need a lot of luck to pull this off. Okay, I'll give you the direct command from here and let each driver pick it up. Do they have headphones?"

"Yes, sir, I thought of that. You know what's funny, Mr. Sutton?"

"No," Jeff said, brushing back his red hair. "At this point I can't imagine anything funny."

"I've been in the air force eleven years and never thought I would be meeting my match driving a truck. That's army stuff."

"Just shows you, Betzig, how much flexibility we need in life."

"Yeah, sure does. It's our finest moment, right, Mr. Sutton?"

"It'd better be."

The CO-2 crash trucks were stationed at various positions along the runway, and the crews were snugged into their metallic-looking asbestos suits. Jeff looked at this hodgepodge of equipment and turned to Laura.

"Even if this fails, they'll have the fire out quickly."

"It *won't* fail. I know it'll work," she said, smiling and squeezing his hand lightly.

Mark Cranston and Hoagy traded smiles.

"You know, Jeff, what you taught me today?" the secretary said.

"That a control tower can be the highest point in hell."

"Might be. But you proved that, despite science and computers like that CORAD contraption over there, life is still one hell of a lot just plain old horse sense."

"But this isn't over yet. We'll see how the horse sense works."

19

Charles Moran had slipped into Lou's left seat and he went through the landing checklist with Cecil, but they decided to do nothing until Lou returned to the flight deck. The Concorde was just out of two thousand feet and lined up with the runway, a slick ribbon in the far distance, pulsating in the light of the afternoon sun. At 1:50 P.M. on the fourteenth, the flight was heading directly west, 270 degrees.

"Lou, we're setting up for final. Better get the hell out of there. Those wheels have to come down."

"Be right up."

Dr. Collins had been pulled through the bay into the Concorde's cabin. Lou turned to Sean and Connie McCafferty. "Please get out of here...please!"

"The children need us," Sean said, his eyes filling with tears. "Who's going to hold the blood pouches?"

"There's *no* assurance that we're going to make this without an explosion or fire. We've got at best a fifty-fifty chance...*maybe*. We're landing on air bags being pulled along the runway. It's never been tried before. If we don't hit the bags, everyone in here will die instantly. At least you have a chance to save yourselves by coming right now."

"We're not leaving the children," Connie cried out, clasping Sean's arm.

"They're not even conscious," Lou said.

"They know we're here," Sean said. "Katie recognized me. She smiled...or tried to..."

"Lou!" Charles barked over the walkie-talkie. "We're closing in on the threshold. Have to get the bloody gear into position."

"God bless you," Lou said to the McCaffertys, as he signaled for the men to haul him up through the inspection-hatch door.

When he reached the cabin, Lou instructed everyone to buckle into the remaining seats. Whatever was movable in the cabin had been assembled aft in order to shift the center of gravity in that direction; the nose had to be held up as long as possible. The forward section of the once-elegant interior looked like an empty cargo hold.

"Listen, everybody, I don't know what will happen here," Lou said, turning to the passengers.

His uniform shirt was torn, his face contorted and confused.

"We tried to get the occupants out of the small plane, but it was impossible. We're heading for the runway and we'll attempt to land on air bags being dragged along by trucks. That should eliminate the chances of fire and explosion. Anyway, thanks for all your cooperation."

Lou started back toward the cockpit amid the flurry of passenger comments, and Honey ran up to him.

"Captain Griffis, are you telling us the truth?"

"As much as I know, Honey," he said.

She nodded. "Well, I think the worst thing is when people don't really know what's going on."

"Honey, I've told them everything. Now, I have to get back to the cockpit."

"Will it work?" she persisted.

"I think so. I mean, we have a chance. It's your father's idea and we're damn lucky he came up with something, because frankly"—he shrugged—"we don't have any other solutions. But it's still risky. Very risky. There could be a fire and explosion. I just don't know. No one can predict these things."

She put her hand on his arm. "May I sit in the cockpit with you?"

"No, dear, you'll be safer aft, away from the fuel tanks."

Honey turned and climbed over the litter of the main cabin toward the rows of forty-two seats starting from the aft galley forward.

"What did he say?" Dame Margaret asked.

"I guess this landing is going to be something entirely new. The captain isn't sure it will work. There could be a fire, Dame Margaret."

The old actress leaned back and tried to straighten her rumpled hair.

She clutched the hand of the young girl and said, "I know we'll make it."

"Well, that's reassuring." Honey smiled at her.

"Yes, you can feel when a play isn't working from the very first act. It's a sense old actresses develop. But I have a feeling this is going to succeed, and what do I know about planes? This is my first time in the air."

Dame Margaret grinned at Honey, and a strange hush fell over the cabin. There was nothing more that could be done, and the panic which had been submerged while the passengers tried to help began to show again. People moved their lips in prayer and held onto each other as the Concorde started down the runway.

The emergency-window hatches were dropped out of the Concorde for fast exit, and the flight attendants arranged pillows in front of the passengers.

In the mangled Helio, Sean clutched his wife with one hand and a jutting structural tube with the other. When Lou moved his aircraft's nose into the high attack angle, the wind which had been slinging in and out of the tiny crushed cabin drew back to a soft whistle.

"I love you, Sean," Connie said. "I know this wasn't your fault...but I really wish you hadn't taken up flying."

"It was something I thought I had to do. I'm sorry, sweetheart."

He leaned over and kissed his wife, then turned away and bit his lips. The accountant saw the buildings around the airport coming up to meet them through the holes in the bottom of his float plane.

In the cockpit Lou Griffis settled into the left seat.

"Here we go! You'd better behave, Concorde," he murmured.

Lou Griffis and all the other SST pilots had come to love the beauty of their bird and she had performed well in every mode of flight. Still, no engineer, no wind tunnel, no in-flight tests could predict what would happen to the landing characteristics of a Concorde hauling another plane around on its nose gear. Would the Helio be an aerodynamic speed brake, pushing the supersonic nose down as they were about to land, or would the burden up front toss the Concorde into a stall, throwing the airliner out of control?

"Baby, if you've got the best set of wings in the business, now is the time to prove it," Lou whispered to his Concorde.

Lou looked out and saw the infinitesimal specks of the five semitractor trucks waiting at the end of the runway.

A couple of elements had swung around in his favor: the weather had cleared; there was a twenty-five-knot headwind, which would slow the landing speed, and, too, the aircraft was lighter and more responsive now, even with the added load on the nose gear.

"Shall we start?" Lou said matter-of-factly. "Gear

down. Snoot down. Retrim fuel for landing. Disconnect auto-stabilizer and auto-throttle."

"You don't want a backup?" Charles asked.

"No. I have to do this by feel. Can't say if we're going to make this, so hang on, lads. How can those bloody trucks establish a constant speed, anyhow?"

"Whole thing might be a fantasy, Skipper, but we have nothing else," Charles said dryly, flipping his hands over the buttons and knobs, setting the supersonic for what might be the most anomalous landing in the history of man's adventure into the air.

"Lou," Jeff called, "I'm going to start the trucks just at the point when you cross the outer marker. Notify me as soon as the O.M. panel light comes on."

"Roger," Lou replied. "Jeff, is this going to work?"

"Can't say. It's a real freak solution."

"But driving our nose strut through a small plane was also freakish," Lou said, letting out a long breath. "I couldn't get those fools out of the Helio...we'll probably lose them, Jeff."

"We're going to try to save everyone. Sixty pieces of fire equipment are on the field, if that's any consolation."

"Okay. Cross your fingers."

"Good luck, Lou," Ralph Caldwell said faintly. "You and I tried everything. My numbers were a bit off...I'm sorry."

"Give it hell, Lou!" George Hornsby chimed in.

"Godspeed, Captain," Smith said.

The first news of the quirk accident had gone out over the AP and the UPI wires at 1:09 that afternoon, about ten minutes after the explosion in the tower. Editors on the English and French desks, who had a special interest in the fate of their transport, wired back immediately begging for supportive backup. They knew, of course, about midair collisions, but midair impaling was new. Verification calls went out to BAC, SUD, Bristol, Air France, and officials at Aérospatiale, the French co-builder of the Concorde, the Air Ministry, the FAA, and various meteorological experts. Everyone was stunned, unable to explain how it had happened; but most of those contacted agreed that such an accident, unprecedented and curious as it was, the million-in-one chance, *could* happen. And it had.

When the story was confirmed and reconfirmed, the news desks, radio, TV, and print media saw the possibilities in this weird succession of events: the tower explosion, the deaths, the impaling, the midair equipment drops to the Concorde, Jeff's emergency-landing scheme—they all added up to a highly promotable aviation news break. It was even better than the fiery landing of the *Hindenburg* or the traumatic midair collision over New York in 1960. This story had what the others did not. There was time to set up cameras and arrange for satellite transmissions. And there was the truly unique opportunity, prized by any newsman, to "feather the audience," meaning they could drag out each step of the real-life documented spectacle with increasing expectancy and terror. It was all true, better than any staged event, better than Evel Knievel jumping his motorcycle across a canyon.

To take advantage of this rare opportunity, news hookups were threaded about the world, cutting into prime time: Télévision Français, the BBC, German TV, and even Russian TV took options on the transmissions beamed to satellites and from there back to various receiving stations.

Tod Wakefield, Miami's skilled veteran newsman from station WTLM-TV, took the lead description of what was happening on MIA's runway two-seven-right. Originally Jeff had barred all news media from the field because of possible interference with the emergency vehicles and procedures, but that order was quickly remanded; the Port Authority was phoned by the president of the Miami *News-Herald,* and certain areas of the field were suddenly opened to newsmen. Ten remote cameras were set up, their combined signals being microwaved to the antenna on top of the News-Herald Building. There were 115 reporters and photographers lining the taxiway to two-seven-right. Seeing them bunch up like bees, Jeff said, "Look at those bloodthirsty asses!"

Tod knew exactly how to handle the story, and over the small black-and-white Sony in the cab of the tower came his commentary beamed throughout the world:

"...and so we are coming to the final moments of this tragic succession of events here in Miami, Florida, on a February afternoon. The Concorde is now in sight, landing with its nose high, beak down, and from the front landing gear we can see the small float plane hanging on. The owner, an accountant from Tallahassee who was flying into Miami to attend a convention at the Eden Roc this evening, is trapped helplessly inside with his wife and two daughters. Sean McCafferty and his family may never attend that convention. The Concorde is coming closer now...."

Jeff ordered, "Turn that off! Captain Betzig, all set?"

"All set. Motors racing, sir. Tell me when."

"How are you doing, Lou?"

"Everything stable. Gear down...all systems are fine. We're coming up on the outer marker. Coming up...coming up...the light's on...we've crossed it!"

"Okay, Betzig, go! Go like scared rabbits!"

The five tractors began their run, the drivers snapping from gear to gear, winding up the turbo-diesels with every pulse of horsepower packed into the large cylindrical heads of the mammoth power plants. The bags bounced and rustled across the runway, making a deep throaty sound. The air-force personnel, roped and prone on the flatbeds, started laying on the trails of mucky CO_2 and the air was choked by diesel whines and the high-pressure surges of the trapped foam.

"Hand me another. Quick, I'm dry!" a tech sergeant bellowed out.

"I'm almost losing mine," another answered as the rumbling flatbeds, insecure platforms at best, began to thump higher and higher, sidewinding back and forth.

The tractors with their trailing bags, each eleven feet across, formed a moving soft pad of about sixty-five feet; thus, there was little danger that the Concorde would miss the cushion. Lou could always make a slight directional correction once he had his main gear planted. The problem was speed: the continuity between the Concorde's roll-out rate and that of the trucks' movements.

"Do you have the rigs in sight, Lou?" Jeff asked calmly, his slow Kansas pace getting edgier with each sentence. He fought to keep his tone calm, routine.

"We have them...but they're not moving very fast."

"They'll pick up speed. Takes them a while," Jeff said.

"I'll overfly the trucks!"

"No, you won't. You're three miles from touchdown; rate of descent fine. Let *us* worry about the rigs. You just paste it in; I'll control the positioning of the trucks."

"Speed's okay," Lou said. "Got a little trim problem here. Dammit! Got the yoke almost in my kidneys...."

"You're looking good, Lou. Lined up nicely. What's your speed, Betzig?"

"Pushing through sixty, Mr. Sutton."

"Pick it up. Skip a few gears."

"Can't. I told you that."

"I'm on the edge of a stall now...everything's shaking," Lou screamed. "Christ, the lorries aren't one-quarter down the runway! Jeff, this isn't going to make it!"

"Set yourself down on the far end numbers, Lou. Take it easy and slow. Routine putdown. Routine. Routine."

"I don't know, with this trim. I'll have to stick on some throttle. Can't lift it beyond twenty degrees. Maybe twenty-two degrees. Don't want to stall...have to add thrust."

"Betzig, what's the matter?" Jeff yelled.

"We're flooring these things, but one of them is out ahead."

"Stay together, whatever happens! Slow that outside truck down."

"Got it. I'm reaching ninety now. That beautiful little needle is goin' and goin'."

There was an explosion followed by a hiss of air as one of the cells in an air bag burst. Jeff saw the black rubber puff.

"Don't worry about that. Keep dragging."

Inside the Helio, Connie and Sean were huddled in the rear trying to hold onto their children and the IV's. Sean leaned over and kissed his wife again.

"I'm sorry, Connie. I love you."

In those horrifying seconds they looked at their girls, realizing that this could be the last time they would see them. With the air screaming by and the ground rising up at them, each sensed that his life was coming down to seconds, final seconds.

In the aft section of the half-gutted Concorde, Dame Margaret wasn't holding onto Honey's hand anymore. She did not need it. They smiled at each other, and then they locked arms together, not so much for emotional support as to celebrate the Englishwoman's courage.

Eighteen crash trucks started their dash, following in the wake of the wound-up air-force semitrailers, which were swaying along now at almost one hundred miles an hour.

Betzig noticed the sway and yelled to his drivers, "Pull away a bit. Pull away! We'll have a big sideswipe."

The air shuffled under one bag. It started to flip up. Then it toppled on its end, dragged along for a while, and overturned, twisting the drag cables. Explosions from the heat buildup began to deflate the soft bags, and the air was filled with hot rubber fragments.

It was not going according to rehearsal.

"The bags are all over the place!" Jeff screamed. "What's wrong?"

"How the hell do I know, for Christ's sake?" Betzig shot back. "This is the air force, not the Grand Prix!"

"What speed are you hitting?"

"One-zero-five. I'm afraid to wind up anymore."

274

"Lou," Jeff called. "They can only hit about one hundred and five."

"I'll just have to yank the reverse thrusts early. But I might lose directional control."

At that moment the Concorde's main gear touched the runway with a pitched squeal, cutting a path through the layer of CO_2. The Concorde, even with its nose load, had remained relatively stable, and Lou took back all his former criticism of the delta wing. The wing had saved them—at least so far. Lou shoved his reverse throttles into position and started to lightly pump the brakes, but the foam layer made traction sluggish.

"We're going to overrun the trucks," Lou said into his boom mike, feeling he was about to enter a high-speed skid. "Tell them to push harder."

"Increase your speed," Jeff yelled into the other mike.

"We might blow more bags."

"The Concorde is on the ground, crawling up your ass! Do you understand, Captain? Do you want your men fried in kerosene?"

The drivers, hearing that, slapped their accelerators to the olive-green floors. The bags jumped higher as the air cushion opened, and soon they were almost flying. The personnel roped to the flatbeds were tossed about, and a few hung onto the stretching lines, unable to supply the CO_2 bottles. The tractors were now at the 9,000 mark of the 14,000-foot runway. Only 5,000 more feet to go, and they were chewing up the hard surface so fast that Jeff feared they might go off the far end of the runway into the turf.

"If the Concorde doesn't slow down, we've had it," he said, turning to the others in the cab.

The tail wheel of the SST was spinning along the runway; it shimmied and collapsed. The tail assembly was now dragging on the partially foamed runway, cutting a neat line through the milk-white layer, and sparks were shooting up.

Lou was almost choking to death. He had sucked in

his tubby midsection and driven the yoke deep into his gut, and when that was insufficient to hold the Concorde's nose off the runway, he yelled, "Throw that goddamn switch, Charles!"

The copilot reached down and pulled the handle. With all the power in his upper legs Lou shoved the seat back. The control yoke flew rearward with a crash. No Concorde pilot had ever held the column that far aft, and old Mr. Caldwell would have said it was impossible.

Yet the nose remained high. So high that Lou could no longer see the truck brigade in front of him, even with his down angle of vision provided by the droop snoot.

With the nose pointing toward the sky, the tail dragging, and the reverse thrusts squealing and the brakes being pumped lightly, the supersonic began to slow down rapidly—too rapidly.

The tractors were racing away. Jeff saw this, even though Lou could not.

"Betzig, you're going too fast. Slow down!"

"Where's the plane?" the captain asked.

"In back of you."

"Goddammit, Sutton, I know that...how *far* in back of me?"

"Two hundred yards. The distance is opening up."

"We'll try to brake."

The boots were lifted from the accelerators as Lou shoved his reverse-thrust levers into neutral position. The Concorde began to pick up speed, but the nose was settling as gravity took over.

"I'm going to run into those lorries!" Lou cried out.

"Hit the accelerator, Betzig," Jeff ordered. "The Concorde has almost caught up with you."

The tractors began to accelerate once again. The captain did not need Jeff to tell him where the Concorde was now, for the air-force officer looked up and saw the spindle nose right over him.

"I'm in position, Jeff," Lou yelled. "I can't see below

me, dammit. Doesn't matter anymore...I'm settling...my nose is landing."

"Hold that speed, Betzig. The nose is about on top of you!"

The Helio plopped into the rustling, popping air bags, which were rising up to make their contact. The edges of the float dug into the first bag, and it exploded into a million pieces of rubber. As soon as it did, the two bags next to it slid over. With a plunging thump and a hissing of air, the floats of the Helio dug into the air bags, and the bottom appendages were almost swallowed up by the soft rubber cushions.

"The nose has settled, Lou," Jeff yelled. "It's in the bag."

"Very funny...shit...I don't feel that my nose is planted," Lou shouted back.

"It's on," Jeff said. "Betzig, now slow down. Don't hit your brakes too much."

The captain swung his head around and saw the massive plane behind and above him.

The Helio was twisted a bit sideways but it did not disengage in the wild ride along the runway, even though the left float, half off the air bag, was making runway contact and sending up a spray of sparks.

The tractors and the Concorde were slowing up rapidly now. Lou got the Helio lined up on the air bags by pumping one brake slightly more than the other.

"We're down to eighty...seventy now...sixty..." Charles called out.

Jeff immediately saw a problem developing: the huge flatbeds could not brake as rapidly as the Concorde. They had built up too much speed, and slowly they started to pull away from the SST, towing the bags after them. The rubber began to rip apart.

The Concorde had slowed to fifty miles an hour and by that time the crash trucks had closed in and were turning their high-pressure CO_2 nozzels on the Helio.

It was suddenly bathed in grayish muck.

The foam entered the cabin of the light plane, and Sean and his family were drenched in a torrent of foam.

They could hardly breathe, but the air pressure around them fell. They were on the runway!

Sean and Connie tried to wipe the blinding foam away, and a sudden surge of joy and relief overtook them. They managed to keep the CO_2 bath off the children, but soon the two of them were blinded.

"I'm coming to a halt," Lou said, "coming to a stop!"

"I can't brake!" Betzig yelled out. "I can see the runway pylons on the end."

"Hit the brakes harder!" Jeff ordered.

"We're trying!" Betzig bellowed in a wild yelp of animal panic.

The Concorde came to a stop 260 feet before the end of the 14,000-foot runway. The layer of foam was so heavy by this time that there were no sparks, no chance of a flip-back or explosion.

But the trucks were in trouble.

They sped on, leaving behind bits and pieces of the ruptured air bags.

"We're going in! We're going in!" Betzig screamed.

The five air-force tractors could not brake in time.

They careened off the runway in a pattern of twisting turns: three smashed through the plyons of the landing lights; two hit each other, overturned, and burst into flames.

The Concorde and the Helio were stopped. There had been no fire.

The tractors and the air bags meshed with the high-intensity landing lights at the far end of runway two-seven-right. Men were tossed off. There was an eruption of flame and most of the emergency equipment sped to the wreckage of the air-force rigs.

"Let's go!" Jeff said, grabbing Laura's hand.

They left the cab with Mark and took the elevator to the ground level, where a Port Authority car was waiting for them.

"Thanks, Jeff," Mark said. "You pulled off a hell of a feat here."

"Well, it didn't quite work," Jeff said despondently.

"Look at that. I was worried about a plane crash, not a big truck pile-up."

He pointed to a column of rising smoke pouring off the wreckage of the air-force trucks.

By the time they reached the runway, the medical and rescue teams were already cutting out the McCafferty family. The side passenger door of the Concorde was open. Lou stood there, his shirt, dripping with sweat, but he was grinning.

"That's some act you have, Captain," Jeff yelled up at him. "When are you going to learn to fly?"

"You screwball bastard!" Lou's big smile broadened.

A couple of seconds later Honey appeared at the open door. She waved and said something, but the wail of sirens drowned out her voice.

Jeff and Laura paused at the crushed Helio as the McCafferty girls were taken out.

"They'll be okay," one of the medics said.

Flames were still roaring over the lump of intermingled tractor-trailers as Jeff and the others ran toward the end of the runway. A man with a singed gray uniform stumbled out of the haze of diesel smoke.

"Are you Captain Betzig?"

"I was."

Jeff placed his arm around him. "What can I say? Thanks."

"Well, we made a mess of it, I'm afraid. My rigs couldn't stop in time. I should have realized what was happening."

"We've alerted Jackson Memorial. How many men did you lose?"

"Five seriously burned. I don't know about some others...they're pinned underneath the wreckage. God, we should have veered off."

The stairs were snug against the SST's fuselage by the time Jeff and Laura returned to the Concorde, and Honey met Jeff halfway up and stepped into his embrace. Minutes later they all rode across the field and out the Thirty-sixth Street gate, where Jeff Sutton had entered at eight o'clock that morning, thinking about his last day at the tower.

"Happy Valentine's Day," Jeff said, squeezing Laura's hand.

"Rather humdrum, wasn't it?" She laughed, holding his hand tighter.

20

Jeff leaned over Nick Cozzoli, who was hooked up to a conglomeration of plastic tubes in the intensive-care section of Jackson Memorial Hospital. Nick recognized Jeff and grinned his usual unshakable smile. "Did we get that big ass bird down, Mr. Sutton?" he whispered.

Jeff nodded. "No loss of life, but the air-force truck drivers banged themselves up. Five are critically burned."

"What air-force truck drivers?" he asked weakly.

"You take it easy and I'll tell you about it later, Nick."

"Okay...."

"Harry's dead and so is Morrison," Jeff said after a pause.

"Um...I'm sorry about Harry. He stayed around too long."

"Yeah," Jeff sighed, "and I let him. But I never knew just how cracked he was. Well I'll be back tomorrow. You get some rest now. You're going to be better than new."

When Jeff entered the solarium, Lou Griffis, Laura, Honey, and Mark Cranston were waiting.

"Cozzoli is going to make it," Jeff said. "And how are you people?" he asked, sitting down and feeling nine hundred years old.

"Oh, they fixed us up quickly," Mark said. "Laura and I were lucky. There's a long-distance call from England for you. The operator's holding it over there."

Jeff stood and shuffled over to the booth.

"Mr. Sutton, Caldwell here. I have Mr. Smith on the line, too. We want to thank you, sir," the old engineer said.

"Yes, thanks from all of us," Roger Smith joined in. "Magnificent work, Mr. Sutton."

"Quite a few anxious moments there," Caldwell added. "Ah...Mr. Sutton, you might want to know where my calculations went off."

"Yeah, I guess I do."

"We didn't take into consideration the degree of saturated air. When the Concorde descended, the burn-off rate went up almost thirty percent. Did you know about it, sir? I mean, was that why you were suggesting alternatives?"

"No, Mr. Caldwell. I just felt we were running out of time."

"Well, you have our gratitude," Smith added.

When Jeff returned to the others, Mark came up to him.

"That had to be Caldwell."

"Yeah, he thanked me. Smith thanked me...Celtic thanks me...it's a little hard to accept all this goodwill, when I might have caused the whole damn thing. I should have yelled louder a long time ago."

"You did, Jeff, but no one listened," Laura said.

"They'll listen now," Mark declared. "I promise you something. We're going to start rebuilding this FAA control system."

Jeff nodded with a patronizing smile. He had heard that before.

The secretary saw the cynicism etched into Jeff Sutton's face, and he moved closer to the retired facility

281

chief, a man who was thoroughly relieved to be departing the agency.

"I'm very impressed with you, Jeff. You used your head today, but more than that, you were the only man who had the courage to speak up about ATC deficiencies. This idea of yours—the cube radar—might be worth studying."

"I think it is, Mark. I wish you luck, and I'll turn over all my research to your office. I don't want it lost in the FAA paper shuffle."

The secretary thanked Jeff with a bow of his head, then spoke again. "Jeff, would you reconsider your resignation?"

"I doubt it."

"I might nominate you for the administrator's post—if you'd assure me that you'd take the job. It's on the sub-Cabinet level, fifty-nine thousand dollars a year. More than that, you'd have the opportunity to do something effective."

Jeff was not quite listening to the secretary, for his mind and thoughts were still fixed on the traumatic events of that day. All he wanted was to leave the hospital and have dinner with Honey and Laura and the man who had so brilliantly landed his Concorde.

"...so, think it over," Mark concluded. "I can promise you that we'll get the necessary budget. A lot was proved today."

"Too much," Laura said.

Jeff agreed with a nod, and then he said good-bye to the secretary. They walked out of the hospital.

Sean McCafferty and his wife, both bandaged, managed to make the cocktail party at the Eden Roc later that evening. They were in a joyful mood because the hospital had informed them that Katie and Hillary would be fine.

Sean had become an instant celebrity, and they had not even been seated when a partner in a major Miami accounting firm came up to Sean and shook hands.

"Ever think of relocating down this way, Mr. McCafferty? Might have something interesting for you."

"No, sir, never thought of it. But I'll listen."

Sean exchanged winks with his wife, and they moved into the private dining room for dinner.

Jeff took his daughter and Laura back to the control tower. It was dark now, and the airport was fully operational. New panes of glass had already been fitted into the cab, and there was very little evidence of what had happened only hours before, except for the wrecking crews still working on the tangle of air-force trucks off the end of runway two-seven-right.

Jeff said good-bye to everyone in the tower, and he asked the deputy chief to send his belongings out to his house. Honey wanted to stay in the cab for a few minutes to watch the planes land, and the former facility chief took Laura downstairs to the door that opened upon the turf at the base of the exotic-looking building.

They walked around on the grass that hugged the "tulip" and Jeff looked up at the ultimate tower, the scene of his success, the microcosmic world which had evoked his failure.

"Can't believe I just arrived here yesterday," Laura said. "Seems like two years ago."

"So much has happened."

"Sure has...a man went wild...killed people...was killed himself...one plane hit another plane. And then there's the part that isn't over yet."

"What do you mean?" Jeff asked.

"Well, I came down here to do a little number on you, and you ended up doing one on me."

"How?"

"You made me fall in love with you."

"I made you?" Jeff laughed.

"Oh, you know what I mean. I just fell in love, and you made me do the first brave thing in my life—tossing the boiling water in Harry's face. I wish I knew if it was really necessary."

"It was...and thank you," he said as he put his arm

around Laura and kissed her. "And how did I know I'd get such a double Valentine?" he said. "You and my daughter...so the day wasn't all tragic. But do you know the best prize?"

"Being with Honey again, I suppose."

"Of course, and I want to be with you, too. But my biggest joy is that I don't have to spend the rest of my life in that building. It was slow suicide."

"Jeff, didn't you hear what the secretary said at the hospital this afternoon?"

"About becoming the administrator?"

"Yes."

"Oh, that was just talk."

"I don't think so. Can't you see that not all government officials are Ed Morrison types? There are good, loyal men up in Washington, and I happen to believe Mark is one of them. So bury that skepticism. Realize something can be done. Running away isn't going to solve a damn thing. From what I've seen, Jeff, they need you."

"Maybe they do," he said slowly, his face lighting up a bit.

They embraced again, and Jeff stared at the tulip, thinking how ironic it would be if he returned there as the administrator after resigning under a cloud.

"How would you like to fly along with me and Honey...I mean, on our trip out west?"

"The plane only seats two."

"But we could charter a different plane and all go together."

"I'd have to pick up a few things in Chicago first."

"All right. You go up there, and we'll fly over and meet you in New Orleans. I just happened to remember a friend there with the right kind of plane, and I know he'll lend it to us."

"Sounds good...because I'm not sure I'm ever going back to my old job now. Been too many changes."

They were silent for a time, and then Jeff said, "You ever thought about living in Washington?"

She grinned. "Well, you know, I might like that."

Laura tucked her arm through his and they walked slowly back to the tower.

About the Author

Robert P. Davis is the author of seven novels. *The Pilot*, the story of an alcoholic airline captain, has just been made into a major motion picture starring Cliff Robertson.

A pilot himself, the author lives in southern Florida, where he is at work on a new novel.

CURRENT CREST BESTSELLERS

☐ BORN WITH THE CENTURY   24295 $3.50
by William Kinsolving
A gripping chronicle of a man who creates an empire for his family,
and how they engineer its destruction.

☐ SINS OF THE FATHERS   24417 $3.95
by Susan Howatch
The tale of a family divided from generation to generation by great
wealth and the consequences of a terrible secret.

☐ THE NINJA   24367 $3.50
by Eric Van Lustbader
They were merciless assassins, skilled in the ways of love and the
deadliest of martial arts. An exotic thriller spanning postwar Japan
and present-day New York.

☐ KANE & ABEL   24376 $3.75
by Jeffrey Archer
A saga spanning 60 years, this is the story of two ruthless, powerful
businessmen whose ultimate confrontation rocks the financial community as well as their own lives.

☐ GREEN MONDAY   24400 $3.50
by Michael M. Thomas
An all-too-plausible thriller in which the clandestine manipulation
of world oil prices results in the most fantastic bull market the
world has ever known.

Buy them at your local bookstore or use this handy coupon for ordering.

COLUMBIA BOOK SERVICE, CBS Publications
32275 Mally Road, P.O. Box FB, Madison Heights, MI 48071

Please send me the books I have checked above. Orders for less than 5 books
must include 75¢ for the first book and 25¢ for each additional book to cover
postage and handling. Orders for 5 books or more postage is FREE. Send check
or money order only. Allow 3–4 weeks for delivery.

Cost $_____	Name _____
Sales tax*_____	Address _____
Postage_____	City _____
Total $_____	State_____ Zip _____

*The government requires us to collect sales tax in all states except AK, DE,
MT, NH and OR.
Prices and availability subject to change without notice.   8215